PRAISE FOR THE NOVELS OF
YASMINE GALENORN

"Yasmine Galenorn creates a world I never want to leave."
—**Sherrilyn Kenyon, #1** *New York Times*
bestselling author on The Otherworld Series

"Erotic and darkly bewitching...a mix of magic and passion sure to captivate readers."
—Jeaniene Frost, *New York Times* bestselling
author on The Otherworld Series

"*Autumn Thorns* mesmerize~~d~~   ~~f~~antastic, perfect blend of myth and modern, ni~~c~~   love and loss. I want to return to Whisp~~   ~~

~~   ~~nes bestselling author

"Those wh~~   ~~ or Rachel Caine's Weather Warden serie~~   ~~ home. Well-crafted fantasy abounds here, along wi   character chemistry and an old-fashioned gumshoe-detective feel."
—*Booklist* on *Witchling*

"Yasmine Galenorn's imagination is a beautiful thing."
—**Fresh Fiction**

"Her books are always enchanting, full of life and emotion as well as twists and turns that keep you reading long into the night."
—*Romance Reviews Today*

"Galenorn delivers suspense, myth, and stunningly relatable characters in her second Fly by Night paranormal contemporary...The suspense builds, layer by layer, as the central mystery is addressed and a wide variety of smaller, more personal issues are teased out, leaving readers with an almost desperate need to know what happens next. Each detail seems specifically chosen to enhance immersion into a beautiful, complicated setting."
—*Publisher's Weekly* (**starred review**) on *Flight from Mayhem*

SOULJACKER

A LILY BOUND NOVEL

YASMINE GALENORN

DIVERSIONBOOKS

Diversion Books
A Division of Diversion Publishing Corp.
443 Park Avenue South, Suite 1008
New York, New York 10016
www.DiversionBooks.com

For more information, email info@diversionbooks.com

First Diversion Books edition March 2017
Print ISBN: 978-1-68230-701-4
eBook ISBN: 978-1-68230-700-7

I dedicate this book to my readers—all of you.
May the journeys and adventures continue.

"Sex is the driving force on the planet.
We should embrace it, not see it as the enemy."
—Hugh Hefner

"The creative habit is like a drug. The particular obsession
changes, but the excitement, the thrill of your creation lasts."
—Henry Moore

CHAPTER 1

I leaned against the side of the sliding glass door, staring out into the cold Seattle night as I waited for Jolene Whitehorse to arrive. A brisk wind was blowing off Puget Sound. Even though the doors and windows were closed, the chill still seeped in through the glass. Beneath the snow that drifted down to cover the world, the streets were busy with people hurrying home before it got too dark. Or hurrying to work before the midnight curfew set in. Everywhere, people were rushing to get under cover before the vampires came out to prowl.

I pushed back my hunger, but once again the gnawing force whispered in my ear, urging me to go out on the hunt. Glistening drops of perspiration clung to my forehead and I wiped them away with the back of my hand, then absently clutched my robe tighter. I should have gotten dressed. Or called Dani or Nate. I should have called Wynter to let her know what was going on. In fact, I could think of a million things I should have been doing but, at that moment, I felt as frozen as the icicles hanging off the eaves of the house.

The Wild Hunt was on the rampage, racing overhead under the new moon. The sound of their horns reverberated through the astral. They were terrifying and yet…they called to me, enticing me to join them. One thing was for sure. When the Fae decided to pull out the stops and ride, everybody felt the world tremor. Especially night demons like me.

Not that I was a true demon. No, I was fully Fae. Fae on the dark side, you might say. I was a denizen of the Winter Court, though I mostly answered to myself. The Hunt would always summon me, though. I was a succubus, and the chase was in my blood.

The satyrs echoed their war cries, howling it up in the Underground. They came out to party when the Hunt was on the move, and I could feel it like a pulse, rippling through the air. Their hunger acted like an aphrodisiac, and I caught my breath, quivering from the cries of the wild boys. I wanted nothing more than to join them, to get down and dirty with the boys of the hood. I hadn't fed in a couple of days, and the thought of a muscular satyr with plenty of chi made me salivate.

But then, like a dose of ice water, the memory of what was waiting in my salon washed over me, and my libido took a nosedive. Because upstairs, Tygur Jones was lying dead on my floor, sucked dry by a vampire who had managed to somehow get through my wards, and there was nothing I could do about it. With one last glance into the icy darkness, I abandoned my thoughts of the rave playing out in the streets of the Blood Night District, and turned, reluctantly deciding to face the dirge sounding through my own life.

• • •

Mr. Whiskers mewed at me as I glanced at the clock. I had called Jolene twenty minutes ago, but after I told her what had happened, the urgency fled from her voice.

"We'll be there as soon as we can, but since this was a vampire execution, it's lower priority. You know that. My partner and I have to corral some of the horny boys first. They're tearing it up downtown and scaring the tourists. Buzz me again if the vampire returns. Otherwise, we'll be there as soon as we can."

Vampire execution. Also known as *VE*, it was the new catchall phrase for any death due to the fangboy brigade. Jolene's answer didn't make me happy, but since the vampire had fled, there was nothing more I could do other than settle into a chair and try to relax.

"So, what should I do, Whisky?"

My nickname for Mr. Whiskers had stuck, but he only put up with it from me. Anybody else, he'd flick his tail at and ignore. And considering Mr. Whiskers's true nature, being ignored was probably safest. Though I couldn't prove it, I had the feeling the cat had retained some of his original nature.

He jumped up and I groaned as the twenty-pound Bengal sprawled across my lap. But as he stared into my eyes, I realized he was trying to tell me something. He seemed concerned, but I couldn't quite read what he was upset about. My ability to do so flickered in and out, depending on the day. He was probably upset about the vampire. Vampires and cats hated each other, because a cat could always recognize one.

"I'm sorry, Whisky, but I don't understand. I guess I'm just too tense to focus."

Fidgeting, I glanced at the stairs leading to the second floor, wondering if I should go check Tygur again. The thought that I might have been wrong preyed on my mind. What if I had missed his pulse? What if he was still alive, but up there, dying right now?

Suddenly panicking, I unceremoniously pushed Whisky off my lap and raced up the stairs. But as I softly approached the open door, I hesitated. I had dealt with death before—far more often than I wanted to admit, but this was different. For one thing, this was in my home. For another...well...*vampires*.

Gathering my courage, I swung into the room.

Tygur was sprawled on the floor, his face powder white, his throat—bloody. The tall, brawny-shouldered weretiger with tawny hair that barely cleared his shoulders was normally hot to trot, and not afraid of anything. But now, he lay pale and still.

Glancing around to make sure we were alone, I dropped to my hands and knees and inched forward until I was close enough to touch him.

Tygur looked so pale. I brushed my hand along his face, shuddering. He had the smoothest skin of any man I knew, but now the texture was that of cracked leather, typical of a vampire kill. The blood on his throat had already coagulated, and two gaping holes marred his neck, but the only sign of blood on the floor was where it had trickled down the side to drip on the carpet. My hopes evaporated. He was really dead.

"Oh, Tygur…" I let out a slow sigh.

I wished I could cry, or feel *anything* except the numb disbelief that welled up. But I was a succubus, and it was a matter of self-preservation to build strong walls. I did my best to avoid any emotional entanglements with anybody I slept with.

The truth was that I genuinely *liked* Tygur Jones. He was a great guy, and we'd had a lot of fun together. But the reality? He was my client. Or rather, had been, until tonight. A wealthy client. A decent guy. But a client, nonetheless. Even after several years of servicing him, I realized that I couldn't call him a friend, and that made me sad.

I started to close his eyes—I wanted to show *some* sign of respect—but then stopped. Jolene had instructed me *not* to touch the body any more than I already had. Not that it would make any difference. More often than not, vampire executions were slapped under the cold-case label as soon as they hit the computer.

Vampires were cunning and powerful, and they pulled all the strings in the Blood Night District. Breathers who chose to live in the area either listened to the old timers, or they learned the hard way. *Buy the wards for your house and business. Travel in groups at night. Keep to the curfews. Stay away from the vampire clubs unless you have a free pass to get in.*

As I stood, I noticed something that had previously escaped my attention. A strip of skin had been flayed from his chest. Grimacing, I bent down to take a closer look. Sure enough, someone had excised a neat rectangle of skin, exposing the raw, glistening muscle below.

"What the hell? Why would a vampire want skin?"

Something niggled at the back of my mind—a memory—but I couldn't quite recall it. After a moment, I gave up. It would come back if it was important. As I turned toward the door, it hit me that there was nothing I could do. Nothing I could say would bring Tygur back, and stalling wouldn't help. I exited the room, shutting the door quietly behind me.

CHAPTER 2

Once I was in the hallway, I texted Nate, asking him to come over. I needed moral support, and I knew Dani—my best friend—was busy.

Whisky was waiting for me. He batted at the hem of my gown, and I realized that I'd better get dressed. He followed me into my personal bedroom and parked himself in front of the closet.

"Come on, boy. You have to move so I can get in there." Disgruntled, I shifted him away from the closet door. Owning a sex salon suddenly seemed more of a burden than a boon. More often than not, I enjoyed my work, but when I really thought about it, most of my clientele were powerful Weres, with powerful enemies, and sometimes those enemies tried to kill them. What if the assassin had managed to succeed his way right into my house?

Or what...what if it was somebody angry at me? I had left a trail of pissed-off people behind me over the years. Angry wives, outraged husbands, ticked-off clients who didn't think they should have to pay my rates. Not to mention the revenge-bent families who had lost loved ones when I was younger and didn't know how to control my hunger.

Shivering, I changed clothes, choosing a pair of black jeans and a purple tank top. I slipped on a pair of leather ankle boots and shrugged on a lace cardigan. Pulling the kanzashi out of my chignon, I swept the shoulder-length strands back into a sleek ponytail. My hair was dark burgundy and was as much a part of me as my steel-gray eyes. I was wearing the silver dragon-scale pentacle that I never took off. I touched it, softly. The necklace was protective, and I realized that it had done its job. Silver alone wouldn't completely ward off vampires. Silver from dragon scales? Yes.

With a last look in the mirror, I felt ready to face Jolene. I headed down to the kitchen to wait.

• • •

Nate knocked on my front door a few minutes after I had finished dressing.

My next door neighbor, Nate was also one of my best friends. He was also my computer guru, and kept my website up to date. Nate was human and I had never slept with him. I never would.

Hell, I had never even offered him a backrub. My touch could spark off my glamour, even when I wasn't trying. All it would take would be one little mistake and he'd be hooked. And since Nate was like the brother I never had, I wasn't about to risk hurting him.

As he bounded up the steps, I motioned him in. "Get in here. I need backup. Life just got weird on me, and not in a good way."

"This, from a succubus? What happened? I thought you were working tonight." His startlingly blue eyes met my gaze, and his tousled hair told me he'd been sleeping. Nate kept odd hours and was always on call for his company—Modal Technologies.

"I was supposed to but…just get your ass in here, *Percival*, and I'll tell you." Nate's first name was actually Percival, but he hated it. I used it when I meant business or wanted to watch him sputter. We were *that* kind of friends. "I need the company right now."

His presence would give me something to focus on other than Tygur's dead body. I busied myself by putting on the kettle and finding the Orange Spice tea.

"So what's up? You look like you saw a ghost." Nate leaned back in his chair, propping his feet up on the cedar chest I kept near the kitchen.

He was tall and lanky with black shaggy hair, and he always had a five o'clock shadow. He had a roguish look that should have won the girls over big time. But Nate was challenged in the romance department and had zero self-confidence in himself as a lover. I had tried to help boost his ego over the years, but it seemed a lost cause. I kept trying, though, because he was one of the good guys. He deserved to find the love of his life and settle down.

"For starters, there's a dead weretiger in my salon. Tygur Jones."

He slammed his feet to the floor, sitting up so fast he almost tipped his chair over. "What?"

"Oh, it gets better. A vampire killed him. A vampire who should not have managed to get into my house because I recently bought new wards. I *have* to keep them up to date given that I'm a business and have to make certain my clients are safe. Do you realize what this is going to do to my reputation?"

"How do you know it was a vampire?" Nate shuddered. He liked vampires about as much as the rest of us. Which was: *Not so much.* Especially among the human community.

I pulled out a bag of macaroons and began to arrange them on a plate. "The two gaping holes in Tygur's neck tell me so. And the lack of blood on the floor."

"How did it get in?"

"That's what I'd like to know. I've called the cops and they'll be here in a few minutes. Meanwhile, I'm going to pour us some tea and talk to you so that I don't start imagining that Tygur Jones is up there, being animated into a zombie or some sort of nightmare like that."

"Can that really happen?" Nate tried to avoid facing the darker sides of the supernatural community unless he was forced to.

"It most certainly could. Someone like Dani could bring him back and run him around like a puppet on a string." I poured the tea and set one of the mugs in front of him, taking care not to spill it. "So, what have you been up to today?"

He stared at me. "You have a murdered client upstairs, and you're asking me what I did today? Lily…"

I shrugged. "Listen, what do you expect me to do? Fall apart? Burst into tears? First, the vampire isn't in the house anymore. I saw it leave. Second, I don't dare touch the body till the cops go over the room. Third, I can't really leave until the cops get here. No, the only thing I can do is try to come down from my hunger, because I haven't fed for a couple days. I was waiting for tonight so I could make it especially…"

I paused, leaning against the counter as I tried to focus. I'd been prepared to feed on Tygur but that wasn't going to happen now. The shock of his death had staved off the hunger, but it would be back soon, harder than before.

"You need to feed." Nate frowned.

"Yes, Captain Obvious." I rubbed my forehead. "I'm sorry, I don't mean to sound churlish. But you're right—I need to feed, however that can't happen for a little while. Until then? Cookies and tea and conversation with you will have to do."

He grinned. "I could be insulted, but I'm not."

"Don't be. You wouldn't survive me and you know it, babe." I gave him a wan smile.

He played with the mug, the corner of his lip tipping up with that quirky half smile he had. "Trust me, I know. You're careful around me and I appreciate it. We don't have the same kinks. I couldn't go where you do. And I don't think I'd want to."

"Good. So talk to me. Take my mind off of Tygur and my hunger. Help me focus."

The wash of energy unsettled me, so strong that I could barely control it. I had never let it go this long before, not for years. Now I realized what a stupid move it had been, even to satisfy a client.

Nate sipped his tea and then wiped his mouth. "Good stuff. Get it at Haverish's?"

Tea. Focus on the tea. "Always. He has the best tea in the market."

"I should go there sometime. But White Tower Center makes me nervous, even though I live in the Blood Night District. I don't like going where humans aren't all that welcome. Would you pick me up some next time you're there?" As I nodded, Nate glanced at me. "Do you have any idea who the vampire was?"

"Not a clue. Tygur was a powerful man, and he had a lot of enemies." I stopped, as the image of the skinned area on his chest flashed through my mind. Maybe this wasn't just some power-hungry assassination. But I didn't want to worry Nate, so I just said, "I don't know. So, tell me about your day."

At that moment, the doorbell rang. Relieved, I answered.

Jolene Whitehorse was a werewolf. Tall and willowy, her short, edgy hair was the brown of soft earth and her eyes were golden, ringed with black. Before entering the kitchen, she took off her hat and dusted the snow off her shoulders where it had accumulated on her walk from the car. Jolene and I went *way* back.

She had joined the Paranormal Investigations Unit shortly after a falling out in our friendship. The cops who worked for the PIU were top notch and they understood the nature of people like Tygur and me because they all lived on the fringe themselves. Meaning every single officer assigned to the unit was either Fae or Were. Though we had patched up our argument, we had never become close again. She didn't approve of my business, and I didn't like feeling judged.

Her partner was a junior member of the force. Another Were, I guessed.

"Hey Lily, it's been awhile." Jolene was methodical. That, I appreciated. She never panicked, just went about her business in a calm, almost taciturn manner. She was good with a gun, hard to startle and, unlike most werewolves, she didn't submit to the alpha of her pack, which was why she'd been kicked out. She was the original lone wolf.

Nate stood when she entered the room. He was always polite to women.

"Jolene, remember Nate Winston, my neighbor and friend?"

Her nostrils flared. I knew what that meant. She had just remembered that he was human. Werewolves were good with scents. But she said nothing, merely gave him a polite nod.

"Hello."

He raised his hand in a polite wave. Nate knew better than

to offer his hand to most of the Weres and Fae who crossed my doorstep. In some cases, it would be taken as an insult. In others, an act of submission. Either way, it just wasn't a good idea.

"So, who's the victim?"

I cleared my throat. "Tygur Jones. He's been sucked dry as dust. I doubt if there's a drop of blood left in his body."

She paled. "Crap. You didn't say it was Tygur. He's big news in the Were community, Lily. This is bad, really bad."

"I know. I have to figure out what to do before word gets out. The minute you lodge an official report, my business might as well be toast."

"Well, it's not like your salon would be the first casualty." Jolene let out a long sigh. "Vampire executions are on the rise and more businesses are closing their doors an hour before sunset. Do you know if Tygur had any bounties on his head?"

I shrugged. "He talked about work, but never anything like that. Tygur liked to leave the details of his life on the doorstep."

She nodded. "Makes sense. So, tell me what happened. The more we know about vampire kills, the better we can design a way to combat them, so don't leave anything out."

I closed my eyes, dredging up the memory. "Tygur's appointment was from seven until nine. He arrived here about ten minutes late—traffic was a bitch tonight. We talked. He undressed and put on his robe. Then, he asked me for a drink. I had forgotten to stock the minibar, so I had to go downstairs to get the scotch."

Jolene glanced up from her tablet. She was taking copious notes. "So you left the room to fix him a drink?"

"Yes. I was here, in the kitchen, when I thought I heard something upstairs. I figured it was probably Tygur. You know, going to the bathroom or something. When I headed back upstairs with both the glass and the bottle, I came to the hall in time to see a black mist ooze out of the room. It headed toward me, but then stopped cold. The temperature in the hall must have dropped twenty degrees in ten seconds. The next moment, the mist vanished through the wall—the one leading to the outside. I caught a whiff of anise. Between that and the mist, I knew it was a vampire."

Vampires smelled of graveyard dust when they first rose, and then their natural scent took on the fragrance of anise. It was rumored their blood tasted like sweet licorice, but I had no clue if it was true, and I wasn't interested in finding out.

Jolene glanced at me. "What about your wards?"

"They're not expired. I just had them redone recently, so I'm totally confused about how it got through."

All the old song and dance about vampires being unable to enter a home without an invitation was just that—an old wives' tale. Vampires could enter any building they wanted, anytime they wanted. Which was why wards were so popular and expensive.

The price went up with the strength. It could cost a fortune to ensure the safety of a shop's customers. Usually, the witches charged less for homes, since everybody had to have them. They made up for the discounts by jacking up the price for businesses. I spent at least 25 percent of my yearly budget on protection.

Jolene set down her tablet. "Then something had to have happened to disturb them. Who do you get your wards from, Lily?"

I shrugged. "Dani makes them for me, and you know how powerful she is. I pay her for quality ingredients too—no cut-rate crap."

Jolene chewed on her lip for a moment. "Right. Well, let's move on. But I suggest you consult her. Get her over here to check them pronto. You have to know where—and how—they short-circuited." She picked up the tablet again. "So, what happened next?"

I stared at the table. "I ran into the room. Tygur was on the floor. I checked for a pulse. That's when I saw the fang marks. He was dead. I checked again just before you came. I panicked, thinking I might have made a mistake but...he's dead." I pressed my lips together.

Jolene waited silently for me to continue.

"There's something else," I added after a moment. "There's a piece of skin missing off his chest. I keep feeling I should know something about that, but I can't seem to remember what."

"Probably because of the shock. When you remember let me know, though I don't know what good it will do. I suppose you'd better take us up to see Tygur now. You haven't called his wife yet, have you?"

The disapproval in her voice bled through. So she still looked down on my lifestyle. I wanted to defend myself, but it was a circular argument for us—no beginning, no end. We'd never agree on the subject.

"Nate, please stay here in the kitchen. Call if you need us." I led Jolene and her partner upstairs. "His wife? You mean he was married?"

"Don't give me that. You *know* he was married, and you know exactly who his wife is. Tygur and Tricia are a major power couple among the Weres. But I assume, by your answer, you haven't done so?"

I sighed. "You'll never understand, will you? Anyway, I don't want to argue. As to telling Tricia…well, given Tygur was murdered in my house wearing nothing but a bathrobe, do you really think I'm going to pick up the phone and call his wife? Give me some credit. I do have some sensitivity. The news will come better from the police. Because while, yes, I *did* know he was married, I'm not sure if he told *her* about *me*."

Most of the Fae were cool with casual sex, but Weres? Not really. Especially the werewolves. Chances were fifty-fifty that Tygur's wife knew about me, but this wasn't the time to find out. And I would never rub her nose in the fact, especially now.

As Jolene and her partner—whose name turned out to be Lucas—examined the body, I wandered over to the window, looking out into the night.

• • •

My house was located in the Blood Night District of Seattle. When the Fae and the Weres had come out of the closet, everything blew up and went to hell. A decade later, the makeup of society was vastly different as we moved to take our rightful place alongside the humans. Met by a minority of vocal and strong humans who hated us, the situation grew bloody and politicians ran for the hills when approached with the subject. Most of them had the foresight to accept the inevitable, and so they generally tried to maintain neutral ground.

Eventually, after a decade of riots, the dust settled. The political landscape had become a very different place. Treaties were set in place, the government grew into a cooperative venture, even though it was an uneasy cooperation, and life settled down for all of us.

Then, the vampires appeared on the scene. And *nobody* was equipped to deal with them.

More treaties were created, hanging in an uneasy balance like the sword of Damocles, but the vamps weren't prone to sticking to agreements. The signed documents might as well have been tissue thin and used to blow a bloody nose on.

In Western Washington, the city of Seattle had absorbed a number of its bedroom communities, forming new districts. Downtown Seattle was routinely called the Blood Night District. Home to the wild-child crowd, it was party central. Unfortunately, the vampires preferred living around us, and it made for an uneasy and dangerous environment.

The Eastside was populated by Fae, with Wynter establishing her court near Woodinville. South, toward SeaTac, was where the Weres tended to congregate. North Seattle was mostly human in makeup, and West Seattle and Alki had gone from being the Ritz to housing the outliers, the poor, and the crazies of all races.

All in all, it was the same city on the surface, with a very different underlying structure.

As for me? I'm Lily Marlene O'Connell, the owner of Lily Bound. My sex salon has catered to the deepest, darkest whims and desires of the paranormal world for years. I get paid to feed on sex—the chi stirred up by lust recharges and energizes me. In return, my clients get anything they desire. A win-win situation all the way around. Except…if I go too far.

There's an old saying: "Bed a succubus, and you'll become her slave. Kiss a succubus, and you'll become a ghost."

Because, truth? I *can* kill with my kiss. My passion is a weapon. I can suck out your breath in a long, luxurious kiss and kill you with a smile on your face. But Weres and Fae? I can drain chi off of them without harming them. They can handle the loss if I stop soon enough.

By opening my business, I ensured that I would be able to feed often, and enough. If I don't, the hunger runs so wild that I can't keep it in check, as it did in most of my past. I have too many memories I'd rather forget, but they added up. Maybe not every month. Or even every year. But my kill list slowly and steadily grew.

So, now, I throw myself into my job. I have to feed in order to keep alive. And to keep the impulse—the urge to take it too far—under control. And so, I give *everything* to my clients.

Unfortunately, with Tygur Jones, my *everything* included a vampire.

CHAPTER 3

"Definitely a vampire kill." Jolene glanced around the room. "You have a measuring tape? I want to see how big this patch of missing skin is."

I nodded, hustling into my bedroom, where I retrieved one from my dresser.

Jolene gave me a long look as she took it. "I never get used to some aspects of this job. The vampire kills are always hard to cope with," she said, a slight tremor in her voice. She measured the wound on his chest. "Five inches by three. Whoever stripped the skin did a clean, neat job of it. This isn't the first time they've done this—it's too clean, professional. Either they have a delicate touch or they were a doctor or a butcher. Whatever the case, *he…she…* our killer has a skilled hand."

"Could it be a woman?" I hadn't entertained that thought.

"Why not? Vampires can mesmerize, remember? The females have as much strength as the males. There's no reason it can't be a woman." She stood up, staring at Tygur. "Can you think of *any* reason why somebody might have wanted a piece of his flesh?"

Shrugging, I sat down on the bed. "I told you, he talks about his job but it's always from the outside in. Never anything that might be sensitive information. I suppose…I should let Wynter know. Some of my people have very odd habits. Stealing flesh might be a fetish for some."

Jolene shuddered. "Oh, *that's* something to look forward to, all right. I don't like to speak ill of your people, but Wynter's a freak and everybody knows it. She's so cold she makes the dead look warm. She also doesn't cotton up very cozy to Weres. Go ahead and talk to her if you want, but I'm not going to be coming along for the ride. I wouldn't be able to convince my supervisor that I should spend the time on it, anyway. Seriously, they've cut the budget for vampire investigations down to the bare bone. We get almost no time allotted to these cases."

"Do you think it's lack of financing, or that the Deadfather might be pulling the strings?"

That was the wrong question to ask. Jolene pressed her lips together and stood, packing her things back in her kit.

"Go talk to Wynter. Find out what you can. But since you saw a black mist and smelled anise, I'm reporting this as a vampire execution. There's no doubt given the holes on his neck and lack of blood. The coroner will verify it, of course." She hesitated. "You can really get an audience with the queen?"

I nodded. Wynter had relocated from the United Kingdom to the US. She lived on the Eastside, near Woodinville. Her sister, Summerlyn, had relocated to Australia.

The Fae Nation was as crazy as they come, and I was part of the whole wild bunch. I loved it, though I tried to keep out of the politics as much as possible. Wynter was manipulative and calculating and not exactly fond of anybody outside of her own realm. But I had a badge to the inner court, thanks to my mother making certain I was received when I was a little girl. I did what I had to in order to maintain my status as one of the insiders.

"I'm recognized by the court."

"Good. Because I doubt if I am." Weres and Fae generally did not get along.

"All right. I'll talk to her and let you know what I find out, but you owe me one. Meanwhile, I'll ask Dani if she knows of any spells that witches use that might require human flesh. I wouldn't put it past them that the answer'll be a big fat *yes*. Dani's kind scare me more than vampires, at times."

Nate was my buddy. Dani—Danielle Halloran—was my best friend. She was a witch who had been married to a man named Greg Fallow, until he had been caught and turned into a vampire.

That had, of course, ended the marriage, and left her teetering on the edge for a long time. It had been several years ago that it happened, but she hated vampires now. She seldom mentioned Greg, but I knew he haunted her dreams and memories.

Jolene let out a snort. "Witches scare the hell out of me, too. Weres don't get along with magic very well. Okay, I'll ask Lucas to call in the body-bag crew. We'll get Tygur out of your house and contact Tricia. This is already headed into the unsolved files. I've noted it as a vampire kill and the coroner will authenticate. That's the best the department can do. Nobody can control the bloodsuckers. We're trying to convince the Deadfather that it's in his best interests to encourage his people to work with us rather than against us, but he's a hard nut to crack. As hard as Wynter. The vamps are slower to change than the Fae."

I walked her downstairs, and offered her a cup of tea. She asked for a latte, so Nate fired up the espresso machine while Jolene asked Lucas to wait on the porch for the coroner.

"Be careful. The vampire might still be around, looking for more. Or it might have called one of its buddies," she said as Lucas headed out into the cold.

The coroner was a formality, really. The moment an execution was labeled as vampiric, the body would be consecrated and buried. A grave watcher would guard the grave to make certain the victim didn't rise, which happened anywhere from immediately to five days after death. After five days, the victim was safe and considered fully dead. There were guardians in every cemetery waiting to put the new vampires down. The Deadfather didn't like it, but he hadn't moved to stop the practice.

Jolene leaned her back against the door.

"I didn't want Lucas to hear what I'm going to tell you next because I still don't know if he's safe or not—too many cops are plants now and I'm walking a thin line due to an incident I really don't want to get into right now, especially with you. But I think you should run this by Archer Desmond. There's something about Tygur's death that isn't tracking quite right to me. My department won't be able to do diddlysquat because…well, vampires. But I think I can convince Archer to take a look into it because of the missing skin."

"Who's Archer Desmond?"

"A chaos demon who runs a PI firm. He does a lot of work on the side for the unit. I'd like you to talk to him, if you will. He'll probably do the first look pro bono, but after that, if you want to continue, you'll have to hire him yourself."

Lovely. Just what I needed—another way to spend money. "I already offered to talk to Wynter, but now you want me to talk to a chaos demon? You really believe in payback, don't you?"

She ducked her head. "You know it's not like that."

I let out a long sigh. "Yeah, I know. But *chaos demons*? They're such a barrel of laughs."

"I know, I know…but he's good at what he does." She softened. "So, how are you?"

"It goes…same old, same old." I hesitated. Maybe it wasn't the wisest thing to do, but I caught her gaze and asked, "So, are you seeing anybody?"

She blinked, then slowly nodded. "Yes, actually. I am."

"A werewolf?"

"No, he's…he's human."

At my double take, she shrugged. "What did you expect?" But there was an edge to her voice that told me she was bristling. No doubt she had taken a lot of flack from her friends. Weres weren't big on interspecies marriage or courtship, either. In fact, Weres made conservatives look liberal.

"I just…I just wondered. I want you to be happy, Jolene. I miss our friendship." And I realized that it was true—I missed hanging out with Jolene, having a beer in the evenings with her while we sat on the porch talking about our day.

She must have caught my mood, because she let out a shuddering sigh. "I miss it too. Maybe…maybe somehow we can get back there. Or to a new place. I'll call you later this week. We'll talk." She glanced over at the window and suddenly, the Jolene I remembered vanished and the cop reappeared.

"Okay, the coroner is here. We'll get Tygur out of your house. Strengthen your wards and find the weak links. If you're interested, call me for Archer's number—I don't have it on me." And with that, she got back to work.

After the corpse wagon had come and gone, and Jolene and Lucas cleared out, Nate and I sat at the table, silently binging on cookies and tea. Nate graciously avoided asking any questions. He had been there during the big blowup, and he knew better than drag it back over the coals.

But seeing Jolene had disconcerted me. I wanted to tell myself our friendship had been a train wreck—and it had been a spectacular one—but it was hard to let go of someone I cared about.

At least the interruption had taken my mind off the hunger for a little while, but now it slammed home again. I needed to feed. If Nate left, I could head into the streets. I was about to ask him to go home when the phone rang.

Relieved, I grabbed my phone and glanced at the caller's name. *Dani Halloran.*

"Dani, thank gods you called. I need to talk to you, the sooner the better."

But she overrode me. "Lily? We have a problem."

Uh oh. She didn't sound happy. Dani was Irish, with a temper to match, and when she was upset, heads rolled. Sometimes, other body parts rolled right along with them.

"Just what I need. What's going on?"

"Rebecca's dead. She's been murdered."

My stomach lurched. Rebecca was a member of Dani's coven. "Dani, come over now."

She paused, then said, "Before I do, I need to tell you something else. I've heard rumors on the street and I think they may play into Rebecca's death."

A premonition swept over me. Whatever she had to tell me

was sweeping in with trouble and mayhem and death. I felt like I did before a thunderstorm hit, when the air was charged.

I steeled myself. "What did you hear?"

"Charles escaped. They think he made his way back here to Seattle. I'll be over in ten minutes." And with that she hung up. I stared at the phone in my hand, very still.

The Souljacker was back. Which meant that a whole lot of people, including Dani, Nate, and myself, were in danger. Because Charles, aka the Souljacker, was stark, raving mad. And the Souljacker? Was a vampire.

CHAPTER 4

The *Souljacker*. My stomach lurched. I slowly set my phone on the table, staring at it like it had suddenly turned into a snake. "Nate, you'd better stay until Dani gets here. She has some news that you should hear too."

Nate refilled our mugs. "Something tells me I'm not going to enjoy this little coffee klatch, am I right?"

I let out a soft laugh. "I'm afraid you're right. Wait here, and don't fall asleep. I want you awake and on your game while I'm in the other room."

I headed into the parlor, ready to open up a long chapter of my life I thought I had left behind. All that remained from a lifetime that seemed so very long ago were my memories, and the mementos in a big oaken chest. After closing the door behind me, I knelt by the massive chest. Four feet long, three feet high, and two feet in depth, the trunk had been a gift from someone I had once loved too dearly. I hadn't opened it for seventy-five years.

I sat down on the floor, cross-legged. The key to the chest dangled from a charm bracelet that I never took off.

As I fiddled with the clasp, Whisky came running into the room. Sleek, with taut muscles, his coloring made him look a lot like a snow leopard, and his eyes were luminous and blue. His name was a misnomer, tricking people into thinking he was just one hell of a big, silly cat.

"You play your part pretty good, bub." I scritched him behind the ears. Mr. Whiskers purred. He put on a good act of being skittish around strangers. Truth was, he had a long history, and a lot of secrets. I'd saved his fuzzy butt on a cold November night six hundred years ago, and he had been my companion since then.

Now, he nudged my leg. I tickled his chin. "Listen, I know what I said about the chest, but we're in trouble. I have to do this."

He let out a *purp* and gazed up at me.

I shook my head. "Sorry, bub. You can't do much good on this one. But do me a favor?" He gazed at me, waiting. "Be careful, please? Vampires don't like being anywhere near cats, but that doesn't guarantee they won't try to hurt you. And…oh, when Dani gets here, hang around and listen, okay?"

With a chattering sound, he padded off toward the kitchen.

I fit the key into the lock and opened it. As I swung back the lid, it exhaled slowly. I stared at the tray lined with red velvet. It was filled with letters, photos, and other mementos, most from the days when I had remained undercover, before the world knew my kind actually existed.

One of the pictures caught my eye, and I froze, staring at the haunted face looking back at me. I had tried to forget him for so long, but he still wandered through my dreams. *Marsh.* He'd been…more than I wanted to remember right now. Biting my lip, I deliberately turned the picture over. Too much baggage and too many heartaches waited down that fork of memory lane. If I was smart, I'd rip up the photograph. But then, if I could bring myself to get rid of it, I would have done so years ago.

Shaking my thoughts away, I felt along the sides of the tray until I found the indentation containing a recessed button. As I pressed it, a *click* sounded, and the tray unlocked from its position. I lifted it out and set it on the floor.

Beneath the tray, the rest of the box was full. And there was what I was looking for, right on top. Slowly I lifted out the black leather sheath, and withdrew a silver dagger from the scabbard, holding it up to the light. The blade gleamed. Forged from the scales of a silver dragon, the dagger sang, the metal smooth and satin-like under my fingers. It had been a long time since we'd talked, but I could still feel the murmur of magic running through the knife into my hands. My mother had given it to me before she died, and it had served me well.

I set the dagger aside to shift through the other items in the trunk. First, the leg strap that went with the blade and sheath, and then wrist cuffs—also forged from silver dragon scales. Together with my pentacle, the dagger and cuffs were a matching set.

I flashed back to the years when the roads had been no more than winding dirt paths through vast fields. When small towns and villages, rather than large cities, were the norm, and women traveling alone learned to journey unseen and unheard. The wrist cuffs weren't particularly protective, but they helped me aim my weapons and strengthened my grip. They had enabled me to survive during a time when I had to protect myself on the road. A time long before cops and locks and wards and the future had become part of my life.

And right now, with the Souljacker on the loose, I needed to jog those memories, to remember what I had once been. Replacing the tray in the chest, I closed and locked it. With a soft *shush*, the chest once again went back to guarding my past, and I was ready to rock.

I strapped the dagger to my thigh, smiling softly. "It's been a long time since we were on this road together," I whispered, unfolding my legs as I stood.

The moment Dani had told me about Rebecca, I *knew* the vampire that had been in my house was the Souljacker. I had no idea why, but with the way he had paused in the hall, I knew that he had been targeting both Tygur and me. I reached for my pentacle, closing my palm around the pendant. He hadn't counted on my dragon-scale pentacle—the one thing I owned that even a vampire couldn't get past.

The doorbell rang and I hurried out to answer it. That would be Dani. It was time to figure out how our past had come to intrude on our present.

• • •

I first met Danielle Halloran the day I moved into the Blood Night District. I ran into her literally and creamed her car. I was usually a good driver, but I was tired that day; I wanted to finally unlock the door of my new home and be done with moving, so I wasn't paying attention.

On the other hand, Dani was barreling down the street too fast. She had a lead foot and admitted to being a speed demon. As I turned the corner, she shot through the stop sign. While technically *she* crashed into *me*, my car survived and hers didn't. Together, we turned her vintage VW beetle into a crumpled mess.

Dani escaped with a broken arm, and somehow, during the mess of medical bills, we realized that we hit it off. She wrote me a check for damages, and we started getting together for coffee several times a week. Within a month, we were best buds. As an added benefit, she stopped driving like a maniac, and I made it a point to look both ways at intersections, even when I had the right of way.

Danielle Halloran was five-three at her tallest. Plump and curvy, she ran the Wandering Eye—a witchcraft shop. Her hair was shoulder length and smooth, black as ink. Irish by blood, she had a temper to match. I often joked to Nate that Dani might look soft and huggable, but woe to the person who laid a finger on her without her permission.

Now she was waiting at the door, a stark look on her face. Dani handled crises well. She was essentially fearless to a fault. But tonight? She looked like she'd tangled with a ghost and had come out on the wrong side of the battle.

I blinked. "You look like I feel. Get your pretty ass in here and sit down." As she shrugged off her velvet jacket and hung it on the peg by the kitchen door, I noticed the new dress. Dani had an eye for fashion, except that she created trends rather than following them. "New?"

"Yes, you like?" Dani slipped into a chair, looking exhausted. She was wearing a shimmering, plum-colored dress. With a deep, plunging neckline on the bodice, and the skirt cinched at her waist and flared out. She'd paired it with a silver-studded black belt and chunky heels. The heels gave her a good four extra inches of height.

"I like it a lot. It wouldn't fit my style, but it's gorgeous on you." I was five-ten, and while I was curvy in my own way, my figure was more athletic than anything else. I envied hourglass figures, but then, I could run without a bra, which Dani couldn't. "Nate, pour Dani some tea?"

As he filled the kettle again and replenished the cookies, Dani set her huge handbag on the floor next to her seat. The smile vanished from her face as, one finger at a time, she removed her gloves, laying them neatly over the handbag.

Nate set the tea in front of her and gave her a quick kiss on the cheek. She air kissed him in return. Dani never went out without her makeup. While her lipstick was smudge proof, she had perfected the art of the air kiss and golf clap for use with some of the social elite who came to her for tarot readings.

"Hey, gorgeous." Nate winked at her.

"How's it hanging, chiphead?" Dani winked back, but her sparkly nature was subdued.

"Low and lonely." He sighed. "Low and luh-ohhhn-leee."

I motioned for Nate to top off my mug and, making sure the door was locked, sat down.

Dani's gaze went directly to my dagger. "You've been in the chest." It was a statement, not a question. While I had never shown her the blade, I had told her about it.

"Yeah, we're going to need all the help we can get. My wards are fucked up, Dani."

"What do you mean? I made those myself."

"There's a problem. Something happened to them. Dani, tonight a vampire got through the wards and killed Tygur Jones in my salon. I saw it leave through the wall when I went back upstairs after getting a drink. It started to come after me, then stopped and fled. I know the only reason I'm not dead too is my pendant. Dragon silver trumps a vampire every time."

Dani paled, and that on top of her porcelain complexion made her look like smooth alabaster. "Vampire? You're certain?"

"I smelled anise. And the black shadow passed through the wall."

"Lily, was there anything...*missing* from Tygur?"

I frowned. "You mean was he robbed? His clothes and wallet were still here—"

"No, I mean was..." She let out a sigh. "When they found Rebecca, a strip of skin was missing from her shoulder. The shoulder where Charles tattooed her spirit leopard. The skin had been carefully excised, and the tattoo was gone." She leaned forward. "Tygur was part of our group, wasn't he? He had a tattoo, didn't he?"

"Damn it, now I remember what I was trying to tell Jolene."

Nate was leaning forward, a worried expression on his face. "Which was?"

"Tygur had a tattoo. And yes, the skin had been flayed from his body. Jolene said a professional had to have done it. Or someone who had a steady hand and plenty of practice. Remember, Tygur was with us when we all decided to get ink during that big party when we were...celebrating Greg's victory. It was his mother's name tattooed on a rose. That was before he became one of my clients."

And *that* was what I had forgotten.

Dani pressed her hands against the table. I suspected my mention of Greg's name hadn't helped matters. "This can't be a coincidence. The Souljacker escaped two days ago. That gave him two days to hide himself in Seattle. And now we have two dead ex-clients of his? Both members of the India Ink Club."

Nate sputtered. "Wait just a minute! Charles is still alive? You told me he was dead, Lily. Where the hell did he escape from and why did you lie to me?" He looked like he might throw up.

"I'm sorry. I just..." There was no good answer except that I knew how terrified Nate had been when Charles was turned. Since he had been locked away, it seemed easier to let Nate believe the Souljacker was dead. After all, WestcoPsi never let anybody out.

"WestcoPsi is the West Coast Psionic Asylum—it's a few hours away from Seattle, toward the mountains. It's for nonhumans who are considered criminally insane. They hardly ever take vampires because they're so hard to contain, so I have no idea why they let Charles in, but once you're there, you never get out."

"Unless you escape," Dani mumbled.

"So they sent Charles there after he murdered that entire family? But the cops stake bloodsuckers who are mass murderers, if they can catch them. Now you tell me that he's not only alive, but on the loose?"

I reached out, about to use my powers to calm him, but stopped myself. Dani noticed his discomfort and leaned over to rest a hand on his arm.

"I'm sorry Nate. We didn't tell you because...well, he was locked up, and we just wanted to put it behind us. I only found out that he escaped about an hour ago." She stroked his arm for a moment and he began to breathe normally again. Dani might not be a succubus, but when she put her mind to it, she could make people relax.

"You said Rebecca is dead, too? And that her tattoo was excised just like Tygur's?" Nate leaned his elbows on the table, staring at his hands, anger crowding out any sign of his usual good nature. "She was nice. I liked her."

Dani ducked her head, her long lashes fluttering softly. "Yeah. She was killed last night, but they just found her about two hours ago." She glanced over at me. "I don't even want to know what he could be thinking."

"This is leading down the rabbit hole. A long, dark, dank, ter-rifying pit. And we really don't want to go tumbling in." I glanced outside at the sky. Though it wasn't full dark—the snow put up too much of a reflection against the silver clouds for that—I really didn't want to think about what was waiting out there in the night for us.

Apparently, Nate didn't want to think about it, either. "Before we jump to conclusions, we need to calm down. Maybe...maybe we're wrong. This could just be one hell of a wild coincidence. They do happen, you know."

"Maybe, but you *know* this isn't one of those times." Dani shook her head. "Face reality now and it might save our skins, because you know the cops won't have any hope of protecting us, even if they had the resources to guard us 24/7."

"Let me think," I said, holding up my hands. "Yes, I do think this is the Souljacker's work, but we have to know for sure. Tell you what. Jolene promised to hook me up with a PI. He might be able to help us out. Because Rebecca and Tygur? Their murders are closed cases. The cops just don't have the ability to handle vampire kills, no matter how much they want to. Jolene pretty much told me that if we want any more answers, the ball's in our court."

"You called Jolene?" Dani's voice was soft. She knew all about my friendship with Jolene and why it had gone south.

I nodded, biting my lip. "It wasn't an easy call to make, either."

I glanced down at my leg. Beneath my jeans, a beautiful phoenix in blue and orange trailed down from the top of my left hip to encircle my ankle with its tail. It brought out my inner self. When I looked at it, I felt like all my masks had been lifted. "So…the Souljacker escaped…"

Silently, Nate pulled up his sleeve. On his left bicep, a brilliant purple skull shimmered under the light, encircled by a sleeping gray kitten. Dani shrugged the shoulder strap of her dress down, exposing a forest nymph on her right breast. It held a bottle of poison in one hand and a glowing orb in the other.

We sat there, tattoos exposed, in silence.

Yes, we *all* knew Charles and he knew us, intimately. He had been able to reach inside, to contact our very essences, and coax them out to blossom on the flesh. That's how he got his nickname. The Souljacker could jack right into your soul. In some ways, he was the one person who would ever know you as well as you knew yourself. Sometimes better.

"You think that the private eye can help us find out what's going on?" She pulled her strap back up and picked up her tea. "I suppose…given Rebecca's death along with Tygur's…you should call him. After you do, we'll try to figure out why your wards failed."

"Yeah. There's just one thing. He's a chaos demon."

Dani carefully sat her cup down, staring at me. "You have to be joking."

"I'm afraid not. His name is Archer Desmond, and he's a chaos demon." Before she could light into me, I put in a call to Jolene to get Archer's number.

"I can't use the department's funds to pay him, but tell Archer I told you to call and that you're my friend. He'll cut you a deal. If he finds out anything…the department could use whatever information you might dig up. I know it's not fair, given you're paying for it but…"

"Sure thing. Hey, Jolene…I found out something." I didn't want to worry her. Jolene had enough on her plate and I didn't like stirring up old memories, but I had to tell her. She was wearing a pair of scales on her back. She was in danger, too. "The Souljacker escaped from WestcoPsi. We think he's back in town. Dani just came over with the news that Rebecca's dead."

There was silence on the other end. Then, "Fuck. Just, fuck."

"Make sure your wards are strong. When they found Rebecca, her tattoo was missing. She had been skinned like Tygur—and I remember that the flesh missing from him? Had the Souljacker's tattoo on it."

Again, silence. Then she said, "I'll see what I can find out. Communication with other precincts is dicey, so I'm not expecting much. We're dealing with a lot of petty power plays. But I'll do what I can. Talk to you tomorrow."

She hung up without a goodbye and I stared at my phone, punching the off button.

Dani and Nate quickly segued into a conversation about growing tomatoes as I punched in Archer Desmond's number. He was out, so I left a message and asked him to call me at the first available opportunity, day or night.

"Okay then." I slid my phone in my pocket. "Let's go check the wards."

And with that, we trooped outside, into the night.

• • •

My property spread across what had originally been four lots. I had close to an acre of land, most of it sprawling in the massive backyard, unheard of in the city. But thanks to my years spent wandering the world, I had accumulated a hefty bank account, and I decided to plunge into the real estate market. I selected a residential area that had held a small, abandoned apartment building. The neighborhood was run down, but at the time I bought it, the vamps weren't out of the closet, and the property values were low, given the rubble and disrepair the riots had left in the area. So I bought the land, tore down the building, and built my house. I'd encircled the entire place with stone. A friend had owed me a big favor and he had access to a quarry, so he'd built the fence to pay off his debt.

The stone wall was four feet high, and to that I had added a thin strand of silver chain encircling the area. It helped in protecting against the vamps, but I'd skimped on the entrance, a simple metal gate. To either side of the gate, on the inside, stood two pedestals. I'd planted garlic bushes around them. During the autumn and winter, I hung braided garlic around the house that I'd picked from them.

After the vamps had come out, and when attacks grew more daring, I began paying Dani to create the wards for my land, including the line of runic wards in the walkway leading from the front sidewalk up to the house. They would sound the alarm if a vamp tried to cross them, but their reach only rose up about ten feet from the ground. In mist form, a vampire could have avoided all the wards until they reached the house. I had long ago faced the fact that there was no way to fully prepare against their attacks.

"It's too dark to look at the wards on the outer gates, but let's check the house." Dani examined the runes on the front-porch wall. "Damn it. I found the crack. Or at least one of them. He must have crossed the wards in mist form till he got to the doorway, because all of the sidewalk wards are still intact. But they end at the porch steps. The back-door ward seems tight. But here… see this sigil?" She pointed to one of the runes by the side of the front entrance.

I leaned in for a look. At first, it looked normal to me, but then I realized there was something amiss with it. The rune had been scratched, by something sharp and big.

"What happened?"

"Somehow, the rune got defaced. See this line here? It doesn't belong there. Whoever carved it into the ward managed to disrupt the magic. This is why I recommended you have me make it in stone and affix it to the wood. It's harder to alter."

I thought for a moment. "But the vampire would have to still be in mist at this point, given the sidewalk runes are still active. If the ward had been intact, in order to deface it, wouldn't he have to manifest in his physical form? To do that, the ward would have had to be damaged already, right? And could he even touch it?"

She scratched her nose. "No, he couldn't have been the one to damage it. So that means that this ward has been out of commission for a while. There's no telling how long, or who did it, but the fact remains that you've been a sitting duck for some time now. Hell, if some delivery guy was carrying a big package that had a hard edge, it could have scraped against it. Or it could be rowdy teens out to raise a little havoc."

I frowned. "Then how did the vampire know he could get in, if the wards at the front are still effective?"

Nate was staring at the door. "My guess is that he wanted in bad enough to check all entrances. And he lucked out and found a weakness."

Dani nodded. "Nate's right. And didn't Charles come to visit at one time? He knew where you lived, and he knew something about the layout of your house. Did you give him a tour?"

I flashed back to the one time I'd had him over to visit. I'd been so proud of my salon, and he asked if he could see the set up of the house. He said he was thinking of working out of his home at some point and wanted to see how I did it.

"Right. I had him over for tea." I stared at the damaged ward. "If that ward hadn't been damaged, he wouldn't have been able to get through. And Tygur would still be alive." I felt horrible. All wards came with the warning that you should check them once a week, but I had neglected to do so. Dani had been nagging me for the past three months to let her come over and recalibrate them if need be, but I kept putting it off, reassuring her that I trusted her work.

"I wonder who was messing around with my wards."

"Kids screwing around. Somebody with a grudge against you…hell, it could have been a squirrel gnawing at the wood. Who knows? The fact is, it happened. I can't replace it right now, but I can patch it. However, the ward will be weak and the magic will dispel within a day or two. Once I go home tonight, I'll start in on the replacements. We'll have to redo the entire network, because they're all interdependent and matching the magical energy is difficult. Nate, we need to check your wards too."

I glanced over at Dani. "Did Rebecca have wards up?"

Pale in the moonlight, she nodded. "Yes. But she and her husband recently renovated their place, and my guess is that it disturbed the magic and she didn't think to fix them again."

Nate glanced across the fence. "Is it safe to check my house now? Shouldn't we wait till morning?"

Dani glanced at the sky, then nodded. "I agree. Let me tighten this ward up, and it should hold through the night. Tomorrow, I'll come out and take a look at your place, Nate. I'll check on mine too. Then we figure out what the hell to do."

We kept watch while she worked her magic. I wasn't sure just what she was doing, but a faint light began to emanate from her hands and flow into the wood surrounding the runes. I looked away, focusing on the surrounding area, hoping that she finished before the vampire came back. If it *was* Charles and he *was* after all of us, then we were in danger till he was caught. Vampires were predators, and once they set their sights on their quarry, they were like bloodhounds—grabbing the scent and keeping a firm hold on their target.

"Done," she said after a few minutes. "It's jury-rigged, but it will hold for the night. He won't be able to get in through the upper floors either; I sent a shot of juice all the way around. But Lily, to make certain, with the new runes I should create a lightning rod—it will bathe your entire house from the rooftop down in protection."

I opened the door and they trooped through. "How much will that run me?"

She shrugged apologetically. "Ten thousand, but it will last a good year or two at the very least. The components are pricey as hell and will take me a few days to gather, so we'll have to keep amping up your wards till I can get the new set created."

"How long will it take to make them?"

She dropped into the nearest chair, looking tired. "Three days to prepare. I need to cast it under the full sun, so I'll have to catch a flight to someplace sunny for a weekend. That's after I order the components. I figure I can have it up and running in a month at the latest. Hopefully a lot sooner. Until then, I suggest you buy premade wards for the doors, hang silver at every entrance, and cook a lot of Italian food."

That made me laugh. After I caught my breath, I said, "I needed that. I'll start a pot of spaghetti in the morning." As I sobered, I let out a long sigh. "If you could start right away, I'd appreciate it."

Dani pulled out her phone and opened her calendar. She stared at it for a moment. "I can start this week. Meanwhile, I think Nate should stay here tonight. It's too dangerous tonight for him to go home, just in case there are problems."

I flashed Dani a murderous look. I needed to feed and having a handsome, sweet human on the premises wasn't going to help matters much.

She caught my look and gave me a subtle shake of the head. "Your pentacle is what saved you, Lily. Silver dragon scales? Strong enough to keep back most vampires. But dragons are scarce nowadays. By the way, while we're on the subject, dragon silver is so precious that I'd make certain you don't tell anybody else what your pendant, knife, or wristlets are made of."

"Yeah, I thought of that. I'd be the target of every person in the world who would either want to sell them to the highest bidder, or who's so paranoid about vampires that they would want them for themselves."

Nate, who had been listening to us without saying a word, chimed in. "I hope you don't mind me crashing at your place. I don't really have any other place to go and I don't remember when I last checked my wards. I'm afraid I don't keep track."

"Doesn't anybody understand that magical runes and spells have a life expectancy? That they can expire?" Dani let out an exasperated sigh.

I really didn't want the temptation of having Nate within arm's reach, but I couldn't turn him out for the night, and I wasn't about to send him home with Dani. If he slept here, I'd slap one of my wrist braces on him for the night to keep him safe. I'd tie it around his neck if I had to.

"You can stay, no problem." Suddenly tired, my shoulders slumped, and I leaned my elbows on the table with a long sigh. The hunger was rumbling deep and I felt wiped out. The need for energy was starting to loom in my mind. Nate was looking better and better. When my hunger got the better of me, it made everybody seem more attractive.

Dani frowned as she watched me, her eyes crinkling at the corners. She motioned to Nate. "I need to have a girl talk with Lily. Go watch sports or whatever it is you men do."

He amenably grabbed a handful of cookies, his tea, and

headed toward the living room. As soon as he was gone, she stood and crossed to stand behind my chair.

"Okay, missy. When was the last time you fed? And I'm not talking about cookies and tea." She leaned down, brushing my hair back as her hands rested gently on my shoulders.

I swallowed—hard. Dani was voluptuous and sexual in a way that I responded to. I turned my head to find myself staring at her boobs. Her cleavage was deep, her neckline low, and I fought the urge to reach out and stroke them.

"I fasted the past few days because Tygur likes it when I'm hungry. He paid for an extra-intense session, which meant I haven't taken any other appointments the past two days. And the last client before Tygur was feeling a little run down so I rationed myself carefully."

My voice felt husky, like when I was servicing a client. Then, I realized where Dani was going with this. She'd done this before, when I forgot to eat and was starting to lose it.

"No, I'm not feeding on you again."

"You damned well better. If you don't take the edge off, Nate won't be safe around you. And you can't go out tonight, dragon-silver protection or not. Not with the Souljacker out there. All it would take is a couple of thugs to hold you down and strip them off you." Her eyes were so very inviting, and her lips shimmered crimson. I couldn't take my eyes off them.

"You're making this very difficult," I whispered.

She lowered her voice. "As I intend. You know I can handle it. We've done this before." She leaned closer, her perfume swirling around me in a tantalizing mist.

"I don't feed off friends." I had made that rule early on in my life, but over the centuries, I'd had to break it time and again in order to keep from losing control and going all succubus on the nearest stranger. Ever since I settled down, I'd managed to keep it from happening except for three times, and Dani had been there for me each time. "Dani, you know how I feel—"

"Yes, and how you feel is all too apparent right now. You're about to go ballistic. When you do, the aftermath isn't going to be pretty."

Abruptly, she walked over to the kitchen door and peeked into the living room. Satisfied, she softly closed the door again and sauntered back over to me.

"Nate's watching television. He won't interrupt us. We have no idea when Archer Desmond will return your call. Don't put Nate in danger."

I knew she was right. I needed to eat, and I needed it now. And if she left me alone with Nate and my hormones raced out of control, I couldn't guarantee his safety. Making my decision, I stood and stalked her back against the wall. She let out a low laugh.

Wrapping my arms around her, I caressed her butt, then leaned down to press my lips against the top of her breasts. She gasped as I opened myself up, letting my glamour run free. I slid one knee between her legs, the smooth folds of her dress making a swishing sound against my jeans.

Sliding her arms around my waist, she sought my lips and I crushed her mouth with mine. As my tongue gently darted between her lips, I began to feed, absorbing the essence of her arousal, radiating in the heat growing between us. The chi flowed from her in a steady stream, slaking my need. There was no need for sex—though I would have happily fucked her right there. Dani ran deep magic, and she was able to channel that magic into her kiss. My mind began to clear, and I realized I'd had enough to take the edge off the worst of my hunger.

Just then, the door opened and Nate entered the kitchen. The moment he saw us, he stopped dead in his tracks, staring. Then, raising one eyebrow, he skirted our tryst and headed over to the refrigerator, rummaging in it till he found a soda.

I broke away, stroking Dani's cheek as I did so. "Thanks." There was no way to make that one word convey how grateful I was.

She smiled, tilting her head to the side. "Not a problem, Lily.

I'm running more than enough mana lately. Though I want some protein now."

Energy, mana, chi…they all came down to the same thing: life force. Witches like Dani ran an extraordinary amount of energy through their systems and bodies and were particularly attractive to succubi and incubi.

I was about to attempt a fumbled explanation to Nate when my phone rang. Grateful for the interruption, I picked it up after glancing at the caller ID. *Archer Desmond.*

"Well, here we go. Let's see if he can help us."

Back to business, Dani soberly returned to the table as Nate handed her a slice of cheese. "Yeah, because we sure as hell need some guidance. And maybe a few prayers."

"You can say that again." And with that, I answered the phone.

CHAPTER 5

The next morning, Nate had already left for work by the time I came downstairs. A box of donuts sat on the table, and the coffee was hot and waiting.

I glanced out the window. We were safe until sundown again. I had made an appointment with Archer Desmond for five that evening—the earliest he could pencil me in.

Archer's voice had been deep and something about it sounded awfully familiar, but I knew I hadn't met him before unless he had been incognito. I made it a rule to steer clear of demons, and chaos demons in particular. They were few and far between, and chaos and mayhem followed them like pins to a magnet. The last thing I needed in my life was more chaos. But if Jolene said he could help, then I trusted her.

I glanced at my calendar. I had no clients today. I never scheduled more than three or four sessions per week, and I always left a day after my appointments with Tygur because he usually wore me out. He was one of the few who could. With a sigh, I realized I had better not schedule any more sessions until the new wards were in place.

I decided to call Dani and ask if she wanted to go shopping with me—a good excuse to make sure she was okay and that nothing had happened through the night. She had texted me when she got home safe, but still, I had slept uneasily.

"You want to meet me at White Tower Center? Tygur's death notwithstanding, I have errands to run, and an appointment with Archer Desmond this afternoon. I'd love it if you came with me for moral support. Call me superstitious, but it feels safer to talk about a crazed vampire during the daylight hours."

"I'll meet you at Little Bart's Food Court at noon. I might as well pick up some of the spell components I need that my own store doesn't carry, so I'll see you there."

Making sure my necklace was hidden beneath my turtleneck, and my dagger strapped to my thigh, hidden by a knee-length leather jacket, I headed out.

• • •

My car was an ecological disaster zone, but I loved the old gas guzzler. It cost me a small fortune to keep it running, but there was no way I was going to get rid of it. The Barrons Impanala was a two-door convertible—black with glittery flames streaking down the sides. Gaudy as hell, and it tore up the roads with gear-grinding speed, but an old friend had left it to me in his will. It was one of my few remaining links to the past.

The Overpass Trains were running at full capacity as I zipped past the stations. I hated the crowding on mass transit, but it *had* freed up the roads. As I sped along the expressway, I thought again about how much Seattle had changed since I first got here. I tried to limit my visits to the past—memory wasn't always a welcome companion—but the Souljacker's escape had brought it to land squarely in front of me.

I'd first arrived in Seattle in 1970. Of course, back then no one knew I was a succubus. I had been as in the closet just like everybody else who wasn't human. Then, many years later, when we Fae and the Weres had made ourselves known, everything went to hell for a decade or so. And it wasn't just in Seattle—no, the turmoil had been worldwide. Now, things had settled into a new normal, but the upshot was that the country felt composed of a thousand different kingdoms, each with its own petty ruler.

The Blood Night District extended over much of downtown Seattle. A mishmash, our district was a haven for those who really didn't belong anywhere else. It was dangerous and gritty, but despite the decay and abandoned buildings, the area felt like it was thriving and alive. We were thrash in an elevator-music society.

As I pulled into the parking lot at the White Tower Center, I tried to shake away the gloom. I felt like a cloud was following me, and the image of Tygur sprawled on my floor had burned itself into my mind. With a shudder, I tried to wipe it away, grabbed my purse, made sure my car was locked, and headed to the market.

White Tower Center. Located below the Underground demarcation line—where the entrance to Underground Seattle was—and directly above the Ports, the shopping center was truly the supernatural Pike Place Market. Some humans came here, mostly to find exotic ingredients and to say they had toured the center, but mostly Fae and Weres shopped in the multitude of stores.

One thing was for sure: shopping centers were just about the same no matter where you went or what your race. Whether you were Fae, Were, or human, you still needed to shop and eat and wear clothes and buy furniture.

I stopped in at Hilda's, a clothing store, to see if she had my new jeans. I liked Limeys, a brand that hugged my butt in a way no other brand could. Woven from dyed hemp, they had been inexpensive until they caught on and became trendy. They were extremely comfortable and flexible. As I approached the counter, Hilda herself was manning the pay station. She smiled when she saw me, but I detected a wary note in her aura, a hint of protection magic.

I leaned on the counter. "My jeans in yet?"

She nodded. "How many pair did you want? I managed to get in seven. They're becoming so popular it's hard to get hold of them. They're a new status symbol, you know."

"Don't remind me." I tended to stay one step ahead of the trends, and just as I was settled in, comfortably liking something, it became so popular that I lost interest. "How much are they running today? And how many do you have in my size?"

Hilda had my size on file. I spent a lot of money at her store. "Four pairs, and I've had to mark them up to ninety-nine dollars."

Crap. That was a good ten dollars more per pair than last time. "Give me all four. They're my go-to jeans." I paused, catching her gaze. She was glancing over her shoulder as though she were nervous. "Something wrong?"

"Just a second." Hilda peeked around the corner. "Just making sure nobody will overhear us."

My curiosity was piqued. "Why?"

"Because I don't want to be spreading this around any further than it's already gone." Leaning close, she said, "My dear, I've been hearing some scuttlebutt with your name attached. I don't know how much to believe, and it's none of my business, but if I were you I'd do my best to avoid Tricia Jones for awhile. I hear she's on the lookout for you."

Oh, hell. Tygur's wife was also a weretiger. Meaning dangerous, and now, pissed out of her mind. Grief had an odd effect on Weres.

"Yeah, about that…" I had expected the news to get out and of course, it had. "Tygur was murdered in my salon last night. Vampire kill. My wards were breached, and I didn't realize it until too late."

"So it *is* true, then."

I caught a glint in Hilda's eyes, and flushed. Hilda, who had never had a bad word to say to me or about my business, had suddenly pulled back and was looking at me like I had a disease. But Tygur had died in my house, and that was enough to convict me in some people's eyes. When you owned a business that was open at night, you were expected to keep your wards up. I had fucked up. It didn't matter that I hadn't let them expire, that somebody else had defaced them. What mattered is that it had been on my property, and Tygur had thought he was safe.

A knot formed in my stomach. I wasn't going to be able to walk away from this, no harm, no foul. No matter how much I tried to prove that it was safe to visit Lily Bound, Tygur's death was going to have far-reaching ramifications for my business.

Dizzy, I realized I needed to sit down and make long-term plans for damage control.

Hilda smiled softly. She reached out and patted my hand. "I hate to say it, Lily, but you're in for it now. Maybe you should take a vacation? Get out of town for awhile." She paused, then added, "Maybe you should rethink the location of your business. Seattle might not be the best place for…your kind."

"I don't like the tone of your voice. You've always been supportive and polite, but now you're branding me? I thought the scarlet letter vanished with the Puritans." I could see the plastered-on politeness in her smile, masking disdain. I laid the package back down on the counter. "I don't think I need the jeans as badly as I thought I did. Thank you for your time." As I turned, she hurried around the counter.

"Please don't run off mad. You've always been one of my favorite customers—"

"You should have remembered that before you decided to judge me along with the rest of the fishwives." And then I remembered: Hilda was a werewolf. Of course she'd take their side once the shit hit the fan. "Goodbye, Hilda."

As I marched out of the door, I could hear her on the phone. No doubt she was spreading the word.

• • •

After a quick stop at Haverish's to pick up some tea for Nate, where luckily I did not encounter the same sort of reaction, I headed to Little Bart's Food Court. Dani was waiting for me in a corner booth. I slid in opposite her, placing my packages on the floor beside me.

I told her what had happened at Hilda's. "Rumors are already spreading. I have to figure out what to do. Dani, this could seriously impact my business."

"*Could?* I'd say it probably already *has*. By the way, while I was at the apothecary, I picked you up a bottle of Zaddul oil. Pour the entire bottle over that rune I fixed last night and it will hold it for another week unless somebody tries to mess up your wards again. It was pricy as hell, but I refuse to leave you vulnerable to another vampire attack when I can put a stop to it. By the way, I still need to check out Nate's wards. I want to do that before we head over to Archer Desmond's." The way she spat out the name caught my notice.

"Do you know him, by any chance? You don't sound pleased."

"What do you expect? He's a chaos demon. Witches and demons don't have a very good history. But no, I don't know him. I did look him up this morning before I left. Archer is a chaos demon, all right. And he has one hell of a history." She picked up her menu.

"Well, don't stop there. Tell me what we're getting into."

"He bought the Space Needle and turned it into Club Z. Then, he seems to have gotten bored and donated—not *sold*, but *donated*—the club back to the city. That's when he opened a PI business. He doesn't need the money, so he's probably just slumming it till he gets bored and goes back to wherever he came from. But, I'll give him credit. He's got a stellar reputation for solving cases. He's also tightly connected with a number of high-powered business types. Be careful, Lily—I have a feeling he could be trouble. He has all the makings of a first-class player."

"I'm already in trouble." At her look, I shrugged. "I promise I'll be careful." I picked up the menu, glancing through the selections. "What are you getting? Have you ordered yet?"

"Don't change the subject on me. Lily, one of these days you're going to meet somebody and lose your heart to them. And chances are it's going to be somebody on the dangerous side. While you're basically a sex goddess, you have no experience in dealing with love."

"You're already pairing me up with him? Give me time to meet the guy first. And I don't fall for players."

"I saw his picture. He's your type, dead on."

I stared at the tangle of choices on the menu, barely seeing anything because I was so preoccupied.

"Quit worrying. I won't let myself fall for anybody. I got too close once and it was a tragic disaster. You know about Marsh. I can't ever go through that again. And why you think I would go for a chaos demon of all people…" I gave her a shake of the head. "Focus on lunch."

Dani shrugged. "Fine. I want a bowl of clam chowder and several of their rolls. I love Bart's chowder." She waved toward a waitress, who immediately turned our way. Dani had a knack for catching the notice of cashiers and service personnel. Whether it was her natural charm or whether she used magic, I wasn't sure, but we seldom had to wait.

She put in her order. I asked the waitress to bring me a double cheeseburger with the works and fries. I also asked for a cup of tea. The din in the restaurant was getting louder as people crowded in for lunch. A mishmash of Fae and Weres lined the counter and filled the booths. A few humans were also in the mix. Bart was famous citywide for his food, and regardless of where people lived, they made it a point to visit his food court.

"So, when do we go see Archer?"

"I have an appointment for 5 P.M. at his office. His building is in a brick walkup across from the Underground. I didn't realize that until he gave me his address. That reminds me, are you working tonight?"

"No, I never keep the store open past four in the winter…in summer I'm open as late as eight o'clock. You want to go out to a club? Maybe go dancing tonight? I know you still need a good long feed." Dani opened the straw for her soda as the waitress deposited our drinks on the table and zipped away again.

I shook my head. "Honestly? No. After what happened last night, I'm not up for much of anything. I'm so glad I don't have any appointments today."

The numbness of Tygur's death had worn off, and the aftermath of it was sinking in. I also was beginning to suspect that I might have liked Tygur more than I let on. Oh, nothing more than friendship, but I realized I was really going to miss his visits. The sex was great, but he was fun to talk to too. I tried to brush away the thoughts—it was never safe for me to like my clients too much—but now that he was dead, admitting it didn't seem to matter much.

"Well, maybe I'll come over and keep you company if you don't mind. My coven was supposed to meet at midnight, but everybody's so freaked that we decided to put off the meeting. So I have the evening free. We agreed to meet in a few days, to discuss what Rebecca's death means for the group."

As the waitress placed our food in front of us, I stared at my plate. "I'm such an ass. I forgot you lost somebody last night, too. I'm so sorry."

Dani shook her head. "We were both in shock last night. And as harsh as it sounds, if the Souljacker *is* the one who killed both of them, we've got more to worry about than the people he's already taken." She stirred her chowder, lips pressed together in a frown.

"Yeah, along with every single member of the India Ink Club. I wonder…if it is Charles, why is he doing this? Did he just go crazy in there?"

"So you really think it's possible that he's the killer?"

"Who else can it be? The question is, what does he want? And whatever he's after, are Tygur's and Rebecca's deaths enough to sate whatever need he has?" I paused. "Can you sense anything? Do you even want to try?"

"Not particularly, but I might as well see what I can pick up." Dani closed her eyes. "I see fury and flame, and hunger…and fear. And there's…a longing so deep that it falls into a dark hole with no bottom." A moment later, she shivered and her eyes flew open. "I hate that I can tune into this. His energy is terrifying, Lily. It's this massive abyss of need and loss. So big I don't think anything can ever fill it. And there's nothing else—no other drive except to fill that void."

Wanting to brush away the concern on her face, I cleared my throat. "Well, maybe Archer can give us some advice. Because tracking down a vampire isn't going to be very easy. And even if we do track the Souljacker—or whatever vamp did this—down, what are we going to do then?"

"You know what we have to do." She spooned her chowder, frowning at it. "We have to stake him, if we can."

I picked up my burger. The line between knowing what we needed to do and being able to do it was a vast chasm. Vampires were strong, and cunning, and top-of-the-food-chain predators. Very few were able to hold onto any semblance of their humanity.

"Let's change the subject, at least for the rest of lunch. There's nothing we can do at the moment, and tomorrow I have to plan a cord-cutting ceremony for Rebecca's funeral. I *really* don't want to dwell on that." She paused, then asked, "Will you go to Tygur's funeral?"

I grimaced. "I rather doubt that I'm on the invitation list. And I'm not going to crash funeral rites. And since I answer to Wynter, if I showed up you know they'd contact her, saying that I did something horribly inappropriate."

"Good point."

As we ate, we focused on anything else we could. Clothes, the weather, an upcoming dance that we were both supposed to attend—it didn't matter what the topic was as long as it wasn't connected to death and vampires.

"Did you hear that Sunny is back in town?" Dani gave me a casual grin over her roll.

I almost choked on my French fry. "You have *got* to be kidding. I thought when she left she'd never come back. Why do you think…" I paused. There was only one reason why Sunny Tramero would return to Seattle. "You think she's getting married?"

"I wouldn't be surprised. She's a prize catch to any social climber. My guess is her parents decided it was time to cement bonds with another powerful family."

And Dani and I were off, speculating about an old frenemy

whom we had both been glad to see the back of. Sunny had a knack for spreading rumors and causing trouble wherever she went, but she was as rich as they come, half-Fae, and—unfortunately—frequently a pawn in her parents' machinations. As we focused on keeping our conversation as light-hearted as we could, we didn't notice the figures standing next to our booth until it was too late.

"Well, well, well. If it isn't my husband's murderer."

I slowly turned. Tricia Jones was staring down at me and she looked pissed.

CHAPTER 6

Tricia Jones was six feet tall and had black hair streaked with blonde that hung down to her lower back. The look in her golden eyes told me she was ready to kill, and with Weres, the look often preceded action. Tricia was also a knockout, dressed in spandex and leather. She looked like a gym bunny. I had only ever seen her from a distance; this was the first time we had met up close.

My thoughts scrambling, I tried to figure out what the hell to do. Could I avoid her right hook? How close was the nearest hospital? And why the hell had Tygur come to me with a dish like that at home? After all, the old saying went, why have steak out when you can have steak and lobster at home? And Tricia Jones was definitely not on the fast-food menu.

"Uh oh," Dani said, scooting further back toward the wall.

Trish was blocking my way out. "Well, answer me, you slut."

I awkwardly slid out of the booth, but she didn't fall back, which meant I had to slide out sideways, which forced me to brush against her. When I managed to get on my feet, we were almost nose-to-nose and boob-to-boob. One thing I could say about most Weres—they weren't afraid of a rumble, no matter how well-armed the other side was.

"If you would let me explain…"

"Explain what? Why my husband was found dead in your salon with his dick hanging out? Or why you were fucking him in the first place? Which question would you like to answer for me, *Lily*?"

It was then that I noticed that Tricia wasn't wearing any makeup. Her face was red and blotchy, as if she had been crying all night long. My stomach sank as I realized I was facing a grieving widow. The anger wasn't for show, which meant it was more deadly than ever. Grief was a dangerous influence.

As I opened my mouth, I stopped. No matter what I said, it would come out wrong. I paused, considering my options. I didn't want to do it, but it might be safest to go on the offense. Weretigers would back down if they thought their opponent was more dangerous.

As she stood there, arms crossed, her long, meticulous nails drumming a beat on her forearm, I gathered my courage.

"Tricia, Tygur told me you knew he was coming to me. I assumed you would take him in hand if it wasn't okay with you." Okay, an outright lie, but the name of the game was "save your own skin." Besides, if she thought he was a cad, it might make her grief easier to deal with.

You're pushing the rationalizations, Lily. But I didn't have the luxury of caring at this point.

She stared at me for a moment. When a big cat—be they a Were or purely animal—stares you down, it's a challenge. If you turn tail and run, they'll follow and boom, you're lunch meat.

So, I stood my ground, holding her gaze. Unfortunately, Tricia didn't find my courage a threat. Before I realized what she was doing, she hauled off and punched me hard enough to whip my neck to the side. I stumbled, falling back onto the seat, scraping my side against the table. It hurt like hell but I scrambled to my feet again, bracing myself against the back of the booth.

"He was *your* husband, not mine. If he lied to *me*, if he lied to *you*, it's not my fault. A vampire murdered him, not me."

"That's supposed to make everything better? I hope you tell better bedtime stories to your clients." She paused, a crafty look entering her eyes. "In fact, I'm *absolutely certain* that all your other clients are going to want to hear how your wards failed. How a vampire not only broke through them, but killed one of your clients right in your house. You might not have been the one who killed my husband, but you left the gate open for the murderer.

And that makes you just as guilty." And with that, Tricia spit in my face and stomped away, her posse behind her.

Everybody was staring at us. Dani handed me a napkin, and I slowly wiped my face. Bart himself came over to the booth. Cheeks blazing, I fumbled for my purse, looking for cash. How could I apologize for the scene? Bart would never let me come back.

But when I silently held out the money, he shook his head. "On the house. You two have been coming here for years. Go get a breath of fresh air and don't let her get to you, girl." With a soft smile, Bart escorted us to the door and held it open as we left the food court.

Once we were outside Dani found a bench and brushed off the snow. I sat down, shaking. At that moment, my phone jangled. Someone was texting me. Another chime, then a third, and a fourth came in before I even could pull out my phone to glance at the notes.

"Crap. Tricia's already been a busy bee. All four texts are from clients, canceling their upcoming appointments. None of them even bothered to make an excuse. They're all Weres."

Dani blinked as a lazy flutter of snowflakes drifted down. "Looks like she wasted no time hitting the phone tree to smear your name." Her eyes flashed dangerously, and I recognized the look.

I shook my finger at her. "*Don't.* Don't even think about it. The woman just lost her husband, and while I didn't cause his death, that fact is that he *did* die in my house." I stared morosely at the texts. "I don't blame her, you know."

"Don't do this to yourself. You weren't the one who killed Tygur."

"No, but Tricia's got a right to be pissed." I couldn't help it. I felt partially responsible. "And the number of notches on my belt just keeps growing. Before I opened Lily Bound…before I decided I could settle down in one place and make a go of it, there was a time when I didn't know how to channel my power. My mother tried to teach me, but she died when I was far too young, so the training didn't take. My father vanished, and I was sent to my aunt's. She ignored me, so I left early and spent centuries wandering the countryside. Along the way, I *fed*."

"You did what you had to in order to live." Dani placed her hand on my arm. "You can't blame yourself."

"Maybe not, but the fact is that I drained so many men I can't even begin to remember the number. I haven't killed anyone in seventy-five years, not since I learned how to siphon the energy off non-humans. Now I can leave someone alive if I'm not in the grasp of the hunger. But Tygur's death? It takes me back to a time I really hate remembering." I touched the dagger on my leg. "It takes me back way too far for comfort."

Dani let out a long sigh and stood. She offered me her hand and pulled me to my feet. "Fine. I hear you. But we don't have time to let regret bog us down. We have to check Nate's wards. Then, we have to talk to Archer. Leave the past where it belongs, Lily. Focus on now. It may be the only time we have."

With that somber thought, we headed toward the parking lot. Dani and I agreed to meet at Nate's. As I sat in my car, staring at the wheel, I flashed back to when I first had met the Souljacker, back when he was just Charles. Back when his art came to life, and he was still a sane, talented man.

• • •

It started one night about six years back. We were all at Fat Bastards, a restaurant, cheering on Greg—Dani's husband. Greg and Dani had wanted to throw a celebration party but they were living in a small apartment that could barely fit the two of them, let alone a group of about twenty. Nate was there, and Rebecca, and Tygur and Tricia—they were only just beginning to date—and a number of other power players in the Supe community.

Most of the people were milling around, chatting, but a core group of us were gathered around the table.

"Here's to Greg, our newest Seattle political power player! Or should I say, Senator Fallow!" Nate stood, raising his glass.

Greg, a tall, lanky man with shoulder-length brown hair, grinned.

"I'm so proud of my husband—he said he was going to make it into politics by the time he was thirty and he's done it!" Dani rested her arm on his shoulder, leaning over to give him a kiss on the cheek. It was obvious the pair doted on each other.

Greg let out a short laugh. "And I didn't even have to buy votes!" He sobered. "Let's face it, most politics are simply a combination of popularity and wealth. And considering the feelings toward the Blood Night District, I was afraid that I wouldn't be able to manage it, given my stance on the vampire rights bill."

While there was certainly a mix of races in the district, it was well known that the vampires were doing their best to control politics behind the scenes. Specifically the Deadfather, who had carved out a large stake in the commerce of the Blood Night District. It was thought his reach extended far beyond Seattle, that he might as well don a crown and call himself the king of the vampires. Money ran the world, and one thing a number of vamps were good at was business. Our district was the best place from which they could try to force the vampire rights bill through, but Greg had managed—by a slim margin—to take control of the seat in an election against the vampires' choice for senator. How he did it, we had no idea, but by a handful of votes, he had managed.

"So, what's going to be the first thing you do when you take office?" I didn't particularly care for political discussions. Over the centuries, I had discovered one thing to be true: even with good intentions, power corrupted. I had never seen a government that truly helped its people rather than hurting them. But I had also learned another valuable lesson, albeit it a jaded one. It was far better to be in the inner circle rather than on the outside. I counted myself lucky to have influential friends.

Dani glanced at me. "Greg's going to immediately start quashing the vampire rights bill. We have to make people understand how dangerous they are."

At that, Greg shot her an irritated look. "Let me speak for

myself, love. I'm going to establish myself...make a few friends, and then see who will work against the bill with me. Killing it will still be a few years off, but eventually, we'll manage. Hell, maybe I'll decide to run for governor next. I've always wanted to make a difference in the world."

Dani frowned, and I sensed some unspoken argument.

I changed the subject. "Well, you'll have Wynter behind you. My people don't like vampires either. Which means courting the Eastside." The politics of interspecies interactions and alliances made for a controlled chaos, but at that point, nobody really had the upper hand. What we needed to do was put a stop to the rising clout of the vampires.

As a heated, yet somehow boring debate on another subject started, I pushed back from my table and wandered over to the lounge, where a lovely woman was singing. Her voice had incredible reach, and I stood, mesmerized. A moment later, Greg joined me. Surprised to see him, I glanced up at him with a smile.

"She's good."

"She's really good. Do you know who that is?"

I shook my head. "No, I've never seen her before."

"That is Isabel Carter. She's Ian Carter's daughter. He's a business mogul that I need to win over. He's wavering right now, contemplating accepting the support of the Deadfather, which would mean he would come out pro-vampire rights. We need to convince him that's not a good idea. The Deadfather can sink a lot of capital into Carter's projects, so it's going to be a tough road." Greg stared at the woman, and I suddenly felt like he had tuned me out.

At that moment, Dani appeared. She looped an arm through Greg's, and he shook his head, smiling down at her.

"We need to celebrate your win, love."

"And how do you propose to do that? I thought we were celebrating." But he grinned at her, and once again I thought they were lucky to have found one another.

"The entire table has decided to get tattoos from the Souljacker to celebrate tonight's victory." Dani walked us back to the table. "I was just telling Greg about our decision."

Nate spoke up. "There's a new tattooist in town. He's down on the corner of Sycamore and Pine. They say he can see into your soul."

I frowned. "Do they now? What do you know about him?"

"His name is Charles, but he's known as the Souljacker. Scary name but damn, the guy is good. I talked to a couple of friends who went to him. They said he's so intuitive that he can reach inside of you and coax out your inner self through his art." Nate leaned his elbows on the table. "He's really incredible. You don't go there asking for something specific. He sees what you need…and makes it happen."

It sounded like a gamble. I wasn't sure I wanted somebody else deciding what artwork would go on my body. But then again, I wasn't entirely sure what I wanted.

"I've heard of him," Dani said. "Nate's right. He's like a shaman with his art. I'm in. We can call ourselves the India Ink Club. Who else is up for it?"

Rebecca and Tygur agreed, along with Jolene, and several of the others. Greg opted out, but encouraged the rest of us to have at it. Tricia bowed out—she liked tattoos but went to one of her Pride's artists.

So that night, we all traipsed down to the Souljacker and scheduled our appointments.

Two months later, Greg was killed and turned by a vampire before he could even take his oath of office. His opponent in the race, Woodrow Blythe, was named senator in his place, and he immediately began pushing hard on the vampire rights bill.

All we had to remember our friend by were the tattoos we had gotten in celebration.

And *that* was how we had met Charles and lost Greg.

• • •

I glanced down at my leg, thinking about the tattoo. The Souljacker had brought the phoenix to the surface. The moment I saw him ink the outline and realized what it was going to be, it felt like the image had always been there in spirit, had always *meant* to be a part of my body.

What had happened to the soft-spoken man who scarcely said a handful of words while he worked on through the night, tattooing my leg as the perpetual buzz of the tattoo needle sounded through the silent shop? Charles had been so quiet; he had seemed so gentle that it didn't compute with the raging monster he had become—with the man who had turned and murdered a family after he had been turned into a vampire.

Had being turned destroyed his mind? It didn't always follow. Some vampires managed to hold on to a semblance of who they had been. But somehow, the lines had blurred, and after the turning, Charles had ceased to be Charles. He had gotten lost.

With a soft sigh, I put the car into gear and—with Dani following—headed for Nate's.

CHAPTER 7

Once we were at Nate's, it took Dani ten minutes to ascertain that his wards were all still intact. She had brought another bottle of Zaddul oil just in case and she left it in his mailbox.

"I'll tell you one thing," she said. "If we don't find some way to cope with the rogue vampires, it's going to be a rough road ahead for anybody left alive."

"All vampires are rogue, even the ones that act like they're trying to fit in."

"You've got that right."

I gave her the address for Archer's office, and we headed out again. Traffic wouldn't be too bad, but still—even with the Overpass Trains, rush hour was rush hour, no matter how you looked at it.

• • •

Archer Desmond's office was in a fourth-floor walkup in the heart of the Blood Night District. On First Avenue, one block above the dividing line leading into the Ports and across the street from the Underground, the building had seen better days. Someone was trying to reclaim it from years of disrepair—the restoration work was obvious—but it still looked run down and tired, as did a number of buildings in the district.

Dani and I found parking spots in a nearby garage. I grimaced as I stuffed thirty dollars in the slot. Fifteen an hour. That's how much parking cost. The city planners had accomplished their mission: it discouraged people from driving to work, so the streets were relatively clear during the day, but the Overpass Trains were jammed full on every morning and evening run. If they didn't think of another way to increase mass-transit options, or add more runs to the lines, there were going to be a lot of unhappy voters at the polls.

Dani glanced up at the building and shivered. "We aren't far from the Underground."

"I know. Right across the street, in fact."

I glanced around. Underground Seattle was no longer a passing tourist attraction. A number of the nightclubs—especially vampire clubs—had cleared out the rubble and shored up the sagging timbers. They had set up shop, and the Underground was a thriving community now. Seattle leaders hadn't cared much for that, but they didn't have much say, given the Deadfather pretty much held the reins.

"So, are you sure about this?"

We headed for the stairs. Elevators in the older buildings weren't all that trustworthy.

"I don't think we have a choice, Dani. We have to do something."

She shook her head. "Chaos demons are freaky. I've met a few. It used to be that some witches were able to summon them, but honestly, nobody tries anymore. There are too many over here as it is, and the old command spells aren't what they were back in the day. Somehow, when all of you Fae and the like came out of the closet, it shifted the web of reality."

"What do you mean?" I seldom talked to Dani about her magic. For one thing, it seemed like a private affair. For another, most of the witches I knew were on the scary side. They were human, yes, but beyond human in a way that was hard to define. The Craft had a way of changing people, especially those who had been born and bred to it. And more often than not, the witches I encountered were from Fam-Trads. They had been brought up in the Craft because it had become acceptable. There had been a time they were as mistrusted as the Fae or the Weres.

"There's so much magic running rampant now that it's subtly altering the structure of our reality. It's hard to explain, but my coven has been conducting some experiments lately and we think we've discovered a parallel world to ours, where the Fae never came out. Our world is harsh, but it's just as bad over there, from what we can tell. The vampires hide in the shadows, and nobody really knows they exist."

I wanted to ask her more, because the concept fascinated me, but we were on the fourth floor and in front of Archer's office by then. I glanced at her.

"Here goes nothing."

"Right…tell me another one." But she laughed as I opened the door.

• • •

Archer Desmond's office was reminiscent of an old movie set. Think film noir from the 1950s, with a touch of tropical. There were two rooms to his office—the main waiting area and then a private office. The bathroom was down the hall. The waiting area was decked out with a worn but comfortable-looking leather sofa, three armchairs, a table with a few magazines on it, a water cooler with hot and cold water, and assorted tea bags. A TV on the wall was tuned to a local news channel, the volume playing at a soft level. Potted palms and something that looked like a bougainvillea brought a spot of color to the room.

A bell next to the inner office door had a sign over it reading, *Ring please, then have a seat until I can get to you.*

I rang the bell and we sat down. I picked up one of the magazines but it was *News Flash*—a political rag that pretty much printed all the scandals it could find, most of them wildly inaccurate.

"Lovely reading material." I thumbed through the others. A home-and-garden magazine, *Fae Weekly*—a local 'zine that listed Fae activities—and a couple others that looked to be generic office-magazine stock.

Dani was about to say something when my phone buzzed. Wearily, I pulled it out and glanced at the text.

"Another cancellation. That leaves the entire next week free. I guess Tricia Jones has more clout than I gave her credit for." I frowned, staring at the terse note. Frasier Wills had been one of my best clients. He was a werewolf, unmarried, not interested in long-term relationships. And he had the money to pay for his liaisons. That meant that Tricia's influence extended beyond just the Were Wives' Club. And *yes*, there *was* a Were Wives Club.

Dani gave me an apologetic shrug. "Yes, she definitely has more influence than you realize. I placed a couple calls on the way over here; over the years Tricia has become the zenith of the were-tiger social elite. And since the Weres all tend to stick together in terms of interspecies politics, it doesn't surprise me that she got to the others. The funeral for Tygur is going to be huge. At least five hundred people there, mostly Weres."

"Hell, the majority of my clientele are Weres."

The Fae were generally so sexual that few of them needed me to fulfill their fantasies. They were quite capable of doing so on their own.

But the Weres were different. Even the ones who weren't monogamous tended to be low-key about any affairs, and they were far more culturally conservative than the Fae. In fact, there was a natural antipathy between the two races. Coming to me served as an act of rebellion for some of my clients, or a freedom they didn't find at home. I had a roster of thirty clients, of which 80 percent were Were. That meant twenty-four potential losses. If rumor made its way through the grapevine that my clients weren't safe in my home, it could tank my business altogether.

I was about to say as much when the inner door opened. As I glanced up, my stomach flipped. There stood Archer Desmond, unlike anything I'd been imagining. I had been thinking some old, behorned, bald-headed demon who looked like death warmed over.

Instead, Archer Desmond most definitely did *not* have horns, and he wasn't old—or at least he didn't look it. In fact, Archer Desmond was smoking hot. He stood about five-eleven, with wavy black hair that reached the nape of his neck and scintillating, emerald-green eyes. With an aquiline nose that was just the right length for his face and thick, full lips, he looked like he should be on the cover of *Gentleman's Monthly*. Trim and athletic, he was dressed in a black suit that screamed designerwear.

"Lily O'Connell? I'm Archer Desmond." Smooth; his voice was velvety smooth.

I glanced at Dani and saw that her gaze was glued to the man as well. So it wasn't just me. Suddenly aware that he had spoken, I stammered out, "Yes, I'm Lily. This is my friend, Dani Halloran." As I reached to take his hand, sparks flew. And they weren't metaphorical. Actual sparks sputtered as our fingers met.

"Must be the carpet," he said with a laugh.

"Must be." Any witticisms I might have at my disposal flew right out the window.

Dani cocked her head, staring at him for a moment. "You look familiar."

"Aren't all demons the same, *witch*?" His voice was pleasant, but the inflection was loaded.

Crap. I hadn't counted on there being any animosity between the two of them. But then again, when I thought about it, witches had been summoning and ordering demons around for millennia. Even though Dani had said it wasn't standard practice anymore, I had the feeling that it hadn't entirely gone out of vogue.

"I'm not sure, why don't you tell me? I've never met any." Dani's reply was equally smooth and cool.

Archer let out a laugh. "So you say. We shall see."

The sparring seemed to end there, because he gestured for us to enter his office.

As we followed him in, the decor continued the film-noir theme. His desk was exactly the big oak desk I would have expected to see, with a massive computer set up on one side, and space to spread out files on the other. It was a huge U shape, with two other tables off to one side, giving him more desk space than I could ever imagine needing. An array of gadgets sat on one of the tables, including a printer and scanner, along with several other items that I didn't recognize. A black leather chair sat behind the desk, smooth and supple from the looks of it.

Three chairs sat opposite, and a daybed was tucked into one corner. A thick blanket was draped over one arm, and the pillows looked like actual bed pillows, not ornamental throw ones. A stand held a minifridge below it, and a microwave on top, along with a coffee bar. It looked like he could set up shop here for awhile, if need be. That, of course, led me to wonder if he lived here, but that was none of my business.

"You say you have a matter of a rather urgent nature?"

I nodded. "Yes, actually. Jolene recommended we call you. She's…a friend of mine. There are a number of us who are in danger if this proves to be what we think it is."

"Do you mind if I record the session?" Archer moved to flip on a switch attached to a microphone, which appeared to be linked into his computer.

"Go ahead. It's all right with me. Dani?"

She nodded. "Not a problem."

As soon as he turned it on and motioned for me to go ahead, I explained what had happened to Tygur. Dani told him about Rebecca, and then we told him about the Souljacker escaping.

"A group of us all got ink from him shortly before he was turned. Rebecca and Tygur were two of his clients. Dani, our friends Nate and Jolene…we all were. We called ourselves the India Ink Club." I paused, thinking of how long ago that seemed now.

"India ink used to be the standard for tattooing until the latter part of the twentieth century." Archer glanced up at us, grinning. "I know that much."

"Right. That's why we picked the name. We were celebrating and all decided to get some ink to commemorate it. The Souljacker had a reputation for being able to reach inside and bring your inner self out onto your body. His talent went beyond mere artistry. It was as if…" I paused, thinking of my phoenix. "It's like he could see into the depths of your soul, into your true nature and freeze it into ink. A couple months after we got our tattoos,

Charles was trapped by a vampire. He was turned and caught. I'm not certain of the whole story, but he ended up being locked away at WestcoPsi. WestcoPsi is supposed to be escape proof but I think that's been proven wrong."

Archer nodded. "Do you know if there have been other victims who were his clients, who weren't in your club?"

I shrugged. "I have no clue. Jolene might know."

"Given he's only been out for three days, I'm not sure how much damage he can have done so far." Dani frowned.

Archer glanced over his notes. "What I'm curious about, Lily, is—if he's after *all* of you, why didn't he kill you that night, too?"

Reluctantly, I reached inside my shirt and brought out my pentacle. "Because of this. Dragon scale. Silver."

If he was surprised, Archer didn't show it. "That would do it, all right." He frowned. "So he managed to get through your wards because one of them had been defaced. Do you have any clue when that might have happened?"

I let Dani answer that one. She was the expert in wards.

"No, it's impossible to tell without a spell that I can't cast. Even if I could, I don't know if we could find out the answer. My guess is that somebody was messing around and scratched it up without thinking about it. By the shape of the marks, it looked like someone could have either keyed it, or they could have scraped against it by accident."

Archer handed me a notepad and a pen. "Can you write me up a list of everybody who was in your club, along with any contact information that you might have for them? Meanwhile, I'll scout around, see if I can find a list of his prior clients. That may be difficult, given the nature of the business."

"I need to tell you something, before we go any farther." Dani leaned forward. "My husband was killed and turned by a vampire. He didn't get any ink from Charles, but…I think he's still out there. His name is…was…Greg Fallow. I think he runs the vampire club, Veek, in the Underground."

I whirled around. "You never told me about the club! I've heard of that. It's infamous among the wild boys set."

"I didn't want to think about it." She lifted her chin stubbornly, tears in her eyes. "Greg died. That's not my husband out there. Not anymore."

Archer stared at her for a moment, then softly said, "I'm sorry, Ms. Halloran. It can't be easy to live with that memory."

Dani let out a slow breath. "It's not."

"Yes, well…" Archer stood. "I think I have all I need to get started. I'll scout around and get back to you as soon as I have anything to report. Meanwhile, I suggest you check with Rebecca's household. See if there was any disruption to her wards that might have allowed the vampire to get through."

"What about payment? I know the department won't pay for it—Jolene told me that much. How much will this cost?"

He cocked his head, staring at me for a moment. "Why don't you let me see what I can find out and then we'll work out the details. This initial consultation won't run you over a hundred for today and the legwork I plan on doing based on our appointment today is included. After that, we'll discuss terms if you want to continue the investigation."

"I suppose you'll want a retainer?" I started to pull out my credit card, but he shook his head.

"Let's see what I find before discussing any more money." And with that, he escorted us to the door.

I turned, as we were about to leave, and my gaze locked with Archer's. Again, a spark. "Thank you. We really aren't sure what to do at this point."

"I suggest you stay indoors, in a heavily warded area, after sunset. In other words, don't hang around outside after dark. If the Souljacker is after you, then he's going to be studying where you go, how he can get at you. In other words, until we know different, consider that you, along with your friends, are being stalked by a deadly hunter."

And with those less-than-comforting words, he showed us out the door.

CHAPTER 8

As Dani and I headed back to the parking garage, I glanced at the clock tower in Pioneer Square. "We don't have long till sunset. I think Archer is right. We should forego dancing or anything else on the town tonight."

Dani frowned. "I hate being corralled because of a vampire. This sucks. No pun intended."

"I know, but the Souljacker is dangerous. Two people that we know of are dead. We're on the potential hit list." I paused, not wanting to ask the next question but deciding I might as well get it over with. "Have you ever thought about visiting Veek? Seeing Greg?"

In a carefully guarded voice, Dani said, "Never ask me that again. My husband is dead. The monster that wears his body? That's not him."

"I'm sorry. I should have kept my mouth shut."

"It's all right." She glanced at the sky. The sun had already set. "You know, we're in danger now, just standing here."

"I just realized that." I pulled my jacket tighter. The cold was seeping in and the parking garage was dark as we exited the stairwell, with the cold florescent lights spaced few and far between. "You don't think he could have followed us here, do you?"

She pressed her lips together, glancing from side to side. "I don't know what to think," she finally said. "I really hate this, you know?"

What Dani hated was being pushed around. She was stubborn as an ox and smart as a whip, but the two didn't always pair well and I could tell she was conflicted. Right now, my fear of dying was stronger than my desire to rebel.

"Come on. Our cars are parked together. We'll check them first, make sure nothing's inside, and then leave at the same time." Stopping, I turned to her and put my hand on her arm. "Dani, I know you're pissed. Neither one of us wants to end up dead. And remember, Charles can turn you into a vampire, and I know you don't want that. So, don't let your temper get away with you, please? I don't want to lose my best friend."

"I know, and I don't want to lose you. I'll be careful. I promise."

"Why don't you come over? We can watch TV, goof around… whatever strikes our fancy."

"All right, you've talked me into it. We'll go to your house, but I'm only going to stay for awhile. I've got plenty of protection in my car and at home. But…hanging out for awhile sounds like it might be fun." She forced a smile, and I knew it was to cover up her nervousness.

We hurried through the garage, eyeing every shadow that seemed to move on its own, every nook and cranny we passed. Finally, we came to our cars and cautiously unlocked them, searching every possible place a vampire could hide, including the trunks. I tried not to think about the fact that if we actually found ourselves facing a vamp, neither one of us was equipped to fend him off. My pentacle would protect me, but it wouldn't protect Dani. And if he had any sort of weapon besides his fangs and hands, well, it wouldn't protect me, either. Instead, I focused on searching the cars and keeping alert.

As we pulled out of the garage—I was close on Dani's wheels—the swirl of snow began to fall heavier, the chill knifing me right to my bones. When Wynter had taken up residence on the Eastside, she brought with her the cold and snow during the autumn and winter months, and all the worry about the greenhouse effect seemed to vanish from the northern half of the world. I wasn't sure what it was like in the southern hemisphere, under Summerlyn's rule. Perhaps the sisters balanced each other out; maybe we were back to a time before the world had begun its crazy swing toward being a perpetual hothouse. Whatever the case, the snow piled up in winter now, and summers were moderate, with few spikes into heat anymore.

As we headed toward my house I said, "Phone. Call Dani." My phone's VOX system put in the call. When she came on the line, I said, "We should stop somewhere to pick up takeout for dinner. What do you feel like? Sen's Chicken and Teriyaki is on the corner of the next street. We can get a bucket, and some fried rice and chow mein if you want. I can call ahead so it will be ready and we can go through the drive-thru."

"Sounds good to me. I'll pull in when I get there and you follow me."

After we picked up dinner, including a quick stop at the bakery next to Sen's for a deep-dish apple pie, we headed directly for my house. As soon as we edged into the driveway, I saw Nate come running out of his house.

"Come over for dinner!" I didn't want him staying alone either. Nate was the least able to fend off a vampire attack, even though his wards were still working.

Nate nodded, then jogged over. As I watched him, I became aware that my hunger was still deep, and I wanted more than just a taste. I needed sex, and a lot of chi to sate the drive. I'd have to go out to feed, possibly tonight, but the thought scared the hell out of me.

I stared into the darkness. The more I thought about it, the more I knew that this was the Souljacker's work, and that he was out there waiting for us.

We headed inside, Nate gallantly carrying the takeout bags while I told him about our meeting with Archer. "He said we shouldn't be alone."

Dani must have caught something in my voice because she sauntered over. "What are you going to do about feeding? You haven't had anything to eat except what little you got from me last night. With no appointments this week, you can't wait it out.

I know what happens. You'll either become too ravenous to care, or you'll resist long enough that you'll be too weak to feed. Which one depends on whether your will power can outlast your hunger."

I hung my head, staring at the table. "I don't know, to be honest. I was just thinking about that. I have to feed. I have to do something."

Nate finished setting the table. He glanced toward me. "I'd volunteer but…"

"Don't even think about it. I can't touch you—I won't take a chance. I'll just have to call over someone from Wynter's court. They'll help me. And Dani, don't you offer. Last night was an emergency, but I need to feed hard. And I'm not going to put you through that." I unpacked the cartons and the bucket of chicken and spread them out on the kitchen table. Who did I know who might be free? Who wasn't a Were waiting to humiliate me or punish me for Tygur's death?

A knock on the door interrupted our dinner preparations. I answered, cautiously peeking through the window. *Archer?*

Wondering what he wanted, I opened the door. "Hi, come on in."

He was looking even better than at the office, now wearing a pair of tight black jeans under the suit coat instead of dress pants. In one hand, he carried a briefcase. In another, he carried a bag. "I brought information and wine."

"You already found out something? Hey, join the party." As I stared at him, I realized I was practically drooling. And then, I felt my body shift, responding to his presence. Archer Desmond would have plenty of chi, and being a demon, he'd be able to handle my needs very well. I brushed past him, resting a hand on his for a moment before taking the wine from him, letting my glamour radiate out through my fingers onto his hand. As the spark flared, he glanced up at me, a curious, knowing look on his face.

Dani, who had seen right through what I was doing, flashed me a cockeyed grin. "Hello, Archer. You can see we're taking your advice and not hanging out where we'll be in danger."

"We're about to eat dinner," I added. "Would you like to stay? There's plenty, though it's not fancy. And we have *dessert*." Maybe I was laying it on a little thick, but I was hungry, damn it. I needed sex and I needed chi, and I wanted him.

Archer glanced at the spread. "Looks good to me. This is what I order when I stay in my office to work on a case." He edged toward me, a shrewd look on his face. "You're *hungry*, aren't you?"

I nodded. There was no use in beating around the bush. "I haven't fed in awhile and it's getting dangerous."

He glanced at Nate and at Dani. "Let me guess—you don't feed on friends."

"Not on humans—not anymore. And Dani…she's human, but she's a witch and can spare the chi. But I won't touch her when I'm this hungry. It's just too dangerous." I stared at him, deciding blunt would be best. "Archer…"

But I didn't have to get into it. His eyes glittered as he looked me up and down. "I've never bedded a succubus before."

"Then it goes two ways. I've never fucked a chaos demon before. You'll help me out?"

"On one condition." He motioned to the table. "If they promise to leave us some chicken."

Nate snorted. "We will. But only if you take it out of the room. It's been too long for me, and I sure as hell don't want to watch."

Dani just laughed. "Go get busy so we can talk over whatever the information is that you found. Lily will be able to think better once she's got her honey pot satisfied."

I snorted. "Nice mouth there."

"You should know; you've kissed it before." And with a wave, she turned back to the table.

Feeling awkward but so hungry that I could have fucked Archer right there on the kitchen floor, I led him toward the stairs. "We'll be back in awhile. Be careful and don't open the door for anybody. If anything happens, feel free to interrupt us but don't worry about any loud thumps or shrieks."

As we headed upstairs, I hesitated. I hadn't allowed any of my clients to enter my private bedroom. My friends had been there, but only to look at clothes or smell perfume. Clients were entertained in the salon. So it felt new…allowing Archer in.

As we entered the room, I paused. "Listen. I don't think the Souljacker can get in now, but keep your guard up as much as possible."

"I hope to keep more than *that* up, girl," he said with a lazy smile. "But set your mind at ease. I brought a ward with me that will secure the house for the next four hours. I'm not about to get involved with this case unless I'm also protected. I may not be on the hit list, but neither am I interested in being collateral damage. And before you ask, you inferred right. There is a hit list, and it *is* the Souljacker after you and your friends."

He pulled a small talisman out of his pocket. I immediately sensed something fill the room—a force that seemed to engulf and shroud the walls. The energy raced along like an electrical streak. As I closed my eyes, I could sense it surround my entire home.

"I want one of those. Permanently."

"That would cost you a king's fortune." Archer turned to me. "So…" He reached out slowly, taking my hand. "You need to feed." His voice was low, and a roiling heat crackled off his body.

"I'm so hungry, I'm almost sick from it."

His proximity made my stomach lurch. He was even more handsome close up and every nerve on my body began to jangle as my breath grew short. His lips, his wonderfully full lips, were close to mine. His gaze slinked over my body, starting at my feet and working their way up to my breasts and then my face.

"Do you like what you see?"

"Yes, I do, but I think I'll like what I feel even better." He laughed, slow and rich, and the sound of his voice rippled through me.

I dropped my head back, moaning softly as he drew me in, anchoring my waist with one hand as he backed me against the nearest wall. He crushed my mouth with his, lips warm and full against mine. I wrapped my arms around his neck and kissed him back, drawing energy from his breath as the chi passed through my lips like a warm gust of summer heat. The strength of his life force was immense and it shook me to the core.

I hadn't been lying when I told him I had never had a chaos demon before. Behind the brute force lurked a dark, cavernous passion. He was brilliant, with a magnetism so strong I wouldn't have been able to stop if the earth opened up and swallowed my house. As the kiss went on, my body began to burn, his lips on mine stoking the fire. My body ached—I needed him. Needed more than his kiss, more than his hands firmly holding my waist.

Archer let go of me, pulling back, a predatory look on his face. He let out a low growl, his eyes lighting up. "Undress. I want to see you naked."

Feeling as crazed as the satyrs in the blind grip of their rut, I slithered out of my shirt, my breasts bouncing free as I unhooked my bra. Archer yanked off his jacket. Another minute and I had managed to strip off my jeans and panties, kicking them over beside the bed. Archer tossed his shirt on the floor as I reached for his belt buckle. But he got there first, whipping the belt out from the loops. With another quick move, he unzipped and, as his cock sprang into view, fully erect and throbbing, I moved to the bed.

As he shed his jeans and approached me, I reached out to draw him down, rolling him onto his back as I straddled his body, positioning myself to slide down his deliciously thick shaft. He stretched me wide as I eased down, inch by inch, growing wetter with every move. And then he was fully inside me, and I leaned over so he could reach my breasts. He cupped one, bringing it to his lips where he worked the nipple with his tongue. With his other hand, his fingers slid down to cup my ass. I groaned, moving a little, but that only made him bring both hands to my waist, where he held me still with a firm grip.

"Don't move," he whispered. "Don't move, don't squirm, just be still." His voice had an authority in it that I couldn't ignore. Demons were powerful; they could mesmerize with their commands. I found myself wanting to obey him.

I shuddered, forcing myself to stop. I couldn't focus on anything other than the feel of him so thick inside of me that it felt like there was no room left. The sensation of his hands on my skin and his tongue on my breast was driving me crazy. I wanted to ride him so hard that it was almost an ache, but he gave me a single shake of the head when I started to squirm, and I stopped.

"Now, first, I'm going to stroke you and you will remain perfectly still." His words were slow, calm, and deliberate. He slid one hand down to between my legs where I was straddling him, and began to circle my clit, tweaking it so that I let out a soft cry—whether it was pleasure or pain, I wasn't sure. I shuddered, trying to control my need to ride his hand, to ride his cock, to go leaping over the edge into orgasm.

"Next, lean down and kiss me. And draw all the chi you need."

I obeyed, leaning down to press my lips against his. As I began to siphon the energy, drawing it from between his lips, he began to thrust upward. I met his movements with my own as the chi flowed into my lungs, satiating me. As he bucked beneath me, I ground my pelvis against him, sliding up and down his shaft, meeting him thrust for parry. We fucked hard and fast as the chi filled my body, bolstering me back to full strength.

And then, so full I couldn't take in another breath, I broke off the kiss. My breasts were slick with sweat as they skated over his chest. I panted, driving him on, grinding against him as fast as I could. His eyes shifted to a brilliant, beautiful ruby color as I rode him like a wild stallion, and the rush from his energy catapulted me higher than I had ever been.

We were a blur of sound, a tangle of motion and then—suddenly—I dropped my head back and let out a low moan as the orgasm ricocheted through me, hard and fast. Archer came only seconds later, arching hard against me, holding me so tight I almost couldn't breathe. He let out a loud moan and then—slowly—I folded down to nestle into his arms, tight against him, clammy and vibrating like a live wire.

...

I slowly shook my head, rolling over to sprawl on the bed beside him. "That…was…"

"Wow." Archer propped himself up on his elbows and gave me a rueful grin. "I had no idea. Thank you."

His smile was infectious. I rested my hands on my belly as I stared at his face. He was a pretty boy, yes, but now I was beginning to see the faint lines on his brow, the worry wrinkle beneath one eye. What I didn't expect to see was the laughter bubbling below the surface.

"You're welcome…but *I* should be the one thanking *you*. The drive to feed was becoming so strong that I was getting scared. And it's rather awkward to take a bodyguard with you when you're on the prowl for chi. Dani would have offered herself, but as I told you, I avoid feeding on friends when I'm this hungry. She can offer me a snack now and then, but this was…"

"A full-fledged three-course dinner," he finished for me. "She's a witch, and she can handle a lot, but this…I'm guessing she would have been weak for days after this. So, does that make me an enemy, since you won't feed on friends?"

I pushed myself up, crossing my legs into the lotus position. I was a yoga aficionado—it made my clients happy that I was so flexible. "No…I don't know what you are, to be honest. I've never dealt much with demons."

"I'll bet you the witch has."

I shook my head. "Trust Dani. If she says she doesn't summon demons, she's telling the truth."

Archer's smile faded, a look of concern taking its place. "I feel for her—her husband taken and turned. I can tell how deeply it wounded her."

I stared at him for a moment. "Yeah, it sliced so deep I know it will never heal." Then, I added. "So, a chaos demon, huh?"

"We're not so bad," he said with a congenial grin.

It was true. Chaos demons weren't the worst of the demonic

realm. Far from it. They were among the least volatile. As a whole, they were appealing. But their curse was that they attracted chaos wherever they went.

"I can't help that I'm trouble." He rolled up to a sitting position, shifting so that he was facing me. "Lily…I really…this was…"

I caught my breath. Once again, a wave of hunger rolled over me, though it wasn't the urge to feed for nourishment. I held his gaze, then slowly reached for him. He leaned me back without a word, sliding between my legs. As he softly entered me again, this time without the frenzy but with a passion so deliberate it almost scared me, I closed my eyes, rising softly to meet him, and once again, lost myself in the sex-colored haze that blotted out the rest of the world.

CHAPTER 9

Dani and Nate had left plenty of food, although I noticed the chicken drumsticks were all gone, as well as half the pie.

"All better?" Dani wiggled her eyebrows as she held out plates to Archer and me.

"Yes, you voyeuristic perv." I filled the plate with chicken and chow mein and a few other goodies that had somehow found their way into the spread. "Where did the pot stickers come from? They're fresh."

"I ordered them. Can't have takeout without them, in my opinion." Nate leaned back, stretching out in his chair. He nodded to Archer. "So you're a private investigator?"

"One of the best in the city," Archer said. He piled his plate high and scooted in next to Nate. Somehow, in the space of an hour, he had lost his aloofness and was looking incredibly comfortable. "I have a long list of clients, and there's never a lull in business. That's either a very good thing, or a very bad thing, depending on which way you look at it. For me? It's a continuous source of fascination."

"Dani said that you donated Club Z back to the city. That's…a big donation." Nate mopped up the last of the sauce with a piece of cheese bread that had managed to join the party on the table. "My company held a retreat there last year."

"I don't have to make a living. I renovated the Space Needle, reopened the club after refurbishing it, and then…I was bored. Call it a creative project. So I decided that, since I didn't need to sell it, and since I don't like a few wealthy businessmen owning the entire city, I'd give it back to the people." Archer piled his plate high and enthusiastically dug in. The demon liked to eat; that much was obvious.

"What's it like? What kind of cases do you work? It can't be the simple ones most humans are trying to solve, right?" Dani leaned forward. "I mean, you don't go out taking pictures of who's screwing who for divorce cases…"

I started to motion for her to keep quiet, but then stopped. She had a point. "Actually, yes. What kind of cases *do* you specialize in?"

He gave us both a quick glance, then looked down at his plate, the smile suddenly cool and reserved again. "I think that's a conversation best left for another time. The clients I work for can be highly dangerous, and those are the ones in the right. None of them are, on the whole, a savory lot. Or forgiving of mistakes. I make sure I do my job and I do it right. That's how I can command the prices I do from them. Then, I donate most of the money where I think it will do the most good, and it's not to the vampire rights movement." And with that, he dug into his meal.

Dani and I shot each other a quick look, but we both recognized the do-not-enter sign he had slapped up. I focused on my food. Now that my other hunger was satiated, my stomach gave the kind of rumble that demanded pizza and chicken and whatever other kind of junk food I could feed it.

The ward Archer had brought with him was sitting on the counter. He had brought it downstairs with us. Dani frowned and wandered over to examine it, but she knew the rules of magic better than any of us and she kept her hands to herself.

"You paid a lot for this one. I can tell. This could only be created by a very powerful witch. I don't suppose you'd care to tell me who fashioned it?" She glanced up at him.

He gave her a quick nod. "You can pick it up if you like. The ward isn't set to sound an alarm unless a vampire comes near or unless somebody tries to deactivate it. I picked it up over on the Eastside. Wynter has some powerful sorceresses in her court. One of them happens to be a friend of mine. I don't know if you've heard of Katarina the Frost?"

Dani abruptly set down the ward and backed away a step. "Katarina? You know the *Frost*? She's Wynter's right-hand witch. She's one of the Calliach's daughters." She abruptly returned to the table.

I blinked, trying not to show my surprise. Katarina the Frost was one of Wynter's best executioners. If Wynter was pissed at you, chances were you wouldn't survive through the next week. Katarina was legendary in the court, both for her knowledge of magic and her ruthless obedience to Wynter. Many of Wynter's enemies had met their end at Katarina's magic.

"How did you meet her?"

Archer shrugged, mulling over a chicken wing. "Long ago, when the world was a much younger place, Katarina summoned me and ordered me to exact revenge on a group of humans. She had managed to learn my real name, which meant I had to obey her. Demons usually like the Fae, but her? No. For ten years I was bound by her spell. She wanted me to overthrow a minor despot—a would-be king who had driven the Fae out of their forest. This was before Britain and the rest of the UK destroyed their woodlands. My chaos was her weapon. I became friends with the petty tyrant. That alone was enough to seal his fate. When it was over and he came to his stultifying end, she set me free. I wanted to destroy her for enslaving me, but by then her powers had increased, and she was riding high in Wynter's court. Frankly, I was more afraid of her than she was of me, so I decided that diplomacy was the best route."

"So that was it? You just let her go?"

He chuckled. "Demons never *just* let old scores remain unset-tled. But did you not hear me? Katarina was terrifyingly powerful by then. Oh, I demanded payment for services rendered, and submitted a bitter bill. I hinted that I might bring an army of my friends to back me up, and Wynter recognized the threat, though I doubt if she really took it seriously. But in the interests of mending fences, the court paid and paid well, which is why I never have to worry about money again, at least in the human world. The matter was settled, and Katarina and I were free to become friends."

"Weren't you afraid she'd come after you again?" Nate asked.

Archer shook his head. "No. I don't know if you realize that—Dani will verify this—once a witch or magician of any sort summons a demon and the task is fulfilled, that's it. The mage is never again able to enslave that particular demon."

Dani nodded her agreement. "That I do know. I've never summoned a demon, but I know the rules."

"Do you work elemental magic, then? Or are you a magical pacifist?" Archer asked. He seemed genuinely interested.

"I do work some elemental magic, rather than ceremonial. And I'm no pacifist. I can hex with the best of them—my family specialized in curses back in the day. But I've just never felt the need to summon demons or elementals. I'm not interested in gaining power over anybody, and I can cause all the havoc I want on my own." Dani laughed.

Archer inclined his head somberly. "You're a lot wiser than many I've met who dabble in magic. I think…you were born to it, weren't you?"

"My mother and father were witches, yes. I'm Fam-Trad in the old-school sense. We can trace our magical lineage back hundreds of years." She paused, glancing over at the ward. "I've always wanted to meet Katarina. The Frost is known far and wide for her ability to create magical talismans. That's something I enjoy doing. I know she probably doesn't need money, but if I could convince her to put a few of those wards in the store on consignment, I could make a fortune on them."

And *that* was the Dani I knew. I let out a burst of laughter. "Oh, Dani, ever practical."

"What do you expect? I'm a Capricorn." But she wriggled her nose back at me, then sobered, glancing over at Archer. "So, you came armed with information, you said?"

I had forgotten, in my hunger and need, that he had something to tell us. "Oh good gods, I'd make a horrible detective. I totally forgot about that."

"No you wouldn't. You were just preoccupied with your hunger—that's something hard to ignore." Archer sobered as he pushed his plate out of the way. Nate began to clear the table as Archer brought out his briefcase and flipped the latch.

"Dani is right. I have information, and it's not what you're going to want to hear. I contacted WestcoPsi and had an interesting talk with a few of the guards and a couple of doctors. I asked them to e-mail over some infomation, including a scanned-in copy of the Souljacker's journal." He set a sheaf of papers on the table once Nate had wiped it clean, then returned his briefcase to the floor. "Apparently he left it behind. My source also dropped the info that the other inmates were relieved to see him go. Trust me, when criminally insane Fae and Were are *relieved* that a fellow prisoner escaped, there's a problem."

"This doesn't sound good." I cocked my head. "All right, tell us what you know—and how did you manage to get hold of this info so fast?"

"Bribes work wonders, and so do threats. Anyway, I found out why they locked him up, instead of destroying him like any normal vampire they catch who's on a murderous rampage. You know what happened, right? When he was turned?"

I frowned. "We know what was in the news, and then Dani and I found out he had been locked up, rather than destroyed. All the papers said was that he murdered a family and the police caught him."

Archer glanced at Dani. "This may hit a little close to home, so I'm sorry if it brings up bad memories, but I think you really do need to hear this—all of you."

She paled. "That's all right. I'd rather know what we're facing—I don't bury my head in the sand."

With a nod, Archer continued. "All right. So as far as anybody can tell, Charles was walking back to his apartment after an evening of work, when he was attacked by a vampire. He was killed—it's thought he had been killed in the early evening. By midnight, a family on vacation happened to be wandeirng through the area. A squad car was also in the general vicinity. The family… father, mother, and three teens, saw Charles struggling to stand up. They thought he had been hurt so they went over to give him a hand. They probably had no clue he was dead."

"A good deed never goes unpunished. Sad, but true, and it's always been that way." I stared at my glass for a moment, then rose to refill it with lemonade. I glanced out the kitchen window at the silvery light. The moon was out, for a change, and its light was reflecting against the snow. It was a silent, ice-filled world out there, beautiful yet filled with deadly creatures.

"Unfortunately, that tends to hold true in all worlds." Archer shuffled through his papers. "All right, so the family went to help him and in less than two minutes, Charles attacked. The police noticed the uproar, but by the time they got there, the whole family was dead and drained. But since he didn't know how to shift into the black mist—his sire had run off without waiting for him to rise—and he was too confused to fight, the cops managed to catch him in a silver net."

"I remember that night." Nate glanced over at me. "I was on my way home from a late shift at work and I saw the cop cars. I had no idea what was going on till the next morning."

"Well, the next part is just as muddy, but it's likely one of the cops recognized Charles."

"Wait a minute." Something wasn't tracking for me. "Why would they recognize him? I mean, he was a famous tattooist but usually the cops don't pay much attention to those of us in the subcult."

"So you *don't* know." Archer nodded. "That fills in a puzzle piece—I was wondering. Okay—so the cops hauled him back to the station instead of staking him. Obviously somebody knew who his father was. The cops called Terrance Schafer to deliver him the news that his son was dead and a vampire. And, according to what I could dredge up, within the hour, Terrance began paying people off."

Bingo. That explained so many things. Charles's father was an extremely wealthy and well-placed politician with more influence than was good for anybody. *That's* why the Souljacker was locked up rather than staked. "Let me guess. These *people* you're talking about were all instrumental in saving his son?"

"Right. Politicians, police precincts…WestcoPsi. We're talking seven-figure donations. Although Charles broke away from his family to become a tattooist, his father is so wealthy that he could buy a good portion of Seattle if he wanted to. And from a preliminary glance at his holdings, he already has."

Charles had always seemed totally focused on his art. Half the time he had looked emaciated. "You mean he had money to burn? But he was always broke."

"He wanted to make it on his own. His father, on the down low, actually paid people to get tattoos so that Charles would have money, until he built up a reputation. He never knew about that and it probably would have killed his ego. The Souljacker was a brilliant artist, but his records show he had no sense for business." Archer flipped through the stack of papers, pulling out one that had columns of figures on it. He slid it across the table so we could all see it.

"Here are the names of the candidates and organizations his father donated to right after Charles was captured. And by *right after*, I'm talking within two hours."

The list of names looked like a who's who of Seattle, and included every community outreach program in every district of the greater Seattle area.

"So Terrance paid them off to keep his son alive, when by rights the police should have destroyed him." Dani tossed the papers back on the table. "And a family of five died without any consequences."

"True, though nobody's ever going to prove collusion. Even if they tried, you know full well all this information would get a brand new spin. The family that died? Their relatives received substantial compensation from Terrance Schafer." Archer shook his head. "Blood money."

I was still at the window, and as I stared out into the yard, I thought I could see a black shadow go floating by. "Fuck. I think—" The shadow vanished.

"What's wrong?" Nate joined me. "Do you see something?"

"I thought so, but now…maybe I'm just jumpy." We watched for a moment but nothing seemed to move. "My eyes playing tricks on me, I guess."

Returning to the table, I said, "Do you think his father thought he could help Charles transition? Some do manage it—there are enough vamps in the business world who navigate society. I mean, look at the Deadfather and the financial empire he runs."

"Just because they can function in society doesn't mean you can trust them," Dani said.

"Right. And Lily, you might be correct, but if so, it didn't work. Charles snapped when he was locked up. Maybe because he was an artist, maybe something else, but being turned cost him his talent. The minute the vampire drained him, he also drained him of his genius." Archer sounded almost melancholy. "He lost everything that made him whole."

Nate was silent for a moment, then shoved the paper aside. "Damn it. He was so talented, and so brilliant. He could look at you and see right into your core."

I nodded. "His artwork is gorgeous. When he tattooed my phoenix, I felt…*complete*. Like he'd reached inside me and raked through the muck to find what made me…special. You know?"

"Yeah, but then he murdered five people." Dani shot me a glare. "The Souljacker who inked my tattoo is not the monster who was thrown in WestcoPsi."

Archer shifted through the papers. "Yes, exactly. Charles couldn't handle the loss. During his time in the asylum, he slipped into madness. In the end, they resorted to locking him in a secure room that was magically blocked to prevent him from changing into any other form. They fed him animal blood and kept him shackled by the ankle with specially formulated chains that vampires can't break."

"It would have been kinder to kill him." I felt a sympathy I didn't want to feel. It was easier to be afraid of him than feel sorry for him.

"Yes, but his father wouldn't hear of it. The files I managed to download show that every time the doctors brought up humane euthanasia, Terrance went ballistic. He paid dearly to keep his son locked up."

"So how did the Souljacker escape?" Nate crossed to the stove and put the kettle on.

"Make me some tea, please?" Archer let out a long sigh. "The facts that were reported are these: Three guards were killed by a vampire the night he escaped, and the keys to the ward were missing. The Souljacker's cell was unlocked. The wards on a window had been destroyed—a fact they discovered the next day when they did a walk-through of the building. I managed a quick hack on the dead guards. One of them has a bank account showing a hefty deposit, all in cash, the day before the Souljacker escaped. He worked on the floor where Charles was located."

"Then he could have been paid to disable the wards in order to let a vampire in. The vampire then turned on him, killed him and two other guards, and freed the Souljacker." Dani frowned. "But what does Charles want? Why is he stripping tattoos?"

Archer tossed a stack of pages on the table. "A printout of the Souljacker's journal. I haven't had time to skim through, but his case file—which yes, I managed to get a copy of—notes that Charles has become morbidly obsessed. He can't shake the thought that when his clients die, his art will decay. He began to talk ceaselessly to the doctors about how he might be able to preserve his artwork if he could just get hold of it."

All of a sudden, I knew where this was going. "Oh man, he isn't..."

Archer caught my meaning. "Yes, he *is*. The Souljacker is out to retrieve his artwork. He seems fixated on the idea that once he does so, it will trigger some magical key that will open the door to his lost talent. Only it won't work because he's crazy. Not to mention, his chosen method of curing himself has the added side effect of killing his clients."

"Cripes. Why can't he just take pictures of the tattoos?" Dani asked, horrified.

"I suppose in his mind, the actual art has magical properties. What he wants…no, what he *needs*…are the originals. The files also state that Charles is in denial about being a vampire. He's convinced himself that if he gets his talent back, it will cure his condition."

"This is just one big can of worms, isn't it?" I shook my head.

Nate handed round cups of tea. I glanced at the clock. It was almost 9 P.M.

"I guess that's that. So, the question is now…where do we go from here?"

At that moment, the phone rang. I glanced at the caller ID. *Jolene.* When I answered, she sounded like she had been crying.

"What's wrong?"

"We've got another one, Lily. You remember Hedge? He's dead. His tattoo is gone. Vampire kill. This proves your theory. This time, a witness caught sight of the Souljacker while he was stripping the flesh. It's Charles, all right. He's back and he's after all of us."

CHAPTER 10

Archer had to leave, but I stepped out on the porch to say goodbye to him, oddly reluctant to see him go. Not only had he slaked my hunger, but I was genuinely growing to like him. He had an easy confidence that wasn't obnoxious, and a gentle sarcasm that wasn't cruel. For a chaos demon, he seemed to be pretty damned normal.

"Are you done, then?" I didn't know what I wanted to ask, but that seemed a good place to start.

He held my gaze. "Done with what, Lily?"

"Done with…your investigation? Do you file your report and we pay you and that's it? This latest murder proves we're all on the Souljacker's hit list. Hedge was another member of our India Ink Club. I'm not sure what more you can do."

He paused. "Do you *want* me to be done with it? I can stop if you want me to, but you're wrong. There's so much more that I can do. I can try to figure out where he's hiding himself in the daylight. I can try to ascertain if there's a pattern to the kills so we have more information. I'll do what I can to try to keep the rest of you safe."

I bit my lip. His offer was comforting, but how much did I really want out of the connection? And why was he so interested? We had just met. Granted, we'd knocked bits but that had been born out of my hunger. I didn't know many in the Fae world who said no to free sex with a succubus. I figured that demons were probably the same.

"How much is your rate? I have money, yes, but unfortunately, every client I had scheduled for this week cancelled on me after Tricia Jones got to them—that's Tygur's widow, in case you don't know. I don't know if we can afford your help." I must have sounded defensive because he reached out and stroked my cheek.

"They're nuts to cancel on you. If you're half as good with them as you were with me, then they'd do well to call on you, whatever the she-tiger had to say." He paused, then lifted my chin so I was looking into his face. "Lily, I'll help you, regardless of my fees. You know I don't need the money. This case fascinates me. And…I'd be lying if I said I didn't want to see you again."

I wasn't sure how to take that. I was used to men wanting to fuck me, but some days, I wanted to hear a different reason. "Because of the sex?"

He stroked my cheek. "No. Though you *are* fantastic, that's not what I meant at all. I *like* you. So, if you don't mind, I'll just keep on digging into the case." He closed in on me, leaning in to gaze in my eyes. "That's all right, isn't it?" His voice was husky; his lips were almost on mine.

But I pulled away. I wasn't sure how to read demons—he might be telling the truth, but he might be lying. I wanted to know which.

"We could use the help." And then, I held out my hand.

Archer took it, softly bringing my fingers to his lips where he gently kissed them, one by one. I shivered as an aching stab of desire raced through me. Not hunger, this time, but pure, absolute desire.

"I'll call you tomorrow." He scanned the sky, and then the surrounding area. "Be careful tonight. Stay inside, where you know it's warded." With that, he slid into his car.

As I hurried back inside, a swirl of snow drifted down. Once again, I could hear the Hunt riding into the night—Wynter was on a roll all right, and the wild boys were chasing her skirts.

· · ·

I hadn't known Hedge very well, but he had been part of our group. He was more Greg's friend than mine. Human, he owned a small diner on the outskirts of the Underground. He had little to no family that we'd ever heard about, and while his death was a shock, it was more because it proved what we were thinking.

Dani shook her head. "I'd better get home and get started on your new wards." She paused, hanging her head. "Hedge was one of Greg's best friends. I wonder what he'd think about this…" She paused, then—her eyes tearing up—said, "I wonder if Greg even remembers him. Would he have cheered on the Souljacker? Sometimes…sometimes when I can't sleep, late at night, I lie awake wondering how many people Greg has drained…killed."

This was the first time she had spoken about Greg so openly since he had been murdered.

When someone was turned into a vampire, usually the families kept it quiet. Greg's turning had been public, widespread because of his political win, and Dani had been hit with an onslaught of questions, reporters, and hecklers until she had slammed the door tight on the subject, refusing to ever talk about it.

Nate was closest. He wrapped his arms around her shoulders and rocked her gently as she stood there, steadying herself by the counter. Tears trickled down her cheeks, and I wondered if this whole mess with the Souljacker would prove too much for her.

"Are you sure you want to go home? You can stay here if you need to. I've got plenty of room."

Dani let Nate ease her back into her chair. "I guess…I have to learn how to talk about vampires without falling apart. I try to keep the subject at arm's length because it hurts so much, but I guess I'm just avoiding the inevitable." She groaned, leaning forward as she rested her arms on the table.

"Vampires are terrifying. And given what happened, you have every right to want to avoid the subject. I can't imagine what it might be like." Nate sat down beside her, taking her hand.

I felt like a hypocrite. I had drained my share of innocents in the past, left mourning families like Dani behind. All I could do now was try to help. "You're both right to fear and hate them. Over the years I've met a lot of vampires. I've been on this planet for a long, *long* time and done a lot of things I'm not proud of. In all that time, I can't remember a vampire who wasn't to be feared. None of them—none—were trustworthy. It's inherent to their nature. That being who owns Veek? You were right, Dani, when you said it isn't Greg. It wears his body, but that's not your husband. Your husband hasn't killed anybody. The vampire who took over has."

She sucked in a deep breath, then let it out slowly. "Thank you…thanks to both of you."

"What do we do about Hedge? Did he leave any family behind?"

"I don't think he had any," Nate said.

Dani looked over at me. "Did Archer say anything else before he left? Are we on our own now?"

I couldn't help it. A warm smile formed on my lips when I thought about the man. "No, actually, we aren't. Archer wants to continue helping us, and he said he would do it for free."

Nate and Dani both brightened. Having a chaos demon on your side was a double-edged blessing, but it was far better than the alternative—facing this all on our own.

"So, what's the next step?" Dani wiped away her tears.

"I'm not certain. First, I need to go talk to Wynter about this. The queen will have to know, because there might be members of the court who visited the Souljacker. If she hears about it through the grapevine, and then finds out I already knew? My neck would be on the block. And, I want to talk to Tricia."

They both looked at me like I was crazy.

"Listen…I have to appeal to her. There's nothing else I can do. I'm going to throw myself on any goodwill that might be hiding under a rock and beg her to ease up on trash-talking me. If she doesn't stop, I won't have any clients left."

Dani flashed me a sympathetic look. "Talk to Shayla Masters instead. She's Tricia's best friend and not as likely to be so antago-nistic. Maybe. I hope."

"I wouldn't count on that," Nate said, his voice glum. "You know the Weres. They're thick as thieves, and they stick together.

Are you sure you want to try this? I'm not just asking rhetorically. You *know* the Weres. They can be a rough bunch."

He was right. Weres put the *v* in volatile. And Nate wasn't kidding when he said they were thick as thieves. Anger one member of a Were pack or pride, and you might as well take out a bounty on your own head because all of them would be up in your business. They held onto grudges like they were a precious commodity.

"What other choice do I have? I can't sit around waiting for her to calm down. If I don't get her to back off, I might as well pack up and move my business to another city." As I spoke, another text came in. I glanced at it. "Oh, for fuck's sake. Another cancellation. Leon, one of my best clients, just cancelled his standing appointment 'until further notice.' The *only* thing I can do is beg her to back off."

The thought rankled. If she didn't like her husband coming to me, fine. But that battle was between the two of them. I wasn't a streetwalker. I didn't go out soliciting business. No mass-mailings or pamphlets or coupons for half-price days. No, I worked strictly on a word-of-mouth basis.

Dani shrugged. "I guess you're right. Do you have enough to live on until you get this straightened out?"

"I sunk a fortune into buying this property and building the house, but at least it's paid off. I'll be fine for a year down the road, as long as I'm cautious. With property taxes and district taxes and everything else, the money will go faster than I want to think... but hell..."

Then, another thought struck me. "Trouble is, I'll have to feed. The salon has primarily been a fun and lucrative way to feed without letting myself get too hungry. I'll have to be cautious, make certain I don't let myself get ravenous..."

"Maybe Archer can help you out there," Nate said.

I stared at him. "Archer?"

"I'm perfectly serious. You two seemed to hit it off. If you both know where you stand, since neither of you has any encumbrances, maybe he can help you cope with your hunger."

Dani's phone rang. She glanced at it. "Damn it. I have to get something started for a ritual—I have to be home by midnight. The moon goes into Capricorn then, and this spell needs to be finished during that time." She stood. "Okay, this has been…real, I guess. I can't say it was the most pleasant evening we've spent together, but at least if this has to happen, we have each other. I'm headed out."

"Let us walk you out to your car." Nate motioned to me. I nodded and we slipped into our coats.

As we walked Dani to her car, we were a silent trio. I stared up into the darkened sky, looking to see if I could spot the mist I had thought I'd seen earlier. The Souljacker couldn't get into the house now—at least not for a few more days. By the time the protection patches wore off, Dani would have my new wards made or I would buy temporary ones. But still, the thought that he might be around, waiting and watching, nagged at me.

Dani let out a long sigh as she opened the door to her car.

"I'll text you when I get home. Please, be careful. I know I'm a little bit fanatical when it comes to the subject, but when you've lost a loved one to a monster, and those monsters are free to walk around in society, you tend to get…paranoid." With that, she slid into the driver's seat, locked her door, and eased out of the driveway.

Nate and I linked arms and headed back to the house. We seemed to share the need to change the subject.

"How was your day?" I asked. "You've heard how mine went."

I rinsed the dishes and put them in the dishwasher. "My boss told me that I should get a bonus this year. I'm up for promotion." He beamed. "I managed to create an automated program that cuts their need for contractors by a third—although that's not going to win me points with the people who lose their jobs. I'm almost hoping someone will find a major flaw in the process so I'm not responsible for layoffs. But the good news is, even if it does work, they can't possibly deploy it for another year. It has to be tested and retested, and the programmers working now have a run-of-the-contract clause. They can't be laid off until their contract is up for renewal."

The run-of-the-contract clause had been implemented, Nate had explained to me, when outsourcing had gotten so bad that unemployment in the US soared to record heights. Now, jobs had to be filled by US citizens first. Only if the employer could prove that there were no qualified applicants willing to take the job could they turn outside the United States. Corporations were still fighting against it, but popular support kept the law in full force and, in the long run, it had been extremely good for the economy.

"I'm sure it will all work out okay. How about your love life? Anybody on the horizon?"

Nate gave me a sideways glance, then slowly shook his head. "I keep looking. I meet a lot of nice women, a lot of attractive women, but I just don't have what it takes…I want a woman who's smart and independent, but I think I'm just too set in my ways to make room for someone in my life."

Nate was a quiet man who led a quiet life, and was fixated on his job. Women didn't like taking a backseat, and even though he was lonely, I suspected that until he found another computer geek to share his life, he'd be sitting alone in his house. He needed someone who shared his interests and could get as caught up in her work as he did his.

I carried the remains of the dinner cartons over to the recycling and garbage cans, trying to think of something encouraging to say.

But at that moment, Mr. Whiskers came up and leaped on the table with a loud *purp*.

Turning around, I took a long look at him. His long fur was fluffed out and the look in his eyes told me that something was amiss. "Great. Now what? Whisky, what's up?"

Nate, who knew Mr. Whiskers's true story, arched his eyebrows. "He can still sense magic at play, can't he?"

I nodded, slowly scanning the room. "Is somebody here?"

Mr. Whiskers jumped off the table and raced into the living room. Nate and I followed. As we entered the place, I immediately saw a sparkle of light that was flickering around the room like a firefly.

"What the hell?" I turned to Whisky. "Someone's here, right?"

He let out a low mew and took a running leap into my arms, almost knocking me back with his weight.

It wasn't a vampire—vampires were anything but sparkly, and they couldn't get through the wards right now. But whatever it was, it was definitely something on the magical side. I put Mr. Whiskers down on the top of the sofa, then cautiously edged over to the light as my hand dropped to unsheathe my dagger.

In a loud voice I said, "Who are you? What do you want? Show yourself."

Nate edged up behind me. "What is it?"

"I don't know," I started to say, but before I could finish, a bright light flared from the sparkle and then Marsh Sheffield appeared in the room, a solemn look on his face.

Unable to believe what I was seeing, I stumbled back.

"Lily? What is it? Is he dangerous?" Nate caught my shoulder, steadying me.

I shook my head, feeling an ache in my heart I hadn't felt in seventy-five years.

"*Marsh*…it can't be you. Can it?"

"Who's Marsh?" Nate asked.

As I stared at the figure in the room, all I could say was, "Marsh is the only man I ever loved. And he died because of me."

CHAPTER 11

"Loved? But you told me…" Nate's voice drifted off. He was looking decidedly confused.

Whisky mewed, startling me out of my paralysis. I glanced back at Marsh. It couldn't be. He was dead. And if it was his ghost, why had he only returned now, so long after I lost him?

"Marsh, what are you doing here?"

Marsh gave me a long look, one that wrenched both my heart and my gut. He looked exactly the way he had on the last morning we spent together, tall with his black hair tousled in curls that hung down to his shoulders. His eyes—the most brilliant green I'd ever seen—still held all the pain and heartache that they had when we'd been together. It was then that I noticed he was wearing the suit he had been buried in.

He leaned against the wall and nodded toward Nate. "So, is he your new lover?"

Startled by the words—and by the fact that Nate seemed to hear them, too—I wanted to shout at him to go away, but I couldn't muster up the heart to do so.

Instead, I stammered out a lame, "Marsh…is it really you?"

"Oh, it's me. Where am I?" He looked around. "I don't remember this place."

I cleared my throat. "Do you…you do realize you're…" How did you ask someone if they knew they were dead? The only way I could think of was to be direct. "Marsh, you know you're dead, right?"

He blinked, then let out a rough laugh. "Oh, I know I'm dead. The last thing I remember is you killing me."

Boom. And the brick wall hit me full force.

I slowly edged over to the sofa, where I dropped to the seat and crossed my arms over my chest. If this was a dream, I really wanted it to end. Now.

"Please, stop. I didn't mean to. I didn't mean to hurt you. I warned you…"

Nate slipped between Marsh and me. "You upset her. I advise you stop or I'll…"

"You'll what? Hire a ghost hunter?" But then, Marsh deflated, shaking his head. "I'm sorry. I…I have no clue what the hell to do. Lily, tell me what's going on."

"I wish I knew." I slowly edged off the sofa again and quietly stepped around Nate. "Marsh, I've missed you so much. You don't know how hard it was for me to move on."

Nate cleared his throat. "How about introductions?" he asked softly.

"Right…Marsh Sheffield, I want you to meet Nate…Percival Nathanial Winston. Nate's one of my best friends. Nate, this is Marsh. Marsh was my fiancé until one night when the hunger grew so strong that…that…" I paused, unable to continue.

Nate grabbed me by the arm. "In the kitchen, Lily. Now." To Marsh, he added, "Excuse us. Wait here. Please."

We entered the kitchen and Nate turned me around, holding me by the shoulders. "Lily, what's going on? Who is he? You were engaged? I take it that he's a…a ghost, but where did he come from and why?"

"I don't know. I really don't." I was feeling more confused every second. It didn't help that my heart was breaking for a second time. I had managed to stop dreaming about him, but Marsh's memory had punished me for decades after his death, haunting my dreams and my waking hours.

"Marsh died seventy-five years ago. I warned him that he shouldn't get involved with me. I warned him I was dangerous but he wouldn't listen. And eventually, I couldn't help myself. I fell in love. I knew it was stupid, but I loved him."

Nate moved me over to a chair and sat me down. I accepted the glass of water he pressed into my hands. "How did he die?"

"We were on vacation in an alpine cabin when a freak snowstorm hit. The first couple days were fine. We had food; we had checked in at a ranger station so somebody would come looking for us when we didn't report our return. But the snow kept falling. I needed to feed. I had explained to Marsh, tried to make him lock himself in the bathroom away from me. But…"

Marsh suddenly appeared in the kitchen next to us. "You explained to me, yes. But how was I to realize just how strong your hunger was? I knew you were a succubus but I never really understood what that meant."

I hung my head, wanting to strike him. But he was a spirit. My hand would go straight through. "I warned you."

"Yeah. But…" Marsh let out a soft sigh.

Nate looked like he wanted to be anywhere but standing between the two of us. "You still blame Lily? You were human?"

"As human as you are, my man."

I bit my tongue, forcing myself to keep quiet. I couldn't let myself get embroiled in a fight with a ghost. Especially *this* ghost. Ever since losing Marsh, I had done my best to keep on an even keel. Fear and irritation, I could deal with. Anger was problematic, given my ability to charm and to feed. But love and regret? They might as well be dynamite in my hands.

I let out a long sigh. "The past is long gone. So tell me, what are you doing here, Marsh? Why return now? Are you out for an apology? Revenge?"

A puzzled look crossed his face, with a touch of hurt thrown in. "Lily, I would never hurt you. Even…I just wouldn't. No, all I know is that I'm here to watch over you. Your guardian summoned me."

That, I was not expecting. "What are you talking about? What guardian?"

Marsh shrugged. "I have no idea. I just have this gut knowledge that someone concerned about you summoned me to do what I could."

My heartache subsiding in the wake of my bewilderment, I asked, "Where were you before now? After…I mean…" The words just felt way too odd in my head, let alone try to verbalize them.

"I don't know. I have no clue how long I've been dead. I don't remember much after I died—in fact, it's a blur, almost like gray space. It's funny though. Now I realize how much I took for granted."

That I could empathize with. "Most people take a good share of their lives for granted. The universe is vast…but most people seem to focus on one narrow sliver."

I stared at the table, wanting to think. Truth was, I worshipped no gods and was indebted to no one. So who was this guardian? Then there was the question of Marsh himself—very few people knew about him. Even fewer knew the full story. Dani did, but she would have consulted me before summoning him. Other than Dani, most of the people who had known about Marsh were long gone from my life.

"How can you not know who summoned you?" I looked up as he stood there silent, waiting.

"It wasn't like being called into the principal's office and told I had crossing guard duty. No, I don't remember anything before I showed up here. I just know…like I know my own name, that I've been sent here to protect you." He sat opposite to me, and I found it disconcerting to see the wood of the chair through his body. He looked so corporeal, and yet he had a vaguely translucent sheen to him.

Again, guilt and regret stabbed at me. "I warned you that it's deadly to love a succubus. I told you to get out of my life—"

"How *could* I, when I loved you so much?" His shoulders slumped. "Leave it. We'll never fully resolve this. What year is it? I don't even have a clue how much time has passed."

"Try seventy-five years. You died seventy-five years ago. I've done my best to forget you. Now that's shot to hell." Feeling raw and broken, I marched to the cupboard and poured myself a good-sized slug of rum. Whisky waited till I sat down again, then jumped on my lap, purring loudly as he rubbed his head against my chin.

"Aw Whisky, what the hell am I going to do?" I scratched behind his ears, the soft tufts of fur tickling my fingers.

Whisky remained silent, his eyes fastened on mine. As he held my gaze he gave one soft mew and then began kneading my chest gently, claws retracted. I buried my face in his fur, hugging him as I fought tears. Everything was unraveling.

After a moment, I sat back with a sigh. "Marsh, do you mind waiting in the other room for awhile? I just…need a minute."

"Sure." Still looking confused, he vanished before I could say another word.

Nate peeked in the living room and then gave me a nod. "He's there. You never told me about him, Lily." He settled in the chair Marsh had been sitting in. "I didn't know you'd been…"

"In love? And with a human? Yeah, my biggest mistake." I slowly raised my gaze to meet his. "I thought everything would be safe. I avoided him but Marsh kept pursuing. I worked out of an apartment in California, playing the high-class call girl for the Fae and Weres, who were still in the closet. I told Marsh what I was. He was the only human who knew. And I warned him about the curse. 'Any human who falls for a succubus will end up dead,' I told him. But he refused to listen. And I liked him, so much…and the more we hung out…"

"You fell in love."

"Right. *Love.*" I spat out the word. The one thing I wanted and couldn't have. "It was like diving into the deep end of the ocean—I just kept sinking. Finally, I gave in. It was lovely at first. But the longer we were together, the harder it got. He hated that I was sleeping with other men, but he tried to shoulder through it. I couldn't deny my nature any more than I could stop breathing. Finally, we went away to the mountains for a winter skiing trip to try to work things out. We were supposed to be gone a weekend. We rented a cabin and took plenty of supplies, but a blizzard roared in and kept us housebound for over a week. We would have been fine except…"

"Except you got hungry."

"As the days passed, I warned Marsh to lock himself in the bathroom at night. He knew what was happening. But he was stubborn. He was convinced that if I fed off him—lightly—that we would be fine. But I knew better. The day before the snow stopped, my hunger grew too strong. I lost control. He refused to believe I would hurt him."

"And you drained him." A look of understanding crept into Nate's eyes. "What happened?"

I shook my head. "I couldn't get out; the snow was too deep. I sat with his body until the forest rangers reached the cabin. Marsh…it looked like he'd just had a heart attack. That's what the medical examiner put down as his death. Everybody tried to console me, to tell me how brave I was. I couldn't stand their pity, knowing I had killed the man I loved. As soon as I could, I left town. That was the first—and last—time that I ever let myself get involved with a human."

"Now I understand." Nate leaned back, resting his hands behind his head. "Now I get why you're so careful."

"I can't let myself love, because I'll destroy everything that is good and beautiful about the person. My nature precludes monogamy."

The truth was, if offered the chance, I'd give up my nature in order to allow myself to be loved. No matter what species I was, I would still be Lily O'Connell. Even if I were to suddenly lose the need to feed, I would still be myself. But there was no power on earth that could strip me of the drive. So I adapted. I learned to live with the reality that I was born for passion, but not for love. Unfortunately, convincing my heart wasn't so easy.

Nate reached out again, but only to lay a light hand on my shoulder for the briefest second. "Are you okay, Lily?"

"I'm lonely, Nate. But I guess that's just my fate in life."

Nate straightened, staring behind me. I turned to see Marsh, watching us.

"How long have you been there?"

"Long enough. Lily, I don't want to hurt you. I should have listened to you. I don't think I realized until now what your life has been like all these years."

I ducked my head, not wanting to see the pity in his eyes. "Yeah, well…water under the bridge. It is what it is. I'm a succubus and I've learned how to keep my heart locked up." After a pause, I asked, "So, how long are you here for?"

"I don't know. I can't leave. Whoever summoned me bound me here for now. Don't ask me how I know. I just do. But I'll try not to get in the way." His lips swept into a tentative smile. "Friends? For now?"

The last thing I wanted was to face my past on a daily basis. But here it was, staring me in the face. "Yeah, friends. But I still want to find out who brought you here. And what you're supposed to be doing."

"All I know is that I'm supposed to follow you around and warn you if anything happens. I'm not sure exactly what's going on but apparently you're in danger."

"You can say that again," I mumbled.

Nate snapped his fingers. "Could Wynter have summoned Marsh? You *are* part of her court."

"Wynter? No, I don't think so, but I can find out. I'm heading out there tomorrow morning, after I talk to Shayla." Yawning, I glanced at the clock. "I need to sleep, and you do too, Nate. Did you want to stay here tonight? I know Dani said your wards are okay but…"

"But two are safer than one? And you've fed well, so you're not hungry. Yeah, I might take you up on that." He stretched. "Mind if I take one of the guest rooms? Your sofa's nice but it's not that comfortable."

"That's fine." I turned to Marsh. "If you're supposed to guard me then I guess we might as well make use of you."

At that moment, I realized that Marsh didn't even know vampires existed. He had no clue about what the world was like now.

"Listen, I don't have time to fill you in on everything that's gone down since you died, but I want you to keep an eye out through the house. If you see anything…a black mist, a figure or a walking shadow…*anything* that seems out of the ordinary, then wake me immediately."

He nodded. "I'm rather looking forward to finding out how the world of today is compared to when we were together. I can't believe it's been so long. Seventy-five years? Really?"

"Marsh, the world has changed in ways you would never have dreamed. I'll tell you all about it tomorrow. Until then, keep an eye out."

After a quick Q&A, I learned that Marsh couldn't manipulate physical objects. I turned on the TV so that he could watch the all-night news station. That would give him some clue as to how much the world had shifted.

And with that, Nate and I headed upstairs. We searched the bedrooms, then without another word past goodnight, shut ourselves up for much-needed sleep. Luckily, the night passed without incident, and by morning I felt a little bit of hope in my heart that maybe, just maybe, I could turn things around.

CHAPTER 12

I had a nightmare that night. I dreamed that Marsh turned into an albatross, sent to weigh me down until I couldn't handle the guilt anymore. In the dream I had been ready to slit my wrists when I woke in a cold sweat that left my sheets damp.

As I showered and dressed, the thought wouldn't go away, that maybe—just maybe—Marsh's presence was a curse, rather than a gift. But I didn't have time to dwell on it. I had to get moving if I was going to get over to Shayla's before I hit the freeway that would take me to Wynter's court.

I opted to dress in a sedate manner—a pair of black jeans and a green turtleneck. No use flaunting my sexuality in their faces. Not that either woman was a slacker in the looks department. Both Tricia and Shayla were gorgeous, but the less I paraded my skin in front of either of them, the better. My hair in a ponytail, I slapped on the barest skim of makeup.

Marsh was in the kitchen with Nate when I trundled in. He was sitting on the floor by Mr. Whiskers's dish. I thought about asking what he was doing, but then decided not to pry.

Nate had fed Whisky already, and the cat was scarfing down food as fast as he could. I often thought about putting him on a diet but the truth was, no matter how fat he got, Whisky would be okay thanks to his nature.

"Morning all." The shock of seeing Marsh had worn off, and I felt more capable of dealing with his presence.

"How many eggs?" Nate was cracking them into a bowl for scrambled eggs.

"Three, please."

While Nate made breakfast, I started a to-do list. Contacting Wynter was at the top of the list, but I decided to wait until after I'd dropped in on Shayla.

I knew the weretiger on an acquaintance-only level, but Dani was right. Talking to her would be better than attempting a détente with Tricia. Nate handed me a plate and I accepted the toast and eggs without comment as he poured me a cup of coffee.

Marsh stood up, dusting off his pants even though there was no dust that clung to them. I supposed habits died hard even when you were a ghost. He wandered over and sat down in the opposite chair. I was still startled by how corporeal he looked.

"I've learned more than I thought possible by watching the news all night long. The world has changed, hasn't it?"

I nodded. "Yes, in some ways for the better. In many ways, not."

"So, vampires."

"Right." I paused, setting my fork down. "Has Nate told you what we're up against?"

"I did, Lily. I hope you don't mind. I figured you'd have enough to deal with today without giving Marsh a rundown on the Souljacker." Nate joined us, plate and coffee in hand.

"Actually, I'm grateful. But yeah…so…vampires. They didn't come out until after the Weres and the Fae did. I knew they existed—most Fae and Weres already knew. But as long as they kept to the shadows, we assumed they weren't a large part of society. Altasociety, that is. We were wrong."

"There are a lot of them, then?"

"Too many. Apparently, the vamps had been massing in the underground areas, waiting for the day when they would be able to walk freely among us. That day has come, however, most of them aren't just walking among us, but hunting." I frowned. "They're dangerous, Marsh. *You* can't be harmed by them—at least not physically—but they are powerful beings and I'm convinced they mean to take over."

Marsh blinked. "You mean, keep the humans and…Weres? Weres and Fae as feeding stock? Horror movie sort of stuff?"

I nodded. "The government says it's all panic, but there are a lot of high-ranking officials who receive plenty of blood money from the vampires. And the more they refuse to play by the rules, the more suspect they are. There are plenty of theories going around that the vampires are planning an organized coup. If we continue allowing them get away with the attacks, we might as well hand over the keys to society."

"She's right," Nate said. "I keep up with a lot of subcult organizations. There's a groundswell movement that claims they have proof that vampires are out to subjugate the living. Part of their strategy is to buy up control over a number of important organizations. Did you know that the Deadfather owns fifty-five percent interest in Tellecom-Via?"

Even I hadn't realized that. "Really?"

"What's Tellecom-Via?" Marsh asked.

"Tellecom happens to be the primary communications company in the United States. They bought out most of the others, one at a time. The mergers started way back when Time/Warner and Comcast and Verizon and Sprint and all the others were waging war for supremacy over the airwaves. Now, it's mostly Tellecom-Via, with a few ragtag startups who are barely managing to stay in business."

"Yeah, not much choice, really," I added. "And trust me, while technology has advanced, customer service hasn't."

"You said a mouthful there." Nate shrugged. "I only found out about the vamps' holdings because I'm a techie and I was poking around, looking for an alternative. I followed enough links to discover that the Deadfather is the shadow behind the primary shareholder."

"Who's the Deadfather?" Marsh was still looking confused.

I finished my breakfast and took a long sip of my coffee. "The Deadfather is the…think of him as the vampire king, so to speak. What he says, goes, among the vamp community. He's officially acknowledged as the leader of the vampire movement by the government. Jolene told me that the cops are instructed *never* to attribute any vampire execution to him because that would only stir up trouble. Anyway, he's terribly wealthy and demands a tithe from most of the vamps over whom he rules. Those who don't pay, don't stay alive long."

Marsh cleared his throat. "Kind of like the old-time Mafias?"

"Only much more deadly. Anyway, the Deadfather is incredibly rich and incredibly strict. You don't want to mess with him."

My lips twitched as I remembered the one time I had actually met the man. It had been at a party—a one-time client had hired me to go as arm candy to a cocktail party. Easy money. I played the part and was a doting, trophy girlfriend. The Deadfather had been there. I hadn't spoken with him for long, but even in that short time there was something so incredibly powerful about the vampire that I had wanted to run as far away as fast as I could. He had taken my hand, turned it over, and gently kissed the palm. The entire time I'd been terrified he was going to sink his fangs into my wrist. The worst of it was that, as strong as *my* glamour was, his had been stronger. I had almost thrown myself into his arms, as terrified as I was.

"You've met him." Marsh said, a glittering look in his eye.

"Once. And I hope I never meet him again. But the Deadfather owns a vast empire, of both wealth and property. I don't know where he hides—it's not in the Underground; that would be too obvious—but wherever it is, you can bet he's got a ton of servants and probably a stable of donors. Though my guess is they aren't volunteers."

There were those who sought out the vampires, begging to be turned or to be used, but the vamps didn't make it easy for the former, and the latter, they willingly took in. Once you pledged your allegiance to the Blood Nation, you pretty much gave up any right to freedom. It was technically illegal, but the cops looked the other way. Once the vampires used you up or grew tired of you, it was easy enough to turn you into a vampire—a slave in an entirely different way.

Marsh blinked, then changed the subject. "I'm supposed to be watching over you. How will I do that when you go out?"

I shook my head. "I have no clue. I'm not an expert in how the ghost world works. I guess…we figure out if you can go with me and hang out in the car."

Nate laughed. "Silent car alarm?"

I snorted. "Whatever. I should get moving. Once I'm done groveling at Shayla's feet, then it's off to visit Wynter. Marsh, when we get to Wynter's court, be careful. The Dark Fae are not for the faint of heart, and there are those who will be able to see you, whether or not you choose to manifest. And some of them can do nasty things to spirits if they decide they don't like your looks." And with that, I dropped my plate off by the sink and grabbed my jacket. "Nate, what's on your agenda today? You have work?"

He shook his head. "Telecommuting today."

And with that, we left the house, all three of us. Nate headed next door, as Marsh walked along behind me, looking around. Since I could see him, and Nate, I wondered who else could.

"Say, how visible are you right now?"

"If someone were to walk by right now, they'd see you talking to a patch of…well…air. I can be seen by those I allow to see me. I don't know how to explain it. Hell, I don't even understand it myself. At least so far." He stared at the car, then he was suddenly inside, sitting in the passenger seat.

I slipped behind the wheel and turned the ignition. "What if someone else gets in the car?"

"This seat will feel incredibly chilly to them. That's about it. I'd just move to the back so you wouldn't get disconcerted seeing me superimposed over them in the same seat." He paused, then asked, "So, Lily…this Souljacker fellow. He's really dangerous, isn't he?"

I nodded. "I wish I could say otherwise. Honestly, I have no idea what to do. I've been out of the battle, so to speak, for years. Since well before I met you. And here? In Seattle? The worst things I have to worry about? Stay out of the vamp paths after dark. Don't rub my business in my clients' wives' faces. Concern myself with being discreet. Nowhere till now did *worry about being murdered by a psychotic vampire out to strip the skin off my body* come into play."

My voice drifted off as I turned onto Onna Avenue. My shoulders felt like one knot on top of another, and the stress was giving me a low-grade headache. It didn't help that it was Marsh I was talking to. Ghost or not, he was still the man I had loved. I felt queasy, like the sky was about to fall and I was the only one who knew about it.

"Lily…" Marsh's voice was soft. "I want to help. I don't know who or what brought me here, but I'll do whatever I can to help you. I've got your back."

I swung into the parking garage beneath the high rise that Shayla lived in. As I circled around, looking for the visitor parking, I managed to shove my fears to the back.

"Do you really not remember anything before showing up in my house?"

Marsh nodded. "I've tried to remember, but the last memory I have…" He paused, then softly said, "The last memory I have is of kissing you, and feeling my breath leave my body. I want you to know something, Lily."

I eased into a parking spot and turned off the ignition. "What?"

"I thought about all of this last night. I watched the news and thought about how the world has changed. My last thoughts were about how much I loved you. And about how I should have listened to you. I was stupid and careless. You warned me, but I put myself in danger and I put you in a horrendous position. I take responsibility." He bit his lip, shrugging. "I pushed you too hard to be someone you weren't. Someone you could never be."

"You weren't the one who killed yourself."

"No, but I didn't do much to preserve my life, either. I could have locked the door against you. I could have locked myself in the bathroom. You would have been furious…but I'd have been alive when they found us." He caught my gaze, reaching a hand out to place it over my own. His fingers went through mine with a gentle chill.

I stared at him. "At some point, we have to stop blaming ourselves. And each other. I'm so tired of carrying the guilt around.

I'm so tired of beating myself up. I have missed you so much, and I never, ever forgot you, even though I tried."

He nodded. "It is what it is, as you said earlier. We made mistakes. I died, but obviously that wasn't the end of me, was it? I'm here now, just in a different form. And if I had lived? I'd be dead of old age by now. Humans don't live forever."

"Neither do the Fae, though it might seem like it to mortals. Okay then. We start fresh. We start here, as friends?"

"Friends. I'll go invisible right now so you aren't distracted by my presence. I'll be behind you, though. There isn't much I can do except warn you if I see a potential problem, but I'll be there."

"If something happens, go to Nate and tell him to call Dani. I don't expect anything to come up, but in case it does, they're the ones to contact." I paused, then for the first time since Tygur died, broke into a wide smile. "Marsh…I'm so glad you're here. It hurts, yes, but I'm glad you're back in my life."

He returned the smile and then vanished. I stared at the empty patch of air, but I could feel him around. Just like when we had been together, only the energy had shifted some. The edge of passion was gone, but I could almost smell his aftershave. With a long sigh, I adjusted my jacket so it hid my dagger and headed toward the elevator.

• • •

Shayla lived on the fourteenth floor. As the elevator doors opened with a soft swish, I stepped out into the tiled hallway. At first I was surprised that it wasn't carpeted, but then thought—Weres. This building was tenanted mostly by Weres, and during the full moon they were out on the run. When they came home, they were often bloody or muddy or roughed up from their nights under the moon. Jolene had returned more than once covered in rabbit blood. Tile was easier to clean than carpeting.

I stopped in front of unit 1405, pausing before I rang the bell. Was this really a good idea? Maybe I should give it a rest. Just let things settle. But before I could make up my mind, the door opened and there she stood. Shayla, Tricia's best friend. I stepped back, startled by her sudden appearance.

Shayla was tall, with long copper hair about three shades lighter than mine, and her eyes glowed with a faint topaz light. She was six-six, towering even for a Were, and lean. I knew that Shayla was a dance instructor, so she had muscle and flexibility, which also meant she could whip my ass. I might still look buff, but I sure hadn't been on a workout schedule lately.

She glowered down at me in her tight spandex pants and halter top. They showed every curve, every inch—and there wasn't an inch to spare. In fact, I could practically see her rib bones through the material. Given her height, I was pretty much staring at them below the gentle rise of her softly rounded breasts—which were small, but perfect in shape. I had the feeling that she'd had body-shaping done at some time. It was a common enough procedure, but it made everything just too symmetrical for my taste.

Shaking my head, I moved my gaze up to meet hers, which immediately seemed to be a mistake. She bared her teeth, letting out a snarl that was unmistakably a threat.

"What the fuck are you doing here, you dumb bitch?" She folded her arms across her chest, moving forward. I stumbled back. It was either that or have her boobs shoved in my face. "Don't you have any shame at all?"

I cleared my throat. I didn't want to get into a fight, but neither was I willing to let her slut-shame me. "Listen, Shayla. I am truly sorry for what happened with Tygur, but come on. Don't you think he should have been the one to remain faithful to his wife? I didn't recruit him, for fuck's sake. *He* came to *me*."

Shayla said nothing, her gaze scorching through me like a laser.

"I wanted to ask you if you could talk to Tricia…to get her to ease up…" I began to stumble over my words as the weretiger snarled again. She began to uncross her arms, and I had the feeling it wasn't because she wanted to shake my hand.

"You want to ask me to talk my friend into forgiving you?

My friend who is burying her husband, because he was murdered with his pecker in your pussy?" Her voice was growing louder, and a couple of doors along the hallway open. The last thing I needed was a pack of irate Weres after me. I decided to forego pointing out that I hadn't been having sex with Tygur when he got killed, and just get the hell out of Dodge.

"Never mind! I'll leave. But if you just think about it—" I didn't have time to get the rest of the sentence out before she smacked me a good one. Her blow was so hard it flung me across the hall, landing me near the elevator. My side hit a garbage can, knocking the wind out of me.

I scrambled to my feet, rubbing my jaw and holding my ribs.

By her stance, it was obvious she was ready to go at it, and I wasn't stupid enough to think I could come out on top. I backed away, one hand held out in front of me. Weres were volatile when they were roused, and she had that look in her eye that told me she had slid into hunting mode. I had no intention on becoming her quarry. Luckily, as I fumbled for the button, the elevator opened immediately and I jumped inside as she started after me. I hit the CLOSE button and, as the elevator started down toward the parking garage, I prayed that she wouldn't be there waiting.

Luckily, there was no sign of Shayla as I cautiously peeked out the doors. I raced for my car. She must not have been interested enough to take to the stairs. Either that or she had managed to cool down enough to let me go. Either way, I counted my blessings on getting out without more than a bruise or two. As I peeled out of the garage, Marsh appeared in the passenger seat again.

"You were lucky," he said.

"I know."

"Where to next?"

"It's time for me to go see Wynter. You better make yourself scarce once we get there." But all the way over toward Faeside, I kept thinking about Shayla and her reaction. I had a very bad feeling I wouldn't be getting my business squared away again for a very long time.

CHAPTER 13

On the east side of Lake Washington, across from Seattle, the area still held a swarm of cities. Most still went by their original names, but the Fae congregated around the Woodinville area, and once she had come out as a force, Wynter had set up her palace in what had once been known as Lord Hill Park, near Monroe. Since then, several of the big industry giants had inexplicably pulled out, along with the military bases that had been stationed around the area, and the population had dropped as the forest reclaimed the outer edges of the developed areas.

Agriculture had become the big thing as of late, and though Wynter kept things pretty chilly, the vineyards had broadened and wine making—which had been an up-and-coming industry in the area before the Fae came out—had taken off. Western Washington was renowned for its wine and spirits.

As I drove through the countryside, Marsh stared out the window. When I had known him, it had been before I came to this part of the country. Given that he didn't remember anything between his death and now, I figured he had probably never seen the area before.

After a time, he cleared his throat. "What are you going to do about your business? That Shayla woman didn't seem very amenable, to put it lightly."

I had been doing my best not to think about it, but realized that denial wasn't going to help matters any. With a shake of my head, I said, "I don't know. They're out to ruin me. I might be able to convince my Fae clients to stick around, but the Weres? Lost cause unless they lift their sanctions. And Weres hold grudges.

Since my clients generally only visit me once a month—I'm expensive—the remaining won't be enough to make a living from, nor to satisfy my hunger. I'm not sure what to do."

"You can't start taking humans as clients." It was a statement, not a question.

"Obviously. The truth is, I honestly don't know what I'm going to do." I paused. "When the Souljacker killed Tygur, he killed more than a client. He took down my business."

"Do you like owning the salon? I know you love sex, but…do you enjoy what you do?"

I frowned. Nobody had ever asked me the question before. They just assumed I was horny all the time. Most people didn't understand the nuances involved in the hunger that drove my kind.

"There are worse ways to earn a living. I enjoy making people happy. Yes, I do envy women who can fall in love without worrying they're going to kill their partner, but truth time? I'm proud of what I do. I give pleasure in a world full of pain. That has to count for something."

"It counts for a great deal, Lily." He flashed me a smile, and I swear, for a moment it felt like the past had been transported into the present.

"Damn it, why do you have to appear so corporeal? Why can't you be all filmy and look like a real ghost?" I was only half joking. "You don't know how much I've missed your laugh. You always could brighten my spirits when I was feeling down."

"I liked making you laugh. Your smile. I always loved it when you smiled." He leaned to the side, staring out the window as we passed by a ravine. "The landscape here is wild and rough, isn't it?"

"You haven't seen anything yet."

"By the looks of those mountains in the distance, I'd say you're right." Another pause. Then, he let out a soft sigh that sounded more like a whisper caught in the wind.

"Lily, I don't know what it means to be dead. If I ever did know, whoever summoned me made sure I have no memory of it. Or maybe I was just…nothing…until they brought me back? Maybe I'm not even real right now, but a construct?"

"Maybe Dani can read the cards for you. She's dealt with the spirit world far more than I ever have." I didn't mention my nightmare, but I intended to ask Dani about that, too.

"Who's Dani?"

"She's my best friend. She's a witch."

If that fazed him, he didn't let on.

Another few miles in silence, and then we were onto the highway that would take us to Wynter's palace. Traffic was light, but the Overpass Train zipped by, crowded as usual. Grateful again that I didn't have to take mass transit, I kept pace, matching it for a few minutes before it rounded a turn and sped up for a straight shot up north rather than following the road.

Another twenty minutes and we were nearing the gates of the Winter Court. I pulled over to the side of the road. "I have to change. I can't be seen in court wearing this get up."

Marsh frowned. "You look fine to me."

"Not for appearing before Wynter, I don't. There's a strictly regulated dress code when it comes to the courts of Fae. Now is not the time to buck it." I eased into a gas station with a convenience store and parked around by the restrooms. "I'll be back in a few minutes."

After getting the key from the attendant, I quickly unlocked the trunk and pulled out a large garment bag. I had worn this outfit exactly fourteen times in my life, though I had owned it for two hundred years. I kept it in pristine condition because it had been terribly expensive. Even now, it would cost a fortune to have redone. As I gingerly opened the bathroom door, I was relieved to see the room was clean. No stains or grime on the floor.

I changed quickly, shimmying out of my jeans and top. Shivering—there seemed to be no heat in the bathroom—I unzipped the garment bag.

The dress made me catch my breath, as it did every time I saw it. Made out of silk, the dress had a fitted corset bodice, with boning down the sides. The neckline was scalloped, low but not immoderately so, and the torso was beaded with clear crystals and sapphires. Embroidery embellished the material, as well as lace—both tone on tone in an icy periwinkle blue. The skirt swept out with a trumpet flare to gather at my feet, while sheer panels of tulle draped from the sides to gather in front, creating a cascading tiered overskirt. Thin spaghetti straps were actually strings of beads—faceted iolite.

Originally, the back had been laced, but when the 1950s hit, I had consulted an expensive seamstress well known for her skill. She carefully altered the dress to include a side zipper, so I could leave it permanently laced in back, yet easily get in and out of the dress without help.

Once I had it on, I gently draped a white fur cloak around my shoulders. I would never show the cloak to my Were friends—that was asking for trouble—but the Fae had no such qualms. It was thick, lush, and hooded, soft mink. I fastened it in front with a Celtic knotwork brooch and was ready to go.

Marsh stared at me, open mouthed, as I tossed my duffel bag of clothes into the backseat.

I gave him a long look. "You don't have to say a word. I love this dress, but I look like I'm going to a period costume ball. Right?"

"I…I just was going to say you look more beautiful than I've ever seen before. It suits you. Really."

I smiled a thank you. Ten minutes later, we reached the front of Wynter's court.

The compound was huge, covering two thousand acres, and smack in the center of the wintry realm sat the palace. Wynter managed to keep every inch of her home trapped in eternal winter, and as I drove up to the gates, a massive amount of ice and snow showed from within the magical barrier.

"You need to vanish for the moment, Marsh, or they won't let you in. Don't show yourself to anyone while we're here."

I opened my window at the gate and flashed my badge to the guard, identifying myself as a member of the court. No one was allowed inside without either a badge or an invitation. Marsh had disappeared, but the guard lingered on his side of the car, staring at the front seat with a long look. After a moment, he motioned for the gates to open. As I eased the car through toward the parking lot—no cars were allowed beyond the outer grounds—the temperature dropped a good forty degrees. My cloak was the only thing between me and shivering.

"Is your cloak warm enough?" Marsh's voice echoed from the seat even though I couldn't see him.

"Yes, actually. I also have a secondary coat in the trunk in case I need it. I keep one handy because of rainstorms. It's just smart to be prepared."

"How did you come to belong to her realm?"

"I was born to it," I said.

And it was true. All Fae, upon birth, were assigned a court, usually by lineage.

Succubi, incubi, and a number of the more predatory Fae belonged to Wynter. Our lighter cousins were no less dangerous, but on the outside they didn't appear quite as threatening. The humans who made the mistake of thinking so all too often discovered their mistake in fatal ways.

The kelpies, for example. Kelpies belonged to Summerlyn's court, but were just as dangerous as I was. They just tended to congregate in warmer areas. While the sirens belonged to summer's domain, the undines belonged to winter. It was a complicated division, but there was some reasoning to it, even if it didn't appear so on the surface.

As I eased into one of the parking spots, I noticed there were few other cars there. Wynter had a limo, but that was—of course—near the palace, brought in through one of the back access roads that was off limits to the general public.

I turned off the ignition and the soft quietude of the compound hit me. Wynter's palace was muffled from the outer world, not just by the magical portal that spanned the gates, but the silence brought about by the blanket of snow and frost that clung to every corner.

Once per month, regardless of the season, Wynter opened part of her grounds to families from all races whose children wanted to play in the snow. Like a theme park, it was an extension of good-will from the Fae to the rest of society. The Weres threw county fairs and rodeos, and the humans staged parades and galas, all three cultures doing their best to honor the treaties.

I glanced over to the passenger seat. "Are you still here, Marsh?"

"I'm here. I thought it prudent to stay out of sight, given your suggestion." Marsh hesitated. I could hear a pending question in his voice. "I never fully realized you belonged to the Fae when we were together. You told me, I know, but you slipped it in so care-fully that I never felt comfortable asking you about it. Why didn't you tell me about all of this? You told me you were a succubus but I don't think I ever fully understood what that meant."

"I didn't dare. We weren't out in the open back then. We couldn't expose ourselves, even to the ones we loved, unless we were absolutely certain that it was safe to do so. There was too much danger of backlash and paranoia."

I dropped my keys in my purse and steeled myself for what was no doubt going to be an unpleasant visit. Wynter's palace was beautiful. Wynter's land was lovely. Wynter herself was gorgeous… and cold as ice.

"I'm heading to the palace. You can either come with me, or stay here."

"I'll stay here. If I follow and they catch me, I don't want any fallout on you."

I nodded, my mind already running ahead to what I would tell Wynter and how I might be able to ask for her help. I slid out of the car and locked it, grateful for the heavy cloak. Fur worked to keep out the chill, and was standard in the court. I had changed into a pair of white walking boots that didn't clash with my dress, so I was ready to go. Ready, and with no more excuses, I slung my purse over my shoulder and headed out to the path that led to the palace.

...

The snow drifted down in a lazy fashion, brushing my hair, my nose, my eyelashes with big, fat, puffy flakes. The walkways were thick with chunky ice, covered with a thin layer of snow. They were slick, but navigable if one was careful. My dress dragged a little, but I paid no attention. The silk was strong, and the snow wouldn't hurt it. The banks to either side were high—three feet in some places. Here and there, various members of the court wandered by, some heads down, intent on their walk, while others strolled by in a leisurely fashion.

Humans still didn't understand us very well. Stories and legends had pegged us generically, as if we were cattle, but not all succubi were the same, and not all of the sirens were alike, nor the dryads. We were as unique and individual as humans, and it had taken some time to get that through society's head.

The Fae, in general, were powerful, but nobody outside of the Fae Nation really understands that to us, Summerlyn and Wynter might as well be goddesses. They were the heart and soul of our people, commanding the seasons and the years.

As I trudged toward the compound's center, I could see the palace rising in the distance. A tall cathedral of what looked like blue crystal, it was spectacular, even from where I stood.

My breath came in little puffs as I realized that I was more out of shape than I had thought. That and my run-in with Shayla were enough to convince me that maybe a little time in the gym wouldn't hurt matters any.

Finally, the gates surrounding the palace came into view. It was impossible to tell merely from looking whether the walls were crystal or ice. I knew from experience that it was the latter, frozen into shape by Wynter's will. Behind the gates, the palace soared five stories high, with minarets spiraling into the sky. Frozen spires, they looked so delicate that any wind might bring them crashing down, but they had withstood intense storms. Like many of the Fae, the minarets were far more resilient than anybody would guess. I had no idea how far beneath the ground the chambers and tunnels led.

Guards lined the frozen turrets, stationed every five yards. They stood as still as pillars of ice, looking neither left nor right, but straight ahead. Every other guard was armed with a bow and arrow, and the rest carried large silver swords. The colors of Wynter were everywhere—from the dark navy uniforms of the guards, to the stark white and silver flags flying from the spires over the palace. Windows gleamed from within with pale light, and against the snow, it looked truly like some faerie-tale castle.

As I gazed at the open gate leading into the palace, manned by still more guards, it occurred to me that I spent so much time with the Weres and humans that sometimes, I lost track of my own lineage. And that wasn't a good thing for anybody. It kept me from remembering where my allegiance lay. Because I wasn't a nomad and I wasn't an outcast. I was a citizen here, a member of the court.

Swallowing my fear, along with my pride—because stepping in front of Wynter was guaranteed to bring even the most resilient Fae to her knees—I stepped into line. As the guards checked my badge and motioned me through, I entered the land of eternal winter.

CHAPTER 14

Three more stops and two hours later, the guards showed me through. Wynter had agreed to grant me an audience, especially after I had stressed it was an emergency.

The guard to my left looked me up and down. "At least you dressed for court. We have so many now coming here who don't bother with proper attire. It's an insult, that's what it is."

The guard to my left gave him an abrupt nod. "That it is. And the queen isn't brooking insults. Come, we'll take you to the waiting chamber."

I didn't bother to tell them that I had considered leaving my court gown at home. But, when you got down to it, I was a traditionalist in that sense. Honor given where due, and Wynter was due my fealty.

The guards escorted me through the bustling courtyard. The courtiers were out in style, dressed in brilliant, outlandish gowns, their hair flowing wild and entwined with snowberry blossoms and holly vines. They were so decked out that I looked positively sedate.

I wasn't noble born, but my mother had been involved in court life, and I had been presented to Wynter when I was barely able to understand what was going on. Having actually been shown at the court proved to be a double-edged sword. It meant I had some standing with Wynter, and I could petition for an audience and carry a badge, meaning I wasn't one of the nameless thousands. But it also meant that should Wynter choose to give me direct orders, I was expected to obey without question.

Once past the inner courtyard, which boasted an indoor skating rink, we headed toward the queen's parlor. Unlike the larger audiences she met in the throne room, she granted private discussions in her parlor.

At the door, the guards motioned for me to stand with my arms out. I handed another my purse, and he quickly sorted through it, making certain I wasn't carrying any weapons. The first guard patted me down, quickly but thoroughly. He then ran a mage stone over my body to pick up any hidden talismans. It let out a chime as it passed my pentacle. I had locked my dagger and wristlets in my trunk. Wynter wouldn't care, but I didn't want the guards getting too interested.

"What have you got here?" The guard motioned for me to lean my head back so he could get a better look at it.

"Pentacle, made out of silver dragon scales. It was a present from my mother. It's sort of a protection charm."

The guard to my left let out a low whistle. "Silver dragon… you don't see much of that around, now do you? Especially in today's world. Where did your mother get it, if I might ask?"

He was being pleasant, although I had a feeling that he was fishing for something he could take to the queen. It never hurt to be in her favor, and the guards knew that better than anybody. But the surprise would be on him, because Wynter already knew about the pendant, dagger, and wristlets.

"Wynter gave it to her as a birth gift for me." I met his gaze squarely.

The guard blinked, then quickly shifted from one foot to the other. This really was a no-win situation for him. If he called me out as a liar and I asked Wynter to prove it to him, she would punish him. If he didn't, and Wynter got on his tail about it, then she would still punish him. I could see the indecision playing over his face and felt a brief flash of sympathy.

"Truly, she did. But if you are worried, go ahead and ask her. I will vouch that you only had her safety at heart."

His cheeks flushed and he ducked his head. "I haven't been on the job long—"

"Shut up. If she said this bauble is a birth gift from Wynter, you will not question it. Any jackass fool enough to lie about something like that will get more than her due from the queen." His companion flashed me a rough look, but it was tinged with respect. He nodded toward the door. "We'll go in now. You've been in audience with Wynter before, I assume?"

I nodded. "I know the protocol."

"All right. Are you ready?" They waited while I adjusted my dress and, with one of them carrying my purse, the other opened the door and stood back. I would enter first, with the guards following behind me.

As I swept through the door, it felt like I had entered another world. I had, actually, when I had come through the gates out front. I had entered the heart of winter, and we were standing between the worlds. I caught my breath. As jaded as I was and as fearsome as visiting Wynter could be, there was a majesty and awe that surrounded her presence.

She was ice and snow, sleet and hail, icebergs and the frozen lands of the world. She was eternal winter and icicles growing like long daggers off the eaves. She was the snow-covered forest and barren realms where only the polar bear and seal existed. Wynter was the fallow Queen of Ice, whose heart burned with blue fury.

As I glanced around the room, the chill austerity struck me. All colors were shades of blue and white, of black and silver. The floor was polished marble, the walls the same chill ice that formed the rest of the palace.

Wynter herself sat beside a table on a throne of wrought silver. She was tall, but not extraordinarily so, and cloaked in a diaphanous gown spun from silver and the pale blue of early morning. It was so sheer I could see her breasts beneath the material, full and round like alabaster porcelain. Her hair was silver, spinning out into a cascade of curls that were piled high atop her head, held in place by a diamond headdress.

As she motioned for me to come forward, the weight of her years hit me. Age did not show on her face, but it crept through her aura, surrounding her with a nimbus that reached back thousands of years. She had seen the long march of time, and while not yet weary of it, there was nothing new that could strike fear or surprise in her heart.

"Lily O'Connell, be welcome." Her voice was a whisper, yet it echoed through the chamber and struck a cold spear of fear through my heart. I realized right then that Jolene had been right not to come. The Fae did not welcome Weres; they thought them uncouth and common in a way that—as hedonistic and savage as my people could be—would never be acceptable. When Wynter's gaze caught my own, she held me fast. Her eyes shone, the irises brilliant silver against a pale blue background.

I sank into a deep curtsey, touching my forehead to my knee.

"Rise, Lily O'Connell, and stand before the Court of the Winterborn." Her voice echoed through the room, ricocheting off the walls. I caught my breath. As jaded as I was, Wynter never failed to strike both terror and awe into my heart. She was ice incarnate, ruthless and cold and chilling, but she was also austere in her beauty.

I slowly rose, and with my fingers pressed to my forehead in a sign of genuflection, straightened my shoulders and spine. I did not speak until she bade me to.

Never, ever speak before Wynter bids you to speak, Lily. I could still hear my mother's voice as she hurried me toward the palace to meet the queen. Different country. Different palace. Same goddess of our people.

Wynter's gaze dallied over my body, moving slowly, as if she were examining every nuance of my stance, my dress, my expression. Finally, she motioned to the chair opposite her. "Sit at my side, young succubus."

I gingerly took my seat, taking care not to tip the table between us. A tea tray sat there, a porcelain pot steaming with what smelled like winterberry tea. Sandwiches were arranged on one side, cookies on another. She motioned for the maid, who was standing well back from us but ever at attention, to pour. The tea was a lovely shade of purple. Winterberries reminded me of spiced blackberries. I accepted a couple cookies and a sandwich. Wynter nodded to me, and I tasted my tea, then nibbled on one of the cookies. A moment later, a dreamy vanilla flavor filling my mouth, chased down by the peppery bite of the tea, I let out a soft breath.

"Now then, tell me why you have come."

"There's a problem you should know about, Your Majesty. While I doubt it will impact much of the court, it's affecting me, and it may well harm others." I cleared my throat.

"Well then, this sounds serious. What's the nature of the problem?" Wynter leaned forward, just enough to tell me she was listening. One thing could be said about her—she didn't blow off the trials that faced her court. She was ever-vigilant, and I had the feeling that was how she had kept her throne for so long. There had to be usurpers looking to take her place, but she wasn't about to let them through the gate without a fight.

As concisely as I could, I laid out the background and problems with the Souljacker. I showed her my tattoo, and her eyes widened as she stared at the phoenix on my leg.

"What an incredible piece of art. Yes, it truly feels alive. I'm amazed a human could be so talented. And if this is truly your inner self, then Lily O'Connell, you have remarkable potential. You say there have been three murders so far?"

"Three that we know of. The problem, of course, is that the police can't do anything about vampire kills. I don't know how many of the court may have gotten tattoos from Charles, but people should be informed and cautioned to guard their wards and make certain they don't disobey the curfews if they live in the cities."

"We shall put the word out. I will also put a bounty on his head." Wynter paused, leaning back to rest against the throne. "Lily, you say your business has been impacted because of this?"

I nodded. "He killed Tygur—one of my clients, in my salon. Now Tygur's widow is out to get even with me."

Her eyes flashing with a dangerous light, the Queen of Winter smiled. "Ah, but in this case, I agree with her. You should not be selling sex in the first place. Among our people, sex is a passion to be enjoyed, and if you need chi, you take it where you can find it. My people are not prostitutes, to be bought and sold like chattel. Your favors should be gifted, not purchased."

Oops...I hadn't seen this coming. What interaction I'd had with Wynter had never come near the subject of my business. I stammered, trying to find something to say. I couldn't disagree with her—that would be stupid with a capital *s*. I licked my lips.

"I don't like killing humans…"

"Whoever said you had to? You know you can feed off the Fae and Weres without killing them. Why bother with humans? Take what you need, but don't demean yourself in the eyes of the court, young succubus. You are not a commodity." She motioned to my tea. "Finish your drink. Eat your sandwich."

I slowly picked up my sandwich, obeying her without a word. But my mind was racing. What the hell did she expect me to do? I had bills to pay; I had to make a living. My worry must have shown on my face, because she shook her head.

"When I first met you, it was long ago, when the world was a far different place. Do you remember the day your mother presented you to court? When she sealed your fortune to mine?"

I nodded. "I do. I was terrified—you were so…you *are* so… brilliant. Like an alabaster statue come to life." I had been so young I could barely look at her without seeing a tall, thin carving of ice and glitter.

"Lily, you are bound to this court. You are bound to me—to the nature of winter. From now on, you work for me. If you must live in the outside world, comingling with humans and Weres, then I'm going to take an active part in shaping your behavior. Your mother isn't here to do it for you, so I will."

I almost choked on my tea. This was outside any expectation I'd had of how the afternoon would go. I slowly set my cup and saucer down.

"First, since you brought him to my attention, I'm assigning you the task of destroying this vampiric leech. Get rid of him. Find him before they can lock him up out of reach once more."

Her words hit me like a sledgehammer. I opened my mouth, but one look from her and I closed it again.

"As you say, the police won't be doing the job. Somebody has to. You have the talent. You did not wear your dagger here today, nor the wristlets, but there was a reason I gifted your mother with those objects, to be given to you when you came of age. I did not envision a life for you as a concubine, but as one of my *Aespions*, one of my agents."

That did cause me to sputter. "You want me to be one of your Aespions? Why have I never known about this?" Nowhere, ever, had any sign been given to me that Wynter had plans for my future.

"I expected for you to return to court after you had gotten your wanderlust out of your blood. But so far, you haven't. This is the perfect time to set my plans in motion. My daughter, I'm reining you in. Especially now that we are out to the mortals, the courts need good liaisons between the world of the Fae and the world of mortals, people who understand both worlds. Who better than one who is from our world, yet lives among the humans?"

I stared at her, uncertain how to respond. What the hell was I supposed to say to that? Very few ever caught the interest of Wynter, and here she had dumped what was supposed to be an honor on my shoulders, but instead, it felt like a terribly fright-ening responsibility. I was an independent businesswoman, but now…I was reminded once again that all of us who owed alle-giance to Wynter were only waiting for the chains to her service to appear. They were always there, even if invisible. If I protested… well…protesting wasn't an option. Not if I wanted to walk out of these halls again. There was no questioning the queen.

With shaking hands, I set down my cup and slid to one knee, bowing my head. "As you wish, Your Majesty. Of course I will serve you, and offer you my life and my heart."

And just like that, within the course of ten minutes, I had a new life, a new job, and a frightening new task.

CHAPTER 15

The magnitude of her orders left me reeling. It'd taken me years to build up my clientele, but only one day for Tricia Jones to destroy 70 percent of it. And one hour with Wynter to bury the rest. I wasn't clear on what the Aespions did, but I knew that it wasn't anywhere near what I was used to—at least not in the present.

Seventy-five years ago I had locked my dagger and wristlets in the trunk, along with Marsh's picture. I swore never to use either again unless in an extreme emergency. They reminded me of days gone by, when I'd had to fight to survive in a brutal world.

Now, Wynter was asking me to pick up a way of life I thought I had long left behind. This time it would be in her service, rather than as a mercenary, but it still hearkened back to the days when I'd held no trust in anyone. To the days where I constantly slept with one eye open and my life had depended on my skill with the blade. My years of owning Lily Bound had given me a breather, one I was grateful for.

Wynter must have sensed what I was thinking. "Lily, be at peace about this. I'm not asking you to be a soldier, nor a warrior. Yes, we still need soldiers and warriors even in today's world, but that's not what I want you to do. I'm not asking you to go back to those days when you wandered from town to town, struggling to stay alive."

As my surprised look, she smiled.

"Do you think that I let any who are bound to my court out of sight? The day your mother brought you to me and you pledged at my knee was the day that your name went in the book. I knew then you would be one of my chosen—one I would cultivate into a vital link in my chain. I didn't know quite how, but even then, I read your stars and saw you were destined for greater things than being a pleasure girl."

"You've been watching me?"

"Not personally, but my eyes are everywhere. You haven't been alone, even though you thought you were. I do not interfere with the journeys of my courtiers unless it proves to be a hindrance to the Crown. My people live and die at their own will. But I keep informed as to what happens to them. I know about your past. I also know there's a ghost sitting in your car right now."

I fought the desire to deny that Marsh was there. There was no use in lying. She already knew the whole truth, I suspected. "He's the ghost of a man I once loved…a man I ended up killing."

Her gaze lingered over my face. "Yes, I know. More the pity you had to destroy him. The hunger makes your kind do things they would normally never do. But he is of no danger to me…or to you."

I paused for a moment. "May I ask you a question?"

"Of course." She gestured toward the teapot. "More tea?"

"Thank you," I murmured. Right now, winterberry tea seemed to be just what the doctor ordered. "My mother died when I was very young—only a few years after she presented me to the court. I was never told what happened to her. My father vanished. I don't even know if he's still alive. Do you know where he is? And how my mother died? When I asked my aunt, she refused to answer. The moment I came of age she gave me the gift you gave my mother, and told me to leave her house and never darken her doorstep again. I don't know what I did, but she seemed to hate me."

Wynter gave me long look. "I've been waiting for the day when you would come to me with these questions. I thought about telling you numerous times, but you had to be ready to ask. Do you know what your father was?"

"I *thought* he was an incubus." Generally, the only ones who could live long term with succubi were incubi. They had much the same nature.

"Correct. He was an incubus. But he was also a maverick. He refused to pledge to me. When your mother insisted on presenting you to the court, he was furious. He had a temper that was unmatched and I warned your mother she should bring you to the palace, and live here under my protection."

"But...she wouldn't?"

"No, she insisted she loved him. Her *love* led her to her death. A year or so after you were pledged to my court, he went off the deep end—I don't know what triggered him, the reasons are lost in time—and he killed your mother."

I stared at her, open-mouthed. My father had killed my mother? As the shockwaves ran through me, the queen continued.

"He tried to hide her body but we knew what had happened. I decreed that your aunt take you. She wasn't happy about it; she and your mother had fallen out when they were young. But she was as bound to my will, as are you. She took you in and she took care of you." Her brow narrowed. "She also knew enough to give you the birth gifts I bestowed on your mother for you. I warned your aunt to keep silent about your mother and father. That's why she never told you. As far as you knew, your mother died in her sleep, because that was the way I wanted it."

I shook my head, unable to take in what she was telling me. "My father killed my mother? I had no idea. I thought he just abandoned me."

"You were too young. My advisors counseled that you be spared the truth, for the world is harsh enough as it is. I would rather you think that he abandoned you, than to know how cruel he truly was."

"What happened to him?" I already knew the answer but wanted to hear it for myself.

"He was executed for his crime. I have ever wished that I had ordered her to leave him. I was too softhearted." Wynter stared at me for a moment, then quietly added, "Since then, I have been more proactive when problems arise. Which is why I insist that you close your doors and take up service to me. I can foresee problems you cannot imagine, if you continue on your path."

I was barely listening by this point. The shock of finding out that my father had killed my mother was reverberating through my core. Then, a sudden fear took hold of me that his blood had tainted mine. I raised my head to meet Wynter's gaze.

"My father, he was a brutal man. If you've been watching me over the years you know how many people I've killed. I didn't mean to, but…"

She seemed to understand what I was saying, and reached out to place an ice-cold hand on my wrist. "Don't worry, Lily. Your father's blood did not stain your heart. You do not carry his nature within yourself. A succubus cannot help her nature. She must feed to live. As much as I don't like the business you chose to open, it was a unique and clever way to handle the situation. But you have learned enough now that you no longer need it. You can move on from this phase in your life. I have faith in you."

"But I have no idea how to serve you in this capacity. I don't even know what Aespions *do*." Truth was, I was dreading the learning curve headed my way.

Wynter gave me a sly smile. "Your training began the moment you walked through the door today. But yes, you will be required to train hard and long. Meanwhile, I will say this: I know of this Archer Desmond you mentioned."

Uh oh. I had no idea what Wynter would think of the chaos demon.

"He's been helping us with the Souljacker. Do you want me to break off my connection with him?" I was hoping she would say no. For one thing, Archer Desmond made a fantastic contact. For another, I could draw chi off of him without a problem and he seems to have no qualms about fulfilling my need in that department. And…I kind of liked him.

She laughed and shook her head. "No, he may be extremely useful in the future. I want you to cultivate your acquaintance with him. And if you need to use him to feed, then by all means do so. It may keep you out of trouble."

"Is there anything else?" She had thrown so much at me that it was going to take quite some time to process everything. I just wanted to go home and crawl into bed and stick my head under the covers. I was praying I could remember everything.

"Yes. A warning." Her smile faded.

I shivered at the look on her face. "What is it?"

"The wife of this weretiger, she is more dangerous than you know, and not only to you. Revenge among the Weres is an art. She will stop at nothing to hurt you—her grief, yes, is driving her on. But also, the desire to make you pay by harming those you love."

My heart sank. "She isn't going to be easily mollified, is she?"

"No, and she's likely to stoop to taking out her anger on your friends. To put it bluntly, warn those you care about to avoid her. Because Weres think in terms of prides and packs and families. And your friends are your family."

"Wonderful. One more problem to think about."

"You'd best think about it, and take what steps you can before she ends up destroying your friendships. Never trust the Weres, Lily."

"Pretty soon, I'll have the whole world after me. At this rate, the vampires don't look quite so bad."

At that, Wynter turned. "Do not joke about the blood fiends. Make no mistake, Lily. Vampires are no longer human—they wear the body they wore in life, but their soul is twisted and they will always be a monster parading as a person." Wynter gave me a long look. "I'm serious. We have our own dangers among our people, but we tend to be open about it. Vampires will lead you to think they are victims. They may have been when they were human. But after the turning? They become the predators."

When I said nothing, Wynter let out a long breath. "I will place your friends under our protection. That doesn't mean we can save them, but if they find themselves in danger, they can come to us. I don't do this lightly, but they play an important part in your life, therefore *they* are important."

Suddenly exhausted, I realized the room felt like it was spinning. I wanted to go home. "So what now? Where do I go from here?"

"You go home and you rest. You destroy this fiend who follows you and your friends. You close your business. I will have Vesper, leader of the Aespions, call you to set up your training. And then, Lily, your new life will begin. Meanwhile, *stay alive*. I will send you home with new wards. They are far stronger than the ones your friend makes. It will free her up from having to do so, as well. Katarina the Frost makes these. They do not take well to being disrupted."

As the guards escorted me to the door, the weight of the world settled in on my shoulders. I had come hoping to give Wynter information that might potentially save others who had been inked by the Souljacker. I was leaving with my world tossed in a blender set on high speed.

One of the guards gave me a sympathetic look. He clapped me on the shoulder.

"Welcome into the service of Wynter. I know you didn't expect this, but how often do things go the way we expect them to? I will find a ride back to your car for you so that you don't have to walk through the snow." He handed me a bag containing new wards—all I had to do was affix them to my fence and house.

As I slipped my cloak back around my shoulders, I thanked him but declined his offer. I had a lot to think about, and a walk through the snow just might help clear my head. As I ducked out of the palace and into the softly falling flakes, I said a soft prayer for my mother. Of all that I had learned this day, the facts surrounding her death were the hardest to swallow. Images of her smiling face filling my thoughts, I began the walk back to my car, under the icy sky.

CHAPTER 16

When I got back to the car, Marsh was waiting for me. He took one look at my face, and said, "What the hell happened to you?"

"I'll tell you on the way home."

I shrugged off my cloak and gently placed it in the backseat, along with the wards. I had a feeling I'd be using it a lot more from now on than I had throughout the rest of my life. Not caring what anybody saw or thought, I retrieved my bag of clothes and, standing next to my car, I changed. I gently placed the dress and cloak back inside the garment bag, zipping it carefully before I slid my jeans, bra, and turtleneck back on. After I carefully locked the bag in the trunk, I climbed back in the car. Turning the ignition, I eased out of the parking lot, flipping the heat on high. Once we were back on the highway, headed to the freeway, I let out a long sigh.

"Are you going to tell me what happened?" Marsh's voice was gentle, as if he could sense my fragility.

"So much that I'm not even sure where to begin. I found out how my mother died. I found out what happened to my father. I found out that Tricia's nowhere near done with me. I was given orders to close my business and take up a new pursuit in service to Wynter. How's that for an afternoon's work?" I knew I sounded bitter but I couldn't help it. Nothing that had happened had left me feeling good.

"Wow. I'm not sure what to say."

I let out a short laugh. "Me neither. Seriously, that was my exact response. Wynter's not at all like I remember her," I added in afterthought. "She is far less...cruel, would be the word, than I expected. I don't think she took delight in anything she had to tell me today. In fact, I had the feeling that she regretted most of what she loaded onto my shoulders."

Marsh waited for me to continue, not prodding or questioning, but giving me the time I needed to gather my thoughts. He'd been like that when he was alive, too. He had never talked over me or pushed me, except when it came to insisting we'd make a good couple—a welcome change to most of the men I had known in my life. In fact, his soft confidence was what had first attracted me to him. I had tried to stem my attraction, knowing just how dangerous it could be for a succubus to get involved with a human. But he had felt the same pull—we were like moths drawn to a flame together.

After a few miles of focusing on the road, I had breathed through most of the shock. Clearing my throat, I told him first about my father killing my mother.

"I had no clue. I thought he just abandoned us. Now, I wish that were true. It was so much easier to live with than the knowledge that he murdered my mother. He's long gone of course; Wynter had him executed. But even that is bittersweet. At least I know he was an incubus—which means my bloodline runs smoothly." When different types of Fae mated, the offspring were often unique in their abilities, and it wasn't always for the best. I had been wondering about myself all my life, and now at least that question was put to rest.

"I'm sorry, Lily. Did she say why he killed her?"

"Not in so many words. I gather he was an angry, controlling man. I don't even know if I want to know. Isn't it easier sometimes? Not knowing? And now I understand why my aunt was so cold to me. She and my mother didn't get along, but Wynter made her take care of me. You know that Wynter's the one who gave me my pentacle, dagger, and wristlets. I have a feeling she knew how this would all work out."

Marsh nodded. He glanced out the window for a moment, and I focused on the series of S-curves that we were winding through. Snow was starting to fall again, light and powdery. The roads would freeze by nightfall. Somehow, the stark whiteness made me feel better. It felt clean and clear, and new to the world.

"You said that Wynter instructed you to close your business?"

I let out a soft snort. "Well, really, she's just finishing what Tricia Jones started. Yes, she did. She conscripted me into her service. Apparently, Wynter does not approve of brothels. I wondered why I had so few Fae clients, although the ease with which the Fae approach sexuality seemed the most logical answer."

Marsh leaned back in his seat, disconcerting me as he passed through the backrest.

"Can you not do that? It weirds me out."

"Do what?"

"Stand in the furniture—sit *in* the furniture? Become part of the furniture? It's unnerving. I'm still not used to the fact that you're a ghost." I paused, uncertain whether even approaching the subject that he was a spirit was proper etiquette. "Marsh, I have to tell you, I don't know how to act around you."

"You think *you're* disconcerted? Try opening your eyes, and the first thing you see is a whole new world. The last thing you remember was being killed by your girlfriend, whom you loved very much. I always believed in an afterlife, but if there is one then I don't know about it."

"That's ridiculous. Of course there's an afterlife. For one thing, you're sitting here in my car and you're dead. That alone is proof of an afterlife."

"I know, I know."

"Anyway, about my business…"

Marsh made a tsking sound. "To be honest, I'm glad she said what she did. Lily, you realize how dangerous your job is? I know—I know, and before you protest, I know you're a succubus and I know you have the potential to put the hurt on people. I understand why you opened your business. I also learned from watching the news that today's world seems far *more* dangerous than the world I remember."

I thought about what he said for a moment, then shook my head. "The world has *always* been dangerous, especially for women and children. I never told you about the hundreds of years that I wandered on my own from town to town, doing my best to stay alive. The world has *never* been safe. But you're right, in one sense. With the growing threat from the vampires, the world grows more dangerous every day. Anyway, life as an Aespion isn't likely to be much safer. That's what she wants me to be, essentially one of her agents. I'm to become a liaison between the world of Fae and the world of humans. After the past couple days, I doubt I'll have much standing among the world of Weres."

"What exactly does an Aespion *do*?"

I shrugged, laughing. "I suppose whatever Wynter orders. Seriously, I have no clue. I guess I'm going to find out, though. I'm scheduled to begin training soon, and I have a feeling I'm going to be sore and bruised by the time I'm done. What worries me most, though, isn't losing my business. And it isn't the fact that I'm supposed to catch the Souljacker."

"You're worried about your friends taking fallout because of you, aren't you?" Marsh always knew how to nail it on the head.

Glancing at him, I nodded. "Tricia commands a veritable army of Weres. The damage they could do, on so many levels… it's terrifying."

"Look out!"

I had gotten so involved in my thoughts that I wasn't paying attention to driving. I jerked my gaze back to the road just in time to see a tree come tumbling down the hill next to the asphalt, a wave of heavy snow thundering behind it. I swerved to the side in the only direction I could—into the oncoming lane. Luckily, there were no cars coming our way, and I managed to swerve onto the opposite shoulder, where I idled the car as I leaned against the steering wheel, panting heavily.

"Don't stop here, get this buggy in gear and drive! The next section may decide to go too!"

At Marsh's urgent plea, I shifted gears and plowed forward,

suddenly aware that the minor avalanche was turning into a bigger one and that we had been sitting directly in the path of another wave of oncoming snow.

As I managed to speed past the thundering deluge, I moved back into the lane next to the hill, even though that was the last place I wanted to be. We couldn't afford to be in a head-on accident. At least, *I* couldn't. It wouldn't hurt Marsh but it could sure kill me. Up ahead was a turnout into a rest area and I sped up, the car sliding on the buildup of slush that was accumulating on the ground. I was able to veer into the parking lot without further incident, and eased into a spot far enough away from the trees to avoid being a target should another one decide to come down. As I turned off the ignition, I let out a soft cry.

"I just want to go home."

"I know, I know. That was a close one." Marsh turned to me. "Are you okay, Lily?"

Clutching the steering wheel with a grip so tight I felt like I could break it, I gave him a short shake of the head. "I don't think I can handle much more today." My voice was shaking so hard that it surprised even me. The sudden avalanche felt like a metaphor for everything that had been happening in my life over the past few days. I felt like I had almost been buried in more ways than one.

"Give me a few minutes, and I'll be able to drive again. I'm going to get out and walk around to catch my breath." I knew I should call the cops about the avalanche, but I figured anybody in the area would have heard it and already done so. As I pulled my jacket tighter and shoved open the door the chill air hit my lungs with a crisp snap. I could see my breath as I tramped around the car, trying not to slip in the falling snow. It was heavy now, thick and wet and piling up quickly.

I crossed the grassy division between the rest area and the road and cautiously stepped out to peer back in the direction we had come. A swath of snow and trees extended all the way across the freeway, completely cutting off access. As the sound of sirens grew, I jumped back onto the snow-laden grass when the emergency vehicles whizzed past. They slowed, stopping a safe distance away from the avalanche. Satisfied that I didn't need to talk to them, I returned to the car and leaned against it.

Marsh appeared by my side. He was staring into the sky, a soft smile on his face. "I know you've had one hell of a day. And I know that you're facing major changes that you would never have chosen had you been given the choice. But life throws us curveballs. And it's how well we respond that make us who we are."

He turned to stare at me, reaching out but then stopping before his hand passed through mine. "Lily, you've got this. You were always the strongest woman I'd ever met. I don't think that's just because you're Fae. I think it's because it's your nature. You aren't cut out to whimper and hide in the closet. You're made of strong stuff, Lily O'Connell. And whoever brought me back to help you, right now I'm thanking them. Because it's given me a chance to see you again. And I'd rather be a ghost standing by your side then just a memory in your heart."

Right then, I knew that I still loved him. The love had changed, and there was no way it could ever be anything but platonic. But I'd settle for that.

"I'm glad you're back in my life, Marsh. However it has to be, as long as you're happy to be here, I'm happy you are. I guess we move forward, huh?"

He laughed and pointed toward the direction we had just come. "I'd say we don't have much chance of going backward, so forward it is. Come on. Let's get you home and ready to face your future."

And with that, we got back in the car, I put her into gear, and we headed back to Seattle.

CHAPTER 17

As I pulled into the driveway, I was surprised to see Archer Desmond's car waiting. I turned off the ignition and looked at Marsh.

"I have to tell you something about the person who owns that car. I know this is a lot to take in, given all you've learned about the world in the past day, but he's a chaos demon and he's helping us with the Souljacker. But there's more…"

Marsh gave me a long look. "He's your lover, isn't he?"

I mulled over the words. "I don't know, to be honest. I fed off him yesterday, and we have incredible chemistry. And I think he wants to see me again. Wynter has approved him. And…I like him." I raised my eyes to meet Marsh's gaze. I had expected to see recriminations or fear because of the word "demon," but instead he met my eyes with an amused look.

"Something happens when you die," he said. "Maybe I'm getting used to being a ghost, or maybe I just realize that my world has become so much bigger than it was when I was alive. But Lily, I'm…I don't feel love the way I used to. It's expanded, become something less possessive. If Archer can help you, then so much the better."

As I climbed out of the car, Archer stepped out of his. He leaned against the hood of his BMW, waiting, his arms crossed against the cold. My heart skipped a beat. After everything that had happened at Wynter's court, I was exhausted and in need of a friendly face.

"Hey, I hope you don't mind me waiting for you. I found out a few more things you need to hear." Archer glanced at Marsh, his eyes flickering over the ghost's figure. He didn't look particularly surprised. "I don't believe we've met. My name is Archer Desmond." He did not extend his hand, which told me he recognized Marsh was a spirit.

"Marsh…Marsh Sheffield. I'm…a friend of Lily's." Marsh ran his gaze over Archer's figure, then he gave a short nod. I could see acceptance in his eyes.

I retrieved my garment bag from the car, along with the new wards. At least Dani wouldn't have to go to the time and expense to make a set. But I'd better get them up now, while there was still light enough to see.

"I have to install these while it's still daylight. Want to help?" I turned to Archer, flashing him a weary smile. I held up the bag. "Wynter gave me a set of Katarina's wards."

"You'll be set for sure." He let out a short laugh. "Let's get to it, then."

"Have you put up wards before?" It was a rhetorical question. Everybody in this day and age had installed magical warding against vampires or, if not, they lived in perpetual fear.

"Katarina's are stronger than the best of them, but they install like the majority. So tell me what the ice queen had to say. At least you came away in one piece." He was trying to stifle a laugh, that much I could tell.

"I'm glad my discomfort causes you so much amusement." I took a deep breath, the cold cutting into my lungs. I might be part of Wynter's court, but I didn't come with antifreeze in my blood. "Actually, I almost ended up a road popsicle. On the way home, I almost got bowled over by an avalanche."

"Well, that's something I don't hear every day. Your car looks all right, so I assume you managed to make it past safely." He took the bag from me as I placed the dress and cloak back in the car until we were done. "Let's get these up now, before we go in for our hot cocoa."

With Archer and Marsh following, I headed to the outer gate. The old wards were on the inside of my fence, spaced every ten feet. Nobody in their right mind ever affixed them to the outside of their gates. It had become a stupid prank to see how many wards you could deface as you walked along the street—so much so that, after a multitude of complaints, the police had made it a misdemeanor, punishable with a hefty fine.

Parents were doing their best to discourage the activity because it cost them a minor fortune, but kids would be kids, regardless of the punishment. If the ward had been placed on the inside of the fence and the vandal stepped onto the property to get to it, the fines tripled, with community service thrown into the mix. That seemed to be enough to stave off all but the most determined delinquents.

Dani's sigils had been painstakingly formed in black ink on a clear adhesive material, but I had no clue how they were made. The ink was magical, but even if I had a bottle, I wouldn't have known what to do with it. Archer tested the corners, then motioned for me to press my fingertips against the center of the ward.

"Now you need to say, 'remove.' These look to be voice activated by the owner of the land. They can be defaced, but their removal depends on you or the witch who made them."

"That's right. To activate them I had to do exactly the same, only I said 'seal.'" I cautiously placed two fingers against the center of the ward and whispered, "Remove." A few seconds later, the ward began to peel back and I was able to pull it off. As soon as it came off, Archer rubbed over the area with a handful of snow.

"I don't think we need to wash the post again, but this should do the trick. Try putting one of the new ones on there. Just peel off the backing and align it against the post and whisper, 'seal.'"

I did as he said and the ward seemed to blend in to the wood of the post. Something shifted in the energy and I realized just how strong Wynter's wards were. We went around the rest of the yard, replacing them all. Then we tackled the house, and I brought out a ladder so we could reach every window. Katarina's set was a lot stronger than Dani's—and covered a lot more area. Lastly, Archer dared the roof, cautiously inching up the snowy incline to slap the final ward at the top. A cascade of energy rippled down to cover my home, and I found myself breathing easier. I stood back and closed my eyes, seeking the magical flow.

There it was—a soft current, a circle of ice and snow and mist surrounding my home, frozen solid against intruders.

"All right. That's better. I feel a lot more secure. I wish I had remembered—I would have gotten a set for Dani and Nate."

"Do you know how much that set of wards would cost if you had to buy it, given they're made by the Frost?"

I shook my head. "No, do you?"

"Yes, actually. You'd pay fifty-thousand dollars. That set will last you for five years, and it's tamper-resistant."

I blinked. I had no clue that it was so valuable. I breathed a soft sigh of gratitude to Wynter. "Okay, next…help me with something else before we go in?"

"Sure," Archer said, "but let's make it quick. My nose feels like it's getting frostbite."

I trudged through the snow on my lawn, over to where my business sign stood, and Archer followed. As I stared at the beautiful signpost that I had commissioned, my stomach lurched. I had owned Lily Bound for years. The business had become my bread and butter, as well as a way to help keep me from losing control. And now it was all coming to an end.

I motioned to Archer. "Give me a hand, please."

"Sure. What are we doing?" He moved to the other side of the sign. "Do you need to move this somewhere else?"

"Not exactly. We are taking down the sign." At his look, I added, "I'll explain after we go inside."

Together, we managed to pull the posts out from the frozen ground and carry the sign around back, where we placed it in the shed. That done, I gathered my dress, cloak, and purse, and we headed inside.

• • •

As I stamped the snow off my boots, and slid out of my coat, I realized that I was freezing. I filled the kettle and set it on the stove to make tea. Mr. Whiskers entered the room and began to wind himself around my legs, purring. I leaned over and picked him up, grunting under his weight.

"You feel like you put on a few more ounces, Whisky. Did you eat all your breakfast?" I glanced over at the food dish to see it was licked clean. "All right, all right. I'll fill it up again."

As I replenished Whisky's chow, Archer motioned to the cupboard. "Do you want me to get out cups and saucers for tea?"

Pleased that he felt comfortable enough to ask, I gave him a nod. "Are you hungry? I'm famished, given the day that I've had. I was going to order pizza for dinner."

"Pizza's good with me. I like just about any topping, so choose what you want. But dinner is my treat." He set cups and saucers on the table, then opened the refrigerator. "Cream in here?"

"Yes, and honey and sugar are on the table. If you take lemon, I'm sorry, but I'm out." I started to put Whisky down, but he scrambled to stay in my arms. So I settled in at the table with him on my lap, scratching him under the chin.

"Say, how is it that you had that cat when you were with me? It's been over seventy-five years. How the hell is he still alive? I *know* that's the same cat." Marsh blinked, cocking his head to stare at Whisky.

I had been wondering when he was going to figure that out, and wondering even more how I was going to explain things. So far, I had managed to pass Whisky off as a regular cat, except to Dani and Nate. Now, it appeared the Bengal was out of the bag.

As I held Whisky with one arm, I pulled out my phone with the other and pressed four on speed dial. "Let me order the pizza first, and then I'll tell you guys Whisky's story."

I placed an order for two large sausage and pepperoni pizzas with extra cheese, then leaned back, cradling the cat in my arms. "Whisky and I have come a long way together. You might even say that our fates are intertwined. It all started about six hundred years ago, in a little English village. I don't remember the name now, or much about the place except that it was a hole in the road even then. It was so far off the beaten path that nobody but the people who lived there knew about it. I only found it because of a storm..."

• • •

The wind had picked up substantially, and it was chilling me through. I was dressed for the road, in woolen trousers, heavy tunic, and a thick cape. My pack was fastened to my horse, Luther, and my dagger was within easy reach. I was picking my way along the muddy trail, having just passed into Cornwall from Devon. The trouble was, I wasn't entirely sure as to my location. I had only a rough idea.

For three days a group of bandits had chased me, intent on robbing me. I had no doubt they had worse ideas in mind, but they knew that I had some money and they wanted it. I finally managed to get away from them by entering a copse thick enough and wide enough for me to hide out in until they gave up.

Luckily, they had no hounds with them, and I had enough food to manage. Unfortunately, by the time I was able to exit the forest, I was starved for chi and the first farmer I came upon ended up being lunch. I regretted killing him as much as I regretted killing any of them, but my hunger drove me forward and though I tried to pull back, there were times I couldn't seem to gauge when the humans dropped so low in their life force that they couldn't recover. I tried to find Fae—or Weres—who would trade me chi for sex, and more often than not, I was successful, but there were times when I had to go after humans, and it never seemed to work out well.

As the wind whistled past, great storm clouds began to roll in, dark and heavy and filled with cold rain. In the distance, thunder rumbled and an occasional flash of lightning blazed through the sky. I sucked in a deep breath, urging Luther forward as fast as he could safely trot. There were too many loose stones and too many mud puddles on the trail for me to allow him to open into a full gallop. Even a trot seemed dangerous at this point. So we trudged along, against the driving rain and wind.

As evening threatened to fall with no shelter in sight, a faint light in the distance lifted my spirits. I was coming to a village.

There was no sign giving the name of the town. And really, the word "town" was a misnomer. The ragtag group of houses surrounded what looked like two or three shops and a small tavern that also looked to be an inn. Hitching posts were stationed in front of the inn, and when I peeked around back, I could see a ramshackle stable. I led Luther back to the stable and tethered him to one of the posts. Then, slinging my pack over my back, I headed through the back door into the tavern.

There were two long tables in front of the bar, lined with benches for patrons to sit and eat. A staircase led to an upper floor where I assumed the guestrooms were. I approached the barkeep and motioned for him to pour me a pint of ale.

"I need a bed and food. My horse is out in the stable. Do you have a stable boy who can take care of him?"

The barkeep gave me a long look. "Don't get many women travelers in here, especially dressed like you. Are you just passing through?"

I nodded, keeping my face shrouded with my hood so he couldn't see my looks. I had dealt with too many horny men as it was. I didn't need another one after me. "I just need a place to get away from the storm."

"I've rabbit stew and bread and cheese, will that do?"

I nodded. "Do you have a room?"

"Aye, I've a room. Do you want your food here, or in your room? I'll tell William to take care of your horse." As he pulled a key off the wall and slid it across the table, I handed him his coins. He gave me my change and filled a wooden trencher with stew, setting a chunk of bread atop it along with a thick slice of cheese.

"I'll have the girl bring up a pitcher of hot water for you. It's cold as sin out there."

I picked up my dinner and headed upstairs to find my room. The maid followed me, carrying a candle and a pitcher of hot water. She set the pitcher down on a rickety table next to a large bowl, then lit the logs in the fireplace. After she brought me a thin blanket and a washing cloth, I locked the door and dropped into the chair next to the fire. Holding my hands out to the flames, I shivered as I realized just how cold I was.

But cold or not, I needed a wash. Before the hot water could cool, I stripped off my cloak and clothes, my teeth chattering as I scrubbed my body with the hot water. Humans had something against bathing that the Fae could never understand. We liked our baths and made frequent use of soapwort. Still freezing, I dried myself in front of the fire and gingerly slipped back into my clothing. I wanted to change, but I had no spare garments with me. I had made the mistake of leaving them with a washing woman in another village two weeks ago. When they found out I was a succubus, I had been run out of town before I could gather all of my things. I was lucky they didn't try to burn me at the stake.

I poured the remainder of the hot water into the bowl and soaked my feet while I sat at the table eating. The heat drew out some of my weariness. By the time I finished my food, I was ready to crawl into bed and sleep for as long as I could manage.

I had been sleeping for about five hours when a racket woke me up. It sounded like someone shouting outside my window. At first I tried to ignore it, thinking it was some drunken idiot. But then I heard something—a *swoosh* that caught my attention. A shiver raced up my spine as I realized there was something more going on than just some rabble-rouser trying to raise hell.

As I padded over to the window and opened the shutters, I was surprised to see a bright flash in the alley below the inn. Magic. And *that* told me that there was trouble in the making.

CHAPTER 18

"So, you lived in Cornwall during the 1600s?" Archer gave me an odd look. "I might have been around there at that time."

I shrugged. "I lived all over, to be honest. I was born in Ireland, long before that. I lived in the Court of Wynter for a while, with my mother and then with my aunt. When I came of age, I left. I took the name Lily O'Connell and traveled all over Ireland, and eventually all around the UK. Although, it wasn't known as the United Kingdom then. It wasn't *uniting* much of anything, to be honest. Anyway, this was around 1560–1580. I don't remember the exact time and it doesn't really matter. I do know that I had bought Luther off of some farmer when he was a foal, and he was with me for a good twenty years. I still miss that horse."

Marsh frowned. "I don't think I ever really asked you how old you were, did I?"

"No. To be honest, I got the feeling that you never really wanted to know. It was rough enough explaining that I was Fae." I grinned at him though, remembering the blank look on his face when I had launched into the explanation of my nature. To his credit though, Marsh had handled the revelation a lot easier than I'd thought he would.

"So what was the racket outside your window?" Archer motioned for me to stay in my seat when the tea kettle started whistling. He poured the boiling water into the teapot, then put the lid on and carried the pot over to the table. The front doorbell rang, and he motioned for me to stay seated. When he returned, he was carrying two large pizza boxes.

I was surprised that Nate hadn't come over and that I hadn't heard from Dani yet, but we weren't joined at the hip, and they didn't owe me a check-in every day. Although, considering we were facing the Souljacker, it would have been nice to hear from them. I had left several text messages for both telling them we needed to talk, but I knew they were busy and tried not to fret when they didn't answer right away. I opened the top box, then crossed to the cupboard where I pulled out two plates. I added silverware. The pizza from Stray Mozz was so thick that half the time you had to eat it with a knife and fork, though I had no compunction to diving in with my hands, even though I did end up with burned fingers at times. Returning to the table I handed Archer his plate and filled my own, giving Marsh a contrite look.

"I'm sorry, I remember how much you loved pizza."

"Not a problem. I can't smell it, and that's half the battle."

As we settled in to eat, I continued my story.

• • •

When I saw that someone was using magic in the alley below, I knew I had better get down there and see what was going on. For one thing, someone could have discovered that I was a succubus and they might be after me. Or, another member of the Fae could be in trouble. There were mortals who could use magic—human witches—and most of them were okay, but a few could be extremely dangerous.

I wiped my feet and slipped my boots back on, leaving my socks in my room to dry. Making certain that what money I had was firmly tucked away inside my tunic, I threw my cloak on and headed downstairs, trying to be quiet. The bartender had apparently gone to sleep, and I could see a night guardsmen sitting in the corner, leaning back in a chair with his eyes closed. I softly tiptoed around to the back door.

Easing the door open, I slipped into the back alley, which ran between the stable and the inn. A few yards away, under my window, I could see two figures tussling in the darkness. Sparks flew, sparks that I knew weren't from any torchlight.

I slipped through the shadows that cloaked the wall until I was a few feet away. Succubi have extremely good nocturnal vision, and I was able to make out both figures. One of them looked to be human, and he was the one wielding magic. The other had a scaly face, reminding me of some snake or reptile. His eyes glowed with a soft yellow light, and I suddenly realized that the mortal was in a fight with a demon. *Lovely.* I readied my dagger, easing it out from the sheath so that I made no noise. Silver dragon scales were quite effective against most demonic creatures. Hell, silver itself was effective against a lot of demons. Add in the dragon part and you had an extremely useful weapon.

I waited until I had a chance, then darted in and slashed at the demon. He stumbled back, letting out a low growl as he did so. The man fell back, stumbling against the wall.

The demon looked at me, his eyes widening as he saw my dagger. "You want to help the mortal so much? Then you take care of him." With a bright flash, the demon disappeared.

I turned to the man. "Are you all right? Did he hurt you?"

With a groan, the man shook his head. "I think I'll be okay. He cut me, but I don't think it's in a vital area. Who are you?"

"You can call me Lily. What's your name? Why was he after you?" It was then that I noticed the splotch of blood spreading over the front of his cape. "You're hurt. Come, let me help you."

He started to protest but then folded over in pain. I grabbed hold of his elbow and draped his arm around my shoulders. I wrapped my other arm around his waist and half carried, half dragged him back to the tavern door. As quietly as I could, I managed to get him inside.

There was nobody in the kitchen as far as I could tell, so I slipped inside and found some old rags that looked clean. I couldn't carry fresh water along with him up to my room, so once again, I half lifted him and eased past the snoring guard. I managed to get him up to my room without alerting anybody and, dropping him into the chair, I locked the door behind us and pulled off my cloak.

By now, he seemed to almost be unconscious. His head was lolling back, and his eyes looked glazed over. I untied his cloak and threw it back to reveal his blood-stained tunic. There was no way to ease it off of him without aggravating whatever wound was under there, so I used my dagger to rip away the cloth. As I peeled the bloody material away, a vicious wound came into sight. It was ragged, trailing down one side, but luckily it seemed to have missed any vital organs. He was bleeding profusely, however, and that alone could do him in.

I was used to sewing up wounds; I had been on my own for so long that anytime I got hurt I was prepared to take care of myself. I kept a needle and thread in my pack at all times, along with healing salve, and a powder that the Fae used to prevent infection. We were miles ahead of the humans in terms of medicine, and though at times our people had offered to share with theirs, most mortals viewed us as demons, in league with the creature they called Satan. And while we Fae all knew demons existed, humans had no clue as to the reality of the situation.

I used the cloth that I had dried my feet with to soak up the blood that was still pouring from his side. After I could see the wound more clearly, I shook the anti-infection powder over the gash, then threaded a needle and began to sew the layers of skin together. Eleven stitches later, the bleeding had slowed to an ooze and I rubbed some of my healing salve on it. Then, I used one of the clean rags that I had stolen from the kitchen and tore it into strips, tying it together to wrap around his waist in a makeshift bandage.

By now, he was starting to come around. I hunted through my pack and pulled out a small flask. Holding it to his lips, I made him drink until he sputtered. The brandy was strong—it was a Fae brew—and brought him around in no time flat. It would also help against the pain, a double plus.

"So, you want to tell me what was going on out there with that demon?"

His eyes grew wide. I noticed they were a brilliant emerald green. His shock of red hair fell to his shoulders. He couldn't be more than twenty-three or twenty-four. A full-grown man, yes, but young in the ways of my world.

"You saved my life. I don't know how to thank you." He started to lean forward, then groaned, easing back against the chair. "How bad is it? Will I live?"

"Oh, you'll live all right. And while it's not life-threatening, I wouldn't plan on running any races if I were you. What's your name? And why were you fighting the demon?"

He let out a long sigh. "They call me Whisky Danvers. I'm from Scotland, and that demon is the bearer of a family curse. It's probably still after me, girl, so you'd best be careful as long as you're anywhere near me. The firstborn son of each generation never escapes the curse."

"What curse is that?" Curses were tricky things, especially if they were placed by demons. They weren't easy to break and family hexes were known to continue for generation after generation, quenched only when the bearer chose to retract the hex.

"Long ago one of my ancestors enslaved that demon to do his bidding. But he didn't do a very good job of controlling it, and the demon managed to break free. He cursed our family line. Any firstborn male in our family tree, especially those of us who have a natural ability for magic, are singled out for destruction."

I blinked. "That's a harsh curse. And it's still affecting your family?"

"You would think the ability would burn itself out with so much death, but so far, it's as strong as it ever was, lass. It passes down through the father." He shifted, looking uncomfortable. "I turned twenty-six three days ago, the age which triggers the curse. I have a wife and a son." He hung his head. "He will be afflicted, as well, being first born."

"What are you doing here?"

"When I realized I was coming to the age where the demon would appear, I headed out. I left them behind. I didn't want them to see me die." Whisky sounded so resigned that it made my heart ache. Curses and hexes were horrible things…I knew too well just how dangerous these powers could be.

He squinted, leaning forward. The pain hit him again and he groaned and fell back against the chair. "Aye, that's a pain. So who are you? Are you a witch? Don't worry, I'm no oath breaker—no warlock who will turn you over to the witch hunters. My family stays well clear of the Inquisitors."

I shook my head. "I'm not a witch, not in the way you would think. My name is Lily, and my bloodline goes back to the Sidhe. I am one of the night folk, one of the unseen."

His eyes grew wide. "I *knew* you existed. My family has known of the Fae, always. We do not have a Bean Sidhe attached to us, but we know of the kelpie and of the corpse candles, and of the black dogs. What are you, Lily?"

I smiled at him softly. "I'm a succubus. Many of your people would think us demons but we are actually part of the Fae."

Before Whisky could say a word, there was a sound behind us and I turned to see the demon appear in the room. I reached for my dagger, which I had placed on the table, but the demon held out his hand and the dagger spun across the room to land in the wall.

"Lily, move. Don't get in the way. This is my fight." Whisky struggled, trying to stand, but he was too weak.

I whirled, facing the demon. "Don't kill him! He's never done anything to you. His ancestor's argument with you is not his fight. Why do you continue this feud?"

The demon laughed and shrugged. "Because it's what I do. You are not mortal. You are of the Fae folk." He stopped, then sniffed in my direction. "I smell you. I smell your sex and your passion. I've heard of your kind. You're a firebrand in the bed." The lust in his voice was thick.

I suddenly realized how I could get Whisky out of the situation. True, it wasn't my fight. But I was tired of death and hexes and curses and all the dark things in the night. It wasn't often that

I got the chance to save a life, rather than take one. Here was a chance to make up for some of the damage I had done.

"I'll make you a deal. You spare him and his son, you allow them to live a long and healthy life—longer than most. And I'll let you taste my fire. You give me some of your chi, and I spread my legs and give you a taste of what I am."

The demon laughed, long and low. "I might take you up on that." And then, he glanced over at Whisky. "You really think he's worth it? You have no idea what he's like, and yet you offer to save the creature?"

I nodded, motioning for Whisky to stay silent. "Do we have a deal?"

"Signed and sealed."

The night was rough. Demons weren't usually gentle, and this demon had a lot of pent-up anger and desire. But finally when he spent himself, and I rolled away, I considered myself lucky. I was getting away with a few bruises and scratches. The sex had been violent and ugly, but I was able to put my emotions on hold and feed at the same time. His chi was potent, though it left me with a case of emotional hiccups. Not too bad for a romp with a scaly freak, but I wouldn't be repeating the act anytime soon.

I hurried over to Whisky's side. He had fallen asleep, but his fever had broken and I could tell he was on the mend.

I turned to the demon. "You will keep your deal?"

He nodded. "On my word, his son will live. And this one? He will live a long and healthy life, *far longer* than most humans could ever dream of." He suddenly smiled, and I had the feeling that he was about to renege on the deal. "But, succubus, note that I *didn't* say what form he would live his life in. You wanted a pet; you've got one."

And with a flash, the demon vanished.

I turned as Whisky let out a shout. He jolted to a sitting position, then a moment later, a large cat sat in his place. I had heard of Asian leopard cats, though most humans hadn't, and that's exactly what Whisky looked like, only smaller.

And that was the end of that.

Whisky never again took human form, and I kept him with me. I wasn't sure just how much he remembered, but most of the time he seemed content enough, and we kept each other company as the years rolled on. Sometimes I wondered about his family and how they were. I finally looked them up without telling him, only to find out that his wife had quickly found herself a rich man and remarried, and his children had turned into spoiled brats. It seemed kinder to leave him in the dark. I told Whisky that I found out his wife had entered a convent and that his children had moved on and were fostering with wealthy strangers overseas. I knew it would hurt him too much to know the truth, and a gentle lie seemed to be the best way to ease his mind and heart.

• • •

"And that is the story of how Whisky came to be with me. He's really a human sorcerer, trapped in the body of a cat. And he's been with me for six hundred years. I trust him and I trust his instincts." I hadn't mentioned finding his family—after all, Whisky could hear and understand me and, after all these years, I still had never told him the truth.

Marsh and Archer both stared at me, then at Whisky. Neither said a word. Archer continued to eat his pizza, and Marsh simply shook his head. Meanwhile, I finished my pizza and then, giving Whisky another pat on the back, began to tell Archer what happened. And why I was going out of business.

CHAPTER 19

Archer listened as I laid out everything that had happened that day. After I was done, he shook his head. "So, how are you taking this?" He seemed more concerned about my feelings than about the specifics of what I had told him.

Even though it had made me blush, I had included what Wynter had said about him. Since he had chosen to entangle himself in my life, he deserved to know what he was getting into.

"I don't know. I don't even know how I'm *supposed* to feel. Today feels like I stumbled into a field of landmines and the explosions just keep going off. I feel horrible about my mother. I feel conflicted about my father. For so long, I've wondered who he was and if I would like him if I met him. I don't remember much about him, and now I feel guilty for ever wanting to. He murdered my mother and I've wasted centuries wishing I could know who he was."

"You feel like you betrayed her, don't you?" Marsh suddenly started as Whisky jumped up on the chair where he was sitting. Now he was superimposed over the cat's form and it was disconcerting, to say the least. As he stared down at his stomach where Whisky curled into a ball a look of understanding came over his face. "I just realized something!" He sounded delighted and confused at the same time.

"What is it?"

"I know who summoned me." He continued to stare at the cat.

"You don't mean *Whisky*? It couldn't be, could it? He doesn't even have opposable thumbs."

"Are you sure about this?" I glanced from Marsh's face to

Whisky's and back again. Whisky gave me a slow blink and I swear, the cat smiled.

Marsh nodded. "I felt a ripple of energy when you asked, and it came from where he's sitting. It was Whisky all right."

I slowly got out of my chair and walked over to Marsh. Picking up Mr. Whiskers—which meant reaching into Marsh's image—I held the cat up and stared into his face. He stared back, his eyes glowing.

"How did you do that? I didn't know you could still practice magic. You never told me."

On one hand, I felt ridiculous having this conversation. Whisky hadn't practiced magic since the day he was turned. And yet…and yet…Marsh insisted. And who else could it be? I had suspected Dani, but now that I thought about it, she didn't know enough about Marsh in order to summon him. She didn't know where he had died, she didn't know about our last moments together and, to be honest, I wasn't even sure she really understood the full nature of the relationship we had had. But Whisky had been there. He had seen everything except those last days up in the cabin. Those, I had told him about, once the shock of Marsh's death was over.

"It *was* you," I said in a soft voice. "Somehow you managed to summon Marsh's spirit here. I wish you could tell me how you did it. I wish you could tell me why."

"We know why," Marsh said. "He wants me to watch over you. He knows what danger you're in and he wants to do whatever he can. Now that I know his story, I understand. That cat loves you like he's never loved anybody."

I jerked my gaze away from the cat. "Whisky and I were never in a relationship—"

"You didn't have to be," Archer said. "Marsh is right. Whisky adores you. Remember, there are many types of love. You've taken care of Whisky since that first night you found him out back in the alley. You helped heal him, then you scared away the demon who was trying to curse him. You saved his son from the curse. The fact that you weren't able to prevent the demon from turning him into a cat? *Not your fault,* and he knows that, too. The truth is, you're probably the only reason he's still alive. He's returning the favor."

The magnitude of what both Marsh and Archer were saying hit me. It had been close to six hundred years since that night in Cornwall, when Whisky and I first met. At first I had been very aware that I had been traveling with a sorcerer in cat form. But as the years and decades and centuries raced by, it was easy to forget that Mr. Whiskers was anything but a dear and constant companion. I realized that if I lost him, I would lose the oldest, dearest friend I'd ever had.

I quietly leaned over and set Whisky on the ground. He flashed me a satisfied look and wandered over to his food dish, where he began to eat. As I returned to my chair, another thought occurred to me.

"Archer, now that you know that Whisky was turned into a cat by a demon's curse, and given the fact that you are a demon yourself…" I paused, not wanting to ask but feeling like I owed Whisky the chance of a normal life again.

Archer let out a soft laugh. "You're as transparent as a crystal. Unfortunately, the answer is no. I cannot reverse another demon's curse. And even if I could, I wouldn't, and I'll tell you why. While the original demon could reverse his hex—if he did? Chances are Whisky would immediately die. Sorcerer or not, it sounds like he was of human blood when you met him. Humans are not meant to live six hundred years, not without magical help. The only reason he's still alive is *because* of the hex. The moment the magic breaks, so will the lengthened lifespan. I'm sorry, but if you want Mr. Whiskers to stay alive, he'll have to remain in cat form."

So much for that. I glanced over at Whisky. "I tried, bub."

He yawned so wide I could have seen his tonsils, if he'd had any. I got the distinct impression Whisky was okay with being a cat. I still wanted to know how he had managed to summon Marsh, but at least we had resolved the mystery. In a way, knowing that much made me feel better. It gave us a little control over the situation. And control was precisely something that felt like it was slipping out of my hands.

"So, on to the more serious subjects. How do I destroy the Souljacker? It shouldn't be too hard to lure him out, but I've never gone after a vampire before. And then there's the matter of my career. At least Tricia Jones is getting her revenge. I wish it were enough to put a stop to whatever she's planning, but Wynter warned me not to count on it." I still had a sour taste in my mouth.

"Lily…I recognize that look." Marsh shook a finger at me. "Don't you go doing anything stupid. When we were together, you always were out to make people pay for their slights."

"I know, and yes, I want revenge." It was true, I was all about payback when someone messed with me or someone I cared about. But reality sank in. "I can't do anything, can I? If I do respond, I'll be pegged as a total bitch. Tricia's a widow and I'm…well…in her eyes and her friends' eyes, I'm the…whore in this little drama. I hate that word, but I know that's how she and her friends see me. I might as well face the truth. She's got me over a barrel."

"Don't ever call yourself that, Lily. The blame belongs with Tygur. He made the choice to step out on her. Or really, she should blame the Souljacker. He's the one who murdered her husband. But never let me hear you call yourself that again, okay?" Archer reached over tilt my chin up, cupping it gently in his hands. With a soft smile, he wiped away my bitterness.

"I promise. I really *don't* think of myself as that but it's hard when you've got an entire community against you. I haven't felt this way since…since before I came off the open road and decided to settle into city life. That was a good hundred years ago."

"We'll deal with the Weres later. Right now, we need to address the Souljacker," Archer said. "I did some hunting around but I have no idea where he's hiding. I'm wondering if his father had anything to do with his escape—if so, maybe that's where Charles is hiding out."

A nasty thought crossed my mind. "You aren't putting yourself in danger, are you? If he does have help from his father…the man is extremely well connected, as we've seen."

Archer shrugged. "To be honest, if I were human? I'd be scared out of my mind that someone might catch onto what I'm doing. But I'm a demon. It's not so easy to take me on when I'm angry, and I have always just left if things got too dicey. But never mind that." He paused. "Are Nate and Dani coming over? It seems to me that they might want to be in on this."

"Yes, but they probably aren't home yet. Let me text them."

Dani replied, saying that she had to make a couple stops, but yes, she needed to come over and would arrive at eight-ish. Nate also gave me the ETA of eight o'clock.

While we waited, I set the leftover pizza on the counter and foraged in the cupboard. A day like today called for chocolate. I found a box of truffles and brought them over to the table.

Archer accepted one of the candies, then gave me a speculative look. "Are you *hungry?*"

The fact that we had just finished off an entire pizza between the two of us, along with a number of chocolates, left no doubt as to the nature of his question.

I was about to answer that I was just tired, when I realized that part of my weariness stemmed from a very different kind of hunger.

"Are you offering?" I asked, only half serious.

But when he said, "I wouldn't ask if I didn't intend to carry through," I realized just how hungry I was. The stress of the day had sapped my energy levels and Archer's voice was soft. The heat in his eyes seared its way across the table. Oh yes, there was a connection between us all right, and it wasn't one that was merely born from the single tryst we'd had.

My breath coming quickly, my hand went to my turtleneck, and I realized that I was playing with the collar. I wet my lips, licking them gently as I leaned my elbows on the table.

"Care to find out if twice is a charm?"

"I don't think there's any doubt about the answer to that." He glanced over at Marsh.

Marsh let out a soft laugh. "I'll hang out here with Whisky. I might have a go at trying to communicate with him, see if I can figure out how he summoned to me here." He shot me a long look. "You need to feed. I promise I won't watch."

I breathed a little easier. He seemed at peace with the thought, and so I stood, holding my hand out to Archer. As I led him upstairs I could hear Marsh talking to Whisky. Secure in the knowledge that my house and land were warded heavily, I let the events of the day go as we entered my private bedroom.

Archer stood in back of me and placed his hands on my shoulders.

"Let me undress you." He brushed my hair away from my face. "Let me take the lead. I have a feeling that most of your clients have always wanted you to be in charge. Let me take that off your shoulders for tonight. Let me be your master."

A ripple raced through my body, as I responded to his words. He was right. I was always the one who led. Usually, I didn't mind, but there was a part of me that needed to let go of control, to let go of the responsibility to make everything work. I was tired of always being in charge, and the day had increased that weariness tenfold.

With a shudder, I leaned into his caress. As his scent swept around me, the hunger began to rise in earnest.

"I need you," I whispered. "I need your chi. I need your hands on my body." I closed my eyes as he reached around to tug the tail of my sweater out of my jeans.

"Stop. Lift your hands."

I obeyed. As he slid the sweater up and over my head, then gently tossed it on the bed, I reveled in the delicious blast of cool air that played over my breasts. I was wearing a lace bra, and he unhooked it, slowly and deliberately. Then, as the straps went slack, he walked around to face me before he removed the bra. My breasts bounced gently as the band caught beneath them, then gave way. My nipples stiffened under his gaze, and a hot flare drove its way down my body, from breast to between my thighs, where it set off a series of minor explosions.

I let out a soft gasp, but he gave me one shake of the head. "Silence."

Closing my mouth, I stood, frozen, as he reached for the zipper on my jeans, easing it down to expose the fact that I wasn't wearing underwear. With a rough laugh, he arched his eyebrows.

"Commando? Brave woman."

I couldn't let that go by. "No, not brave. Just…being me."

"Being you is a good thing." He tugged on the belt loops, lowering my jeans until I could step out of them. They landed atop my sweater and bra, and I was truly naked except for my pentacle. That, I had no intention of removing.

He must have sensed my thoughts, because he shook his head, placing his finger to his lips to kiss it, then touching my own to transfer the kiss. "I will never ask you to remove your necklace. It protects you. It will burn me if I touch it, but I've been burned before."

I didn't want to hurt him. "I'll take it off for you."

"No. Don't. I will never ask you to lower those defenses which keep you safe." His voice grew serious, the play vanishing. "I will never ask you to endanger yourself for pleasure. Or for food. I'll wear my shirt. The cloth will take the brunt of the heat from the silver."

"Archer, be sensible—" I started to say, but he swept me to him, crushing my mouth with his in a kiss that went on forever. I moaned, frantic for his touch, frantic for the heat to consume me. With one hand, he reached down and began to finger me as I let out a low growl and—unable to wait—grabbed for his belt buckle.

I shoved his jeans down as he walked me forward to the bed. As I fell backward onto the mattress, he kneed apart my legs and thrust into me, hard and thick, demanding entrance. The fire between us flared, stronger than the first time, and the haze of passion began to overwhelm me as he covered my face with kisses.

Returning his lips to mine, he whispered, "Feed…feed on me…"

As he continued to drive himself into me, I began to feed. I inhaled deeply, drawing his breath—his life force—deep into my lungs. With every second, the charge grew stronger.

He arched, grinding against my pelvis, so deep inside he was touching my core. With one hand, he pinched one of my nipples so hard that I let out a cry that was mingled with his breath. The pain drove me higher. I was hooked to a live wire, a direct current to life itself. The glow of his touch, of the shimmering nimbus that made Archer who he was flared with wild abandon, and I drank it down.

Suddenly, unable to soak up any more, I realized that I was about to come. I called out his name as I came hard and fast, pleasure and pain mingled to where I could not separate them. Tears sprang up as I wrapped my arms around him. Archer followed suit, arching into my embrace as he closed his eyes and groaned. Then, spent, he fell against me and lay still, murmuring soft words that I couldn't quite understand.

From a long way off, the doorbell chimed. Neither one of us moved, but a moment later, Marsh appeared in the bedroom.

He stared at us, still coupled, for a long moment. "I don't mean to interrupt, but Dani's downstairs. She let herself in. She's hopping mad, Lily. You'd better come down."

And with that, playtime was over.

CHAPTER 20

Crap, what had happened now? I threw on a nightgown, then slid a silk robe over it, belting it firmly. Archer grinned at me as he jammed his legs into his jeans and yanked them up.

"Good thing we were finished," he said. "Otherwise, she could wait." As I started for the door, he caught my arm. Pressing his lips to my forehead in a gentle kiss, he whispered, "I could get used to this, you know? I could really get used to this."

I gazed up at him. Once again he took my breath away. What was it about him? I barely knew him and yet I wanted him in my life. I had been so relieved when Wynter told me to keep him around. It wasn't just because I could feed off of him, either. That was a big plus, but below the surface, I realized there was so much I wanted to know about him.

"What are you thinking?"

Startled, I almost answered and then stopped myself. I couldn't just blurt out that I wanted him to stick around, at least not the way I had been thinking. That was a one-way trip to stalker city. Plus, it didn't seem fair to lay my expectations on his shoulders. Not when he had been so helpful. I pressed my lips together and shook my head, smiling.

He frowned. "Do you want to know what *I'm* thinking?"

Again, I had no good answer. I wanted to shout out, "Yes," but something stopped me. Maybe it was fear, maybe it was just shock from all the changes that had gone on through the day. I wasn't sure that I could handle anything that I might not want to hear at this point.

"I'm going to tell you, whether or not you ask." He pushed

me back, facing me directly. "Lily, this…*arrangement* we seem to have…it means more to me than just helping you out. I like being part of your life. That's all I'll say for now on that matter, but please, never feel you are using me. Okay?"

I nodded, drinking down every word he was saying.

"I also think that I know what you can do, now that you have to shut down the salon." Before I could ask, he continued. "Work with me. I can use a partner in the business. It also seems to me that this would be a good way to fulfill Wynter's orders, at least regarding the Souljacker. And this way, I can tell you the things that I need to tell you, but that confidentiality prevents me from revealing."

Startled, I took a step back. That was the *last* thing I had expected him to say. "But I don't know anything about being a detective or an investigator. Won't I just be in the way?"

"Not at all. Let's face it, you have to do something. I have more than enough work—it would help to have an assistant. I just haven't found the right person yet. I have the money to pay you, and this would mean that when you grow too hungry, even if it's during the day…" He didn't have to finish the sentence. I already knew the end.

I jammed my hands in my pockets and stared at him. There was no subterfuge in his voice, and I couldn't detect any hidden agenda behind his expression. That didn't necessarily mean one didn't exist, but if there was one, Archer was doing a good job of keeping it under wraps.

"I suppose if you think I'm capable of learning the job…And you're right, there are perks, aren't there?"

At that moment Marsh appeared again. He looked irritated. "Can you *please* hurry it up? Dani is roiling mad, and quite frankly, she's taking it out on me. I don't want to find out what she can do to spirits when she's in a bad mood."

I turned to Archer and nodded. "I'll do it. Thank you for the vote of confidence. And…thank you for everything else."

Marsh let out a snort. "I'm not even going to address that, but please—"

"We're coming." And with that, Archer and I headed downstairs.

• • •

Dani was sitting at the table, the look on her face cold enough to freeze water. Something had happened, all right. Before I could say anything, a knock on the back door announced Nate's presence. I refilled the kettle and set it to boil. We could all use a hot cup of tea.

Nate glanced at Archer, giving him a little wave. "Hey, how's it hanging?"

Archer's lips crooked into a gentle smile, lifting ever so slightly. "It's been an interesting day. And you?" He included Dani in his question.

Nate shrugged. "Rough day at work. I had to let one of our better programmers go because we found out he was embezzling money via his expense account. He was also leaking sensitive information. I don't see how this is going to end well. He's the type who might show up at work with an automatic and mow down the whole office. Security's on high alert." He glanced over at Dani. "And don't *you* look like you want to set the world on fire. What's going on?"

Dani let out a sputter. "Well, for starters, when I got to my shop, I find it's been trashed. Someone broke in and totally destroyed half my inventory. The cops came and dusted for prints, but unfortunately, whoever did it took the film from my security cameras before smashing them to pieces. This is going to cost me a fortune to fix. I won't be able to make your wards, Lily, but then again, I noticed when I drove in tonight that you have a new set—they're nice, by the way. I assume Wynter gave them to you? Good deal, because I'm going to be spending the next two weeks shoveling out the mess in my shop." She paused to take a breath.

"Crap. Who the hell do you think did it?" Nate asked.

"I don't know, but I'm ready to kill. And then, I got a call from Rebecca's husband. He's blaming me for her death. He says I was a bad influence on her and that it's my fault she got the fucking tattoo. He can't do anything to me, but damn it all—Rebecca was my friend. She is...was...an adult. And then..." She suddenly ran out of steam.

So it was already beginning. "I think I may know what happened to your shop. I could be wrong but..." I glanced at Archer, who inclined his head.

"If you do, tell me because I'll throw a whammy on them so fast they won't be able to sit down for a week. I lost a lot of money."

I let out a long sigh. "While I was out at Wynter's today, she warned me that Tricia's not done with her revenge. She's out for my blood, and if it means hurting my friends, that's what she'll do. I—along with anybody associated with me—am on her shit list. She's got revenge on the brain and you know how Weres hold grudges."

"Fuck. That explains something else. The cops found a patch on the floor where somebody peed. They said it was strong—very strong. Ten to one, whoever she had in there was marking their territory to let me know they had been there." She motioned to the refrigerator. "Can I grab something to drink? Some lemonade if you have it?"

"I'll get it." Archer moved to the counter to pour her a glass. As he set it on the table, he said, "We have some pizza left. Would you guys like it cold or hot?"

She accepted the soda, drinking half of it before answering. "Hot. Nate?"

"Hot's fine with me. Pizza's good no matter what." He frowned. "So, your security cameras were tampered with? Did they steal anything?"

Dani shrugged, staring morosely at the glass in her hand. "I don't know yet. I think so, though. Several of my expensive crystals are gone. But Weres don't like magic, so I doubt they took any of my scrolls or spell components. They made a mess of them, though."

Archer slid the pizza onto a pan and put it in the oven to heat. "I guess she wasted no time, did she. What did the police say?"

"They said that I should keep my eyes open, call them if any troublemakers come into the shop, and that they would analyze the urine to see what they can find. All so much talk meaning they haven't a clue who did it and they have better things to do than waste their time on a break-in. Seriously, they can't stop the vampires, and now they're writing off burglaries. What *are* they good at?"

It occurred to me that maybe I could confine the damage, if I talked to Tricia. I didn't want my friends taking the brunt of her anger for me. As Archer, Nate, and Dani discussed the break-in, I slipped into the living room and looked up her number on my phone's InfoPages. I decided it would be safer to text, and sent her a message, asking her if she would meet with me privately for a talk—that I wanted to apologize and do what I could to make amends. I knew that it would never make up for what happened, but I couldn't sit around and do nothing.

That done, I took a deep breath and returned to the kitchen. Maybe I could at least take care of one problem without too much collateral damage.

CHAPTER 21

Dani and Nate were deep into the pizza when I returned to the kitchen.

As I settled back in my chair, Dani asked around a mouthful of mozzarella, "So, tell us what happened out at Wynter's."

"What didn't happen?" I gave them the rundown of my visit. "So, in effect, in one day, my entire life has been turned upside down. I'm no longer self-employed, that's for sure." I couldn't decide if I felt more grumpy because I had been forced to close my business, or if it was because I hadn't been given a choice in the matter.

"We've all had one hell of a day," Nate said. "What about you, Archer?"

"I was waiting till everybody was here to tell you what I managed to find out today. I decided to try to find out who might have been helping the Souljacker escape, and why they did so. The most logical suspect is his father. So I started there. And that's when the trail opened up into a rabbit hole, and I went tumbling down."

That didn't sound good. "Is it really that bad?"

"I think that I found out a number of things we'd all be safer off not knowing." Archer wasn't smiling. He spread out a series of file folders on the desk. "I printed off the information just in case somebody decides to go in and try to delete it."

We settled in to listen.

"First, you have to know that Terrance Schafer and the Deadfather go way back. Terrance helps out the Deadfather politically, the Deadfather invests in Schafer's businesses." Archer looked up from the paper he was holding. "Got that?"

"Yeah, and that sounds about right. Big business and vampires are becoming synonymous." As much as I didn't like the fact, I wasn't going to refute it.

"Okay, well here's where it gets dicey. Terrance's wife—Charles's mother—is petitioning the court for power of attorney over her son. She wanted him staked. She's also a major power player in the political scene, so it's feasible she could win the case. She and Terrance are divorced, you know."

Light-switch time. I snapped my fingers. "So Terrance asks the Deadfather to help him smuggle Charles out of WestcoPsi. He couldn't ask the authorities to release Charles—he did murder that family, and if he's let out he'll automatically be under penalty of death."

Dani paled. "But, why would the Deadfather let Charles go free? Why didn't he turn him over to Terrance?"

Archer scratched his nose, looking very much like he was about to tell us something we didn't want to hear. "Because something went wrong. Dani, I don't know how to tell you this, so I'll just come out and say it. There were two witnesses to what happened the night Charles escaped—they managed to stay out of sight. They described the vampire who broke in and killed the guards. I did a little more digging and sure enough…this vampire works for the Deadfather. He's his right-hand man, so to speak."

Dani hugged her stomach, grimacing. "You don't mean…"

"I'm afraid so. The vampire who broke into WestcoPsi and freed the Souljacker was supposed to take him back to Terrance and the Deadfather. Something happened along the way, and he lost control of Charles after he got him out of the institution. I found out today that the name of that vampire is Greg Fallow. Dani, your late husband is the Deadfather's right-hand man."

• • •

Between Dani crying, and Nate and me shouting, the kitchen was a free-for-all for the next few minutes. Finally Archer let out a loud whistle.

"Enough. We have to talk about this. I know it comes as a shock, and I'm sorry I had to tell you like this, but I only found out this afternoon."

Dani wiped her eyes with a napkin. "I'm just…I don't know why I should be shocked. After all, it's not like he's the Greg I married. I just…I didn't expect for him to be involved." Straightening her shoulders, she inhaled deeply, then let it out in a slow, even stream. "All right, get it over with. Tell us everything you know about him."

Archer gauged her cautiously. "You sure?"

"Yes, go."

"All right, here it is. Greg has been working for the Deadfather since shortly after he was turned. Your husband was always smart and that didn't change when he died. He was ambitious, correct?"

Dani nodded. "Yeah, he was never content to just *be*. He was always working toward the next new thing…new stage in life, new job, new…whatever came his way."

"Okay, so now that the fundamental shock is out of the way, here's what I found out. The Deadfather owns Greg. I mean *owns* him, lock, stock, and barrel. The Deadfather funded Veek."

"Is that how he got the money?" Dani asked. "I wondered about that. We weren't rich when he was alive, and he hasn't had that much time to amass the amount it would take."

"So, what does Greg *do* for the Deadfather?" I didn't want to know—it couldn't be good, whatever it was, but we had to find out.

Archer paused again. I could tell there was more unwelcome information coming. "I can't be 100 percent sure about this, but I think he's one of the Deadfather's hit men."

Dani said nothing. The shock seemed to be all wrung out of her. She just stared at Archer with a morose look on her face.

I rubbed my head. "You mean he's basically a gun for hire?"

"I'd call it a fang for hire, but essentially, yes."

I slumped back in my chair. Greg worked for the Deadfather. He not only worked for the Deadfather, but he killed for him. I let out a shaky sigh and glanced over at Dani. She was on the edge of breaking down, that much I could tell. The trauma of discovering her shop had been trashed along with discovering that her ex-husband had helped spring the vampire who was stalking us had taken its toll. I motioned for Archer to cut the discussion.

"Dani, stay here tonight. You don't have to go home, do you?" She silently shook her head.

"Stay here, let me give you something to help you sleep." Then, I used the oldest lie that every friend had used at one time or another. "Things will look better in the morning."

After a moment, she finally relented. "All right. But I know I won't be able to sleep."

But I was determined to make sure she got a good night's sleep. I gave her a sedative guaranteed to eliminate nightmares, and walked her up to the guest room. She was so tired that she immediately crashed. Once I was certain she was fully out, I headed back to the kitchen. The day had been extraordinarily long, and Dani wasn't the only one who had been through hell.

While I was gone, Nate had cleaned up and a fresh batch of oatmeal-raisin cookies was baking in the oven. Archer was poring through his files, studying them carefully.

I dropped into a chair. "Do I smell cookies?"

Nate let out a small laugh. "You know as well as I do that when I'm upset, I cook."

"Much to my advantage. Without you, half the time I'd be eating takeout. So what are we going to do next?" I still hadn't mentioned my text to Tricia, and I wasn't planning to. What I wanted to do right now was to tromp down to the Underground and drive a stake through Greg's heart. His death had cost Dani so much. Now, like a bad penny, he kept turning up.

After removing the cookies from the cookie sheet with a spatula, Nate set the plate on the table, wiped up the crumbs on the counter, then slid into the chair opposite me.

"Well, I can tell you what you are *not* going to do next. You are not going to head into the Underground to stake Greg. I know you were thinking it, because that's what *I'm* thinking. You do that and you'll get yourself killed."

Archer spoke up. "He's right. Leave him alone. If you try to destroy him and fail, he'll take it out on Dani. Vampires are cruel beasts. Dani will survive this news. She's stronger than she thinks, or than you think. But if you pique his interest, Greg just may come back to haunt her in a way none of us wants."

I held up my hands. "Okay, I give. I was thinking about it, but I know I don't have what it takes. And anyway, it would be suicide, given how close he seems to be to the Deadfather."

Archer was studying something on his tablet. "The Souljacker seems to have focused his attention on clients in the Blood Night District so far. Do you know if he ever traveled? Did he work the convention circuit? If he leaves town, we're screwed as far as tracking him. And then you'll always be watching over your shoulder."

I squinted, thinking. "Let me see. I don't know, but there's someone who might. A tattooist in White Tower Center who was a friend of his. What the hell was his name..." I tried to remember. Charles had mentioned the guy a couple of times. "Ray—Ray Bender. That's it."

Nate pulled out his tablet and, after a moment, said, "Here he is. Bender Skin Art. He's open from 6 P.M. till midnight every day. He must pay for protection, given his location. He's not open tonight, but tomorrow. Want me to call for an appointment?"

"Would you?" Archer said. "That's one place to start. Without the cops behind us, we're going to have to tackle this on our own, and very carefully, given how powerful Schafer's father is. With support like the Deadfather behind him, the Souljacker might as well be a grenade, set to explode on touch."

A thought crossed my mind. "But won't they be out looking for him too? If Greg screwed up, the plan wasn't for Charles to be set free. Maybe he was supposed to deliver him to Terrance, who would probably hide him away. Which means, if Charles is on the loose, my bets are that he isn't in contact with his family."

I bit into one of Nate's cookies, closing my eyes as the fragrant flavor of oatmeal and raisins melted on my tongue. They were hot enough still to burn, but the heat of the caramelized brown sugar added to the taste.

"You're probably right." Archer tossed the paper on the table. "Enough for tonight. We'll exhaust ourselves. Lily, tomorrow you start working for me."

I nodded. "Sounds good to me. I think during the day might be a good time to go hunting around in the Underground. Maybe there's somebody there who's seen something."

That brought an immediate response from Nate. "Wait a minute, that sounds dangerous."

"What else do we do? Sit here and wait for Charles to pick us off once we're outside a warded area? We have to go on the offensive." I turned to Archer. "What do you think?"

"I think both of you are right. Before you head down to the Underground, we'll discuss the best way of doing so and I will go with you. But leave that for tomorrow. It's been a volatile, emotional day for all of you. Even I'm tired from just hearing about it. I suggest we take a break. Do you have any beer?"

Nate warmed up to that idea. "I could go for a drink."

Marsh laughed. He had been listening quietly, sitting in the rocking chair that I kept near the heating vent. "I wish I could join you. I feel like I've entered the Twilight Zone here."

Both Nate and Archer gave him a puzzled look, but I laughed.

"You have, essentially. As for beer, none in the house, no. But my liquor cabinet is well-stocked. Nate, what would you like?" I crossed over to the liquor cabinet and unlocked it. Archer was right. We needed to unwind, and with Dani out like a light and the new wards firmly affixed to the house, we could take a few minutes to relax.

Nate grinned. "You know my poison. So, spill it. By the way, I noticed your sign's gone. Did you take it down already?"

"Yeah, I did." As I pulled out the bottle of peppermint schnapps and three shot glasses, I caught my reflection in the window. I looked tired. Giving myself a rueful grin, I turned around and set the glasses on the table, filling them to the brim.

I raised my glass. "Here's to new beginnings, and hopefully, a long life for us all."

"*Skol!*" Archer said.

As we drained our glasses and refilled them, I began to let go of the day, hoping the alcohol would turn it into a soft blur for just a little while.

CHAPTER 22

Groaning, I tried to open my eyes, but the lashes were glued shut. My head was pounding like a Were hopped up on jackhammer sex. I tried to sit up, only to fall back against the pillows. My stomach let out a protest at the sudden movement, and I clutched the bed sheets, holding on as the room spun in a lazy circle.

"What the hell happened last night?" Archer's voice echoed in my ear.

I managed to reach up and pry the goop off my lashes enough to separate them. Squinting against the light shining through the window, once again I tried to sit up, this time taking it much more slowly. I managed to prop up on my elbows and realized just how sick I felt.

"I feel like I ate a peppermint plant." My voice was scratchy, and I had the vague memory of singing very loudly, for a long long time. "Please tell me we didn't go crash a karaoke joint."

"That's weird. I feel like I turned into a cinnamon stick. I don't think we left the house." Archer didn't look much better than I felt.

I tried to remember what had happened, but the next moment I found myself off the bed and racing for the bathroom, the jarring strides making it even more imperative that I reach the toilet. I managed to fall on my knees in front of it and raise the lid before everything in my stomach came rushing out. When I finally finished, I was relieved to see that I had managed to aim correctly. I flushed, then spent a long time rinsing out my mouth, although I couldn't even look at the toothpaste without feeling queasy. Instead, I used an antiseptic rinse. By the time I returned to the bedroom Archer was racing past me, presumably on the same mission I had just finished.

I dragged myself back to the bed and gently lay down, pulling the blanket over me. It was icy cold in the room, and as I looked around I realized where the chill air was coming from.

"Whose bright idea was it to open the window during the night?"

Archer mumbled something from the bathroom that I didn't catch.

"We're just lucky we put the new wards up." Grumbling, I stumbled over to shut the window, then turned up the heat. I glanced at the clock on my way over to the closet. It was only 8 A.M., which surprised me given how drunk we had all gotten the night before.

"Do you want to take a shower together?" Archer stuck his head out of the bathroom.

Struck by how comfortable we had suddenly gotten, I flashed him a smile, albeit a queasy one. "I really do need a hot shower. Start up the water and I'll be right in."

Archer was naked and standing by the shower when I padded in, carrying both our robes. I looked him up and down. He was lean and fit, his abs firm, and a flare of hunger raced through me, but I was way too queasy to think about sex. And somehow, I didn't think it would be a good idea for either of us to French kiss until we had brushed our teeth and our stomachs had calmed down.

He stood back, letting me get into the shower first, then stepped in behind me. When I had my house built, I had made sure the master bath was almost as big as my bedroom. It contained a giant soaking tub, a massive walk-in shower with built-in benches and room for three, a double-vanity sink, and everything else needed. And today, I was extremely grateful that I had planned ahead. I inched over and slid down onto one of the stone benches. The water shot out from three sides and it was warm, soothing my aching muscles.

"Did we get into wrestling last night? I feel like I took a shot to the side."

"My guess it was Shayla's punch that is causing the ache. With all the adrenaline and changes going on yesterday, I doubt you noticed it, but you've got several good bruises there, and I happen to remember that we weren't that rough in bed." He pointed out the bruises that were all purple and blue on my body. Sure enough, they were right where I had slammed against the wall and floor when Shayla backhanded me.

I winced, gingerly exposing them to the hot water. Archer lathered up his hair, and he leaned back to let the water pour over him, washing away the shampoo. His body was slick and wet, and once again I wanted to brush my hands over his skin.

"You know, sex is supposed to heal me up some." I said, but just then, my stomach twinged again. "Never mind. Bad idea after a night of schnapps."

Laughing, he shook away the water. "I can't believe how much we drank. I haven't partied that hard in a couple decades."

"Really? Don't you get together with friends and just let it all blow to hell every now and then?" It occurred to me, aside from his business and that he was great in bed, I knew almost nothing about Archer. I figured now was as good a time as any to find out.

He shook his head. "To be honest, I don't have a lot of personal friends. I'm not proud of the fact, but the truth is that most people are skittish around me. You know the reputation chaos demons have." He sounded rather melancholy, and I realized that succubi weren't the only ones judged by the reputation of their race.

"Yeah, I guess I can see that. I'll be honest here. When Jolene suggested that I contact you, it made me nervous. While I hadn't heard a lot about chaos demons, what little I had made me wary. I'm glad that I changed my mind."

He flashed a look at me, and I couldn't tell whether he was irritated or not. "So what *have* you heard? Maybe I can put your mind at ease."

I forced myself to stand so the water could pulse full force down on my back. "Well, for one thing, that chaos follows you like a magnet. That wherever a chaos demon goes, mayhem follows. Rumors are that it's one of your natural attributes, that you can't help it."

Archer gave a little shrug. "That much is true. As much as I hate to admit it, I suppose you can think of me as your personal Pandora's box. It's not that I want to cause havoc in peoples' lives; it just happens. Believe me, it makes dating difficult. Humans are out of the question. If I dated a human, chances are they'd end up dead through some terrible catastrophe. And it wouldn't be by my choice. I suppose you should be careful when you hang around me, given what could happen."

The tone of his voice made me want to gather him in my arms and reassure him that I wasn't afraid. But the truth was, it did make me leery, even though I liked him a great deal.

"What else do you want to know?" He flipped off the water and opened the shower stall door. As we stepped out onto the bath mat, I thought about his question. What *did* I want to know?

"Have you ever been married? Have you ever been in love? Where is your family and are you close to them? And why did you choose to become a private investigator in the mortal world?" That should be good for a start.

He laughed and held up his hand. "Slow down, slow down. One question at a time. First, no. I've never been married, or even close to it. Yes, I have dated even given the difficulties involved. As to the second question, I was in love once but it was a long time ago. Unfortunately, she died. Not my fault!" he hurried to add. "At least, it wasn't deliberate. I can never be sure, but I think it was the chaos factor. She was hit by a runaway steer at a country fair."

"I'm sorry. What was her name?"

"Deidre. She was Fae." He tossed me my robe and I slid into it. "It was a long time ago, before the Skirmish Years. We lived in Spain. As for my family, I haven't seen any of them in centuries. Chaos demons don't tend to band together. I'll be surprised if I ever see someone I'm related to again. As to your last question, I like humans, as strange as it may sound coming from someone like me. I like the world of mortals and I enjoy interacting with both humans and the Fae. I'm not keen on the Weres, but they can be okay. They get testy. Anything else?"

I bit my lip, thinking. "Okay, then…Where do you live? And how did you meet Jolene? You know, she and I used to be an item until I realized how easy it would be for me to hurt her. Well, until I realized that I was already hurting her. Werewolves tend to be monogamous, and I'm a succubus. Those two factors don't work well together."

"I thought it was something of the sort, but I decided to let you tell me in your own time. As for where I live, I own a penthouse on the border between north Seattle and the Blood Night District. I met Jolene when she joined the force. I was already helping out the PIU. Anything else, or is that all for now?" He laughed, and I realized with relief that my prying wasn't offending him.

"What's your favorite color? Food? Do you like to read?" I grinned, just playing now.

"Orange, a cheeseburger dripping with mozzarella, and I have a huge library at home. I read just about everything. And now, we should get downstairs, eat breakfast, and then get to work. Remember, I'm your boss now!" He snapped the towel and hit me on the butt.

I darted back into the bedroom, realizing that even though I was still queasy, I was starting to feel better. I pulled out a pair of jeans and a thick, cowl-neck sweater. One look outside told me that it was blowing snow like crazy. The room had finally warmed up, and as I slipped into my clothes and pulled my hair back into a French braid, my stomach rumbled.

"Believe it or not, I think I need some breakfast."

As Archer dressed, he nodded. "Me too. Just nothing greasy and nothing fried. Toast and jam would be good if you have it."

"I've always got bread, I'm not so sure about the jam. Let's go find out. But first, I'm going to drop in on Dani and see how she's doing. Do you remember if Nate stayed the night?"

"Yeah, I recall seeing him passed out on the living room sofa before heading up stairs. You do realize that you performed a strip-tease for the two of us last night? But he was too drunk to notice. I'm not sure where Marsh took off to; he had vanished by the time we managed to make it to the living room."

Mortified—the last thing I wanted to do was make Nate uncomfortable—I opened the door to the guest room and peeked inside. Dani was sitting on the edge of the bed, dressed, her face ashen white. She moaned and rubbed her forehead.

"What the hell did you give me? I feel like somebody took a sledgehammer to my head."

"I gave you Beladonacia. That's the only side effect unless you take too much. How are you feeling otherwise?" I sat down beside her and took her hands in mine. "I know last night was a horrible shock. I'm so sorry."

Dani raised her eyes to meet mine. "There's nothing to forgive. I woke up about half an hour ago, and I've just been sitting here trying to sort things through. It's not your fault that Greg's popped up again in my life."

My spirit took a nosedive as the pain in her voice filtered through. "For what it's worth, he loved you, Dani. You were the golden couple. He died loving you. And you're right—the creature wearing his body? That's not Greg. Please, don't ever start think-ing it is."

She gave a halfhearted shrug. "I won't. I can't let myself."

"What are you going to do today?"

"Go to my shop. Clean up some more. Figure out how much damage has been done. See if the cops know anything. And maybe get some bars put on the windows and door. I've avoided that route—I hate feeling like I have to make my shop a jail, but damn it, I can't afford this sort of crap. I don't make that much to begin with. At least I shouldn't lose customers. Weres hate magic as it is, so they aren't in my client base. Generally, they buy their wards through an intermediary, and I know they won't skimp on protec-tion just to spite me. So, what are you doing today?"

I thought about asking her if she wanted to poke around the Underground with me during the day but squashed the idea the moment it flashed through my mind. Veek was down there, and that would be rubbing salt in her wounds.

"I'm going down to Archer's office to get all signed up. Then…I guess we start work on trying to pinpoint the Souljacker. It occurred to me last night that, given he escaped from Greg, it means that he's out there on his own. If he goes back to his father, Terrance would probably lock him up for his own safety and Charles doesn't want that. He wants to get his art back. Tonight, we're going to go talk to Ray Bender—remember him?"

Dani squinted, then recognition filled her face. "Right, I do. You think he might know something?"

"We can hope." I groaned. "Oh, my aching head. Come on, let's get downstairs and find some breakfast." I took her by the hand and pulled her to her feet. "At least you don't have a hangover like the rest of us. We decided on some stress release, and apparently peppermint schnapps fit the bill just perfectly. I seem to remember we polished off an entire bottle between the three of us."

Dani laughed. "So I assume you have the hangover from hell?"

"Well, apparently there was karaoke, and I did a striptease. The window in my bedroom was open this morning, and it was freezing." Before she could say a word, I held up my hand. "Archer said that Nate was passed out by the time I decided to take it all off, thank gods."

As we headed down the stairs, the smell of toast and eggs wafted up and my stomach rumbled. Whether it was the hunger or the queasiness talking, I wasn't sure. All I knew is that I needed some food, and I needed it quick.

CHAPTER 23

Over breakfast, Nate was looking decidedly the worse for the wear. Archer had managed to find the eggs and bread, and was cooking. Nate was staring at the table, mumbling something under his breath. Mr. Whiskers was marching around looking decidedly put out, and I realized his breakfast was overdue. As I pulled out the cans of cat food and the dry kibble, Marsh appeared in the room.

"I see you all went on a bender," he said. "Get it out of your system, then?"

I let out a grunt as I filled the cat bowls with food. "More or less."

Nate snorted and slid the peppermint schnapps bottle—now empty—onto the table. He added another, a half-empty cinnamon schnapps bottle. "Apparently, we decided to have ourselves quite a little party."

My cheeks flaming, I decided to come right out and ask. "Do you remember me doing a striptease?"

Nate arched his eyebrows. "I *wish*. But the last thing I remember is…We were having an impromptu karaoke party. Archer was singing *Got That Girl*. Then you and I tried to sing a duet. I seem to remember it was *Ride Me like Magic*, but I wouldn't testify to it. After that everything is a blur, until sometime earlier this morning when I woke up in the bathroom with my head over the toilet."

Archer slid the platter of scrambled eggs and toast on the table. He added a pot of coffee, and a teapot that was steaming with the fragrance of rose. I started out of my seat to get plates and silverware, but Dani motioned for me to sit back down.

"I may be a little drowsy from the sedative, but I'm not hung over. Let me do that."

As she passed out the plates and tableware, she let out a long sigh. "I got a message from the cops. The urine is Were, they can tell that much, but that's all they have to go on. I've contacted a window company to come replace the windows and put up bars. So much for goodwill in the neighborhood."

"I'm sorry. Tygur's death is hitting us all, it seems. I'll pay for your window if you like—it's essentially because of me that Tricia's posse went after you."

"No, that's all right. I've got insurance. But damn it, I'd like to slap that girl upside the head." Dani held out her plate as Archer scooped scrambled eggs onto it.

I stared at my dish, my stomach unsure of what it wanted to do, but finally, I attacked the food, which tasted surprisingly delicious. I felt like I hadn't eaten in days.

Archer nodded. "I put in a call to a friend who runs a shop in the Underground. He's agreed to meet us there tomorrow. That's the earliest he can be available. He'll play tour guide, and he knows a lot of about the Underground that few others do. Today, first thing, Lily—you and I should go down to the office and get everything set up, since you'll be working for me."

I was about to answer when the chime on my phone sounded. I glanced at the text. Tricia had answered. "Excuse me, I need to take this in private." I hurried into the living room.

Meet me at White Tower Center, back entrance. I'll be waiting right inside Level Two. Be there at four or don't come at all.

I stared at the message, debating whether or not to go. But I'd been the one to ask for the meeting, and I felt like I had to try something. Maybe I could reach her. And if not? I'd be no worse off than I already was. I texted back, *Four. See you then.*

That done, I headed back to the kitchen.

"I'm confused," Marsh was saying. "If the Deadfather is so dangerous, why do the authorities let him live? He's a vampire, and according to what you said, they don't have rights. If they took him out, it wouldn't be like assassinating a foreign country's ambassador or king, would it?"

"Oh, it would be worse. Given the number of vampires in the world, we'd be up against a legion out for revenge." I shook my head. "While in theory, it would be nice to be rid of him, unless there's a crackdown on vampires and what they can get away with, it would only make things worse."

Dani cleared the table for us. She wiped her hands on the dishtowel. "Consider him the king of vampires. In fact, a good 80 percent of vampires claim they happily support him. The Deadfather is tremendously wealthy and until recently he remained in the shadows like all the other vampires. But as they grew more bold, so did the Deadfather."

"More than that," Archer added, "the Deadfather has been around for thousands of years. He's probably the oldest vampire alive at this point. Or one of them. I've been doing some research into him, although superficially until now. Do you know that the oldest vampires refer to themselves as the elder gods? That's how they see themselves—immortal, almost invulnerable. And truthfully, unless you find one in his lair during the day, fighting and killing one that old is almost impossible except for the strongest and most cunning of hunters."

And with that sobering thought, we prepared to start the day.

• • •

Nate promised to call me if he found anything. He was going to delve into whatever he could find about the Weres and what they might be planning. "The rumor mills will be active, given how popular Tygur was. I'll see what I can find out about Tricia's plans. Maybe I can help out Dani, too."

"Stay here while you work—it's safer than your place."

"The vamps are asleep during the day, remember?" But he shrugged. "I'll keep Whisky company, sure."

Dani also promised to call us before the day was out, to let us know how things were going at her shop. "I don't intend to open today at all. It's just going to be cleaning up and making an inventory of what's missing." She paused at the bottom of the back porch. "By the way, I'd love to examine your wards, if you don't mind. The chance to look at Katarina's work is like…like what viewing a Picasso is for an art student. She's brilliant. I can feel the energy zinging around your yard like a Ping-Pong ball. At least we can trust your place to be a safe haven from the Souljacker, along with any other vampires that might take it into their heads to come after us."

I knew she was talking about Greg, but said nothing.

After Dani left, Archer and I headed out for his office. Now *my* office too, when I thought about it. For almost seventy-five years now I had played the part of lover and mistress. Today would be different.

I took my car rather than ride with Archer, because I would need it later on. As I passed through the Blood Night District, I found myself looking at the city in a new light. I had grown so used to my surroundings, they had become a backdrop—but today something seemed different. I felt more like an outsider. For decades I had belonged to the city and been content with my role. One thing I knew for sure: working for Archer would be a whole new experience. And if I was honest with myself, it felt like a breath of fresh air had blown into my life in the shape of a chaos demon.

My phone rang as I sped past White Tower Center. I instructed the car to answer.

"Lily? It's Jolene. Do you have a few moments?"

"Anything for you, doll." Then I paused, thinking about why she had called the last time and I suddenly grew sober. "Has there been another murder?"

"I wish I could say no."

"I know it can't have been Dani or Nate or myself, because they were both at my house last night. Who, then?"

As I waited for her to pronounce death sentence on another

one of the Souljacker's clients, the weariness of the past couple days hit me full force.

"This is someone I don't think you knew. His name was Peter Trent. Does that name ring a bell?"

I thought for a moment, going over everybody that I could remember meeting in the past few years. "Not really," I finally said. "If I did meet him, I don't remember. He wasn't part of the India Ink Club, which tells us that the Souljacker is after *all* of his clients. Where did you find him?"

"Down in Pioneer Square, near the Underground. Sprawled on a park bench, no less. Drained dry as a bone, and half his skin missing. The Souljacker had tattooed over half of his body, and every tattoo was missing except for one. We verified with his sister that the remaining tat had been his first, inked by a different artist. It seems Charles isn't interested in any artwork but his own."

I wanted to tell her what we had learned about Greg freeing the Souljacker, but it wouldn't do any good. Greg was a vampire too, therefore they wouldn't touch the case. If he had been human—if Terrance had gone there himself to let Charles out—he might have been arrested as accessory to murder.

You're kidding yourself, a voice inside me said. *Terrance Schafer's home free because of his connections to the Deadfather.*

"Jolene, do you have any clue as to where the Souljacker is hiding?"

She paused, then cleared her throat. "Sorry, Lily. We aren't even looking. Vampire execution, remember? Not on our radar. We're putting out warnings throughout the city that if you were tattooed by him, to beef up your wards, but in terms of actual investigations, our hands are tied."

And there was another beef we had always gotten into. I had a headache and my filters weren't working so well. "Seriously, you still sit there and say that? Not you, personally, but your department? What if the vamps start killing people in waves? What then? Are you still going to turn a blind eye? Or maybe, just maybe, can you get your men on the street with stakes and go hunting? There's a lot of rumbling about this, Jolene. I wouldn't want to be on the other side of a badge if you guys continue to let this happen."

"We do what we can to make the city as safe as we can." She sounded put out now, and I recognized the code for *we really don't want to upset the powers that be.*

Feeling huffy, I decided I might as well get off my soapbox. It wasn't going to do any good. "Were there any witnesses?"

The irritation in her voice died down a little. "Actually, that's where we come into a bit of luck. There were two witnesses who saw the Souljacker attack Peter. When they realized it was a vampire, they took off and called the cops. By the time we were able to get there, he was gone, along with a sizable layer of Peter's skin. But they said they saw him come out of the Underground. One moment they saw him across the street, the next he was standing by Peter. He moved so fast there was no time for Peter to react."

"What was Peter doing in Pioneer Square?"

"According to the witnesses, he was just sitting on the bench, high as a kite on Uthanol. You know we have a simple finger-prick test for the drug now. From what I could gather, when I called his family, Peter's been strung out on Uthanol for two years now. I hate to sound this way, but if the Souljacker hadn't gotten to him, the man would have died within five months from the side effects."

I stared at the road, thinking. "Was Peter terminal? Uthanol is most often used by terminal patients."

"No, he wasn't sick at all. At least not physically. Apparently he started using the drug when his mother was on it for pain control. She had an incurable blood disease. It helped her avoid most of the pain. Peter started stealing her pills. She died seven months ago, and by that point, he was hooked. He drowned his sorrows by falling into the drug. He was a hard-core user." Jolene sounded so sad that I wish I could reach through the phone and give her a hug.

"That's rough. Thanks for letting me know, and if you have any clue where we can find Charles, call me. I'm checking on a few things myself, and once I find out whatever there is to find out, I'll let you know."

"I hate to bring this up," Jolene said, "but I've heard through the grapevine that Tricia Jones has put a hit out on your business and that some Were tore up Dani's shop. You guys okay?"

I let out a sigh. Maybe Jolene could help after all.

"Tricia and I got into it the day before yesterday. Let me tell you, it wasn't pretty. Then her BFF left me bruised up yesterday. But you heard right. Most of my clients have canceled and I put away my shingle for now. I imagine *you* think that's a good thing."

I paused, realizing how bitchy that sounded. "Sorry, this whole mess has just fucked up my life in so many ways. I have to change professions. No matter what happens now, Tricia's made certain I'll have a bad reputation for safety. Since most of my clients were Weres, there's no use in fighting back."

"What about Dani?"

"Tricia's got it in for my friends, too, according to Wynter. Is there anything we can do on a legal level to stop her?"

Jolene paused, then said, "A restraining order, but between you and me, those are about as good as a wet tissue. You have to understand, we Weres are an insular community and a lot like a hive mind. Oh, not literally, but when one branch of the tree takes a hit, we tend to rally around the wounded party."

My filters slipped again. "Are you defending her?"

"Not at all. This is ridiculous, and she doesn't have a legal leg to stand on. But…I'll ask around, see if I can figure out a way to help diffuse the situation. I'll call you later if I find anything out."

That didn't sound all to promising. I let out a long sigh. "Thanks. Anything you could do would be appreciated."

"Okay, well, I have to get back to work." She sounded reluctant to hang up. "Is there anything else you need to tell me?"

"Not right now, but I'll talk to you soon. And Jolene—thanks for hooking me up with Archer. He's been extremely helpful." And with that, I ended the call.

. . .

As I pulled into the parking garage beneath Archer's office, it occurred to me that I'd be coming here every day. I decided to insist on parking as part of my perks. The cost was astronomical, and I had no intention of using the Overpass Train to get work.

Archer was waiting for me as I entered the waiting room. He locked the door and then motioned for me to follow him into his office. As I took a seat, I wondered where I was supposed to do my work, given there were only two rooms.

He had anticipated the question though, and jerked his finger over his shoulder toward the side wall. "Next door, there's a second office suite for rent. I just called my landlord and agreed to take it as long as I can build a door pass-through between the two suites. We'll have you in an office of your own within a week. That particular suite includes a small bathroom, so we won't have to share the hall restrooms. Until then, you can just work out of my office." Archer seemed delighted with the prospect and my impression that he was lonely increased.

"Jolene called. The Souljacker struck again." I told him about Peter.

"That doesn't give us much to go on, although it makes me more determined to search the Underground. My friend will meet us tomorrow morning at ten. We'll have to be discreet so we don't put him in danger, but maybe we'll be able to find something. Jo-Jo knows the Underground like a bee knows how to find its hive."

I had brought my planner and now I jotted down *Jo-Jo* under the 10 A.M. slot for the next day. It felt good to see *someone's* name on my calendar, considering I had erased almost every appointment I had booked.

Archer pulled out a piece of paper. "I've accumulated a list of as many of his client names as I could come up with. At least we know it's not just members of your India Ink Club that he's after. So a lot of potential targets."

"Yeah, and I'm one of them." I didn't want to think about that, so I changed the subject. I tossed my planner on the desk and wandered around the room, stopping in front of the bookcase.

Archer was well-read, by the number of titles I recognized. "Tell me, what kind of cases do you work on?"

"Before I answer that, you need to fill out these forms. The moment you sign those, then I can tell you all of my confidential information."

Looking very pleased with himself, Archer shoved a clipboard across table with several pages on it. Even though most transactions were done electronically, there were still some cases that called for an actual signature—in ink. I flipped through the pages, skimming over the documents. Standard NDA, authorization for a background check, the usual. As I filled out my name, address, national identification number, and a few other choice pieces of information, I thought this had to be one of the strangest weeks of my life.

Archer sat a cup of coffee in front of me. "Cream? Sugar?"

"Lots of cream, a little sugar. Vanilla sugar, if you have it."

Once we settled the formalities, he leaned back in his chair.

"Okay, here's the deal. A number of my cases concern political intrigue. Some of them are dangerous and those, I will take care of for the time being. I won't put you in danger, at least not until you're brought up to speed. Which brings me to another matter. I know Wynter wants you to be her liaison. But anything that happens in this office remains confidential. You'll have to impress that on her, or this isn't going to work. If she balks, remind her that I can be a valuable asset to the Fae."

I could see his reasoning. "I have to make another trip out this week. For one thing, the leader of the Aespions is supposed to contact me about my training. While I'm there, I'll talk to Wynter about all of this. Somehow I doubt she'll object."

"Does it bother you that she doesn't approve of your former business?"

I shrugged. "I don't like being made to feel like I'm doing anything wrong. But I also understand that, in my culture, sex is thought of as a gift, not a commodity. It may be a pastime, or something to share. But it isn't for sale."

"How does marriage work? I gather the Fae are primarily polyamorous."

"Most marriages are matters of convenience and of—for lack of a better word—social networking. Economics, heritage, breeding—it all plays into the choice of a spouse."

"What about love?"

"Love…and lovers…are a totally different matter. The only thing that matters in a marriage is that you produce an heir and that you do not disgrace your spouse. And even that only matters among the nobles and those who have court status. Since I'm bound to the court, it will play into my life, if I ever decide to marry. But lovers? They are a choice of the heart. In a sense, marriage is the commodity rather than sex. So does it bother me that she was upset about my choice? On one level, yes. But on another level, I understand."

Archer glanced at the clock. "I'd better run. I have some documents to file with the court, and I have to meet with an informant on another case I'm working. Why don't you start using the spare laptop over there. You can start with the cases that directly impact you—Tricia and the Souljacker. Go ahead and look up any information you need. The password is written on the notepad beside the keyboard. Or you can go home and start your official work tomorrow, if you like."

If I left for the day, I could easily make it to my meeting with Tricia without arousing suspicion. "Can I do some of the research at home? Thanks to Nate I have a highly encrypted network. It's been a rough past few days and I didn't expect to feel so shaken from everything."

Archer frowned, squinting for a moment. Finally he gave me a noncommittal shrug. "I suppose that won't hurt. You still meeting me at Bender's shop tonight?"

"Yeah, I'm good with that."

"I'll swing by and pick you up. Text you later about the time." And, with a quick peck on my cheek—which surprised me—Archer hustled out the door.

As I headed back to my car, I looked around for Marsh, but he wasn't there. "Oh Marsh, where are you?"

As I unlocked my door and slid into the driver seat, he appeared in the passenger seat.

He laughed. "Miss me? And how's your head feeling?"

"Like it's full of cotton. And of course I missed you." And with that, I turned the ignition and eased my car out of the parking garage.

CHAPTER 24

Nate was waiting for me, grinning from ear to ear. "Get everything squared away with Archer?"

"Well, don't you look like the cat that caught the canary, and ate it, too." I dropped my purse on the table and slid out of my coat, stamping the snow off my boots. "Yeah, I signed all the forms and filled out all the information. Now he can tell me all about his cases without any problems. Did you find out anything yet? So you decided to work from my house after all?"

"It made sense when I thought about it, so I called in sick. With this hangover, there is no way I'm going in. Besides, I heard on the weather that we're due for a whiteout. The storm is packing in heavy, and it's going to get worse as the day goes on. You might want to consider rescheduling the meeting with Bender."

I shook my head. "No, we have to find out everything we can. Besides, it's not that far to White Tower Center."

"I've never been there," Nate said.

That didn't surprise me. Most humans didn't frequent the area—White Tower Center was in a dangerous area, even for those of us in the Supe Community. "I have to go there this afternoon on an errand. I'll scout out where his shop is so we can park close." I sat down, pulling off my boots and setting them by the back door. "Jolene called. The Souljacker struck again. I don't think you knew the victim. I didn't. His name was Peter Trent."

Nate frowned. "No, I don't recognize the name. Where did it happen?"

"Pioneer Square. And this time, he took several patches of the man's skin. Apparently he had given Peter a hell of a lot of tattoos.

There were witnesses, but you and I know that's not going to do any good. But one thing could help us: they saw the Souljacker come out of the Underground."

Nate pushed back his chair. "Tea?"

"Please."

He emptied what was left in the teapot and began a fresh one. "There are a lot of vampire clubs down there. Including Veek."

"That occurred to me too, but I doubt he's hiding there. He managed to ditch Greg, so he's not going to go running back to him. My guess is that Charles found out his father was probably planning to lock him up somewhere privately, where neither the cops nor Charles's mother could get to him. Being locked up wouldn't sit well with someone with delusions of regaining his mortality if he regains all his artwork."

"Yeah that occurred to me too. So you say you and Archer are going hunting through there tomorrow morning? Be careful. Not all those who are connected with the vampires sleep at night. And there are other dangers down there—just as deadly as the vamps." Nate was frowning. "I don't think I'd want to get caught in there, even in the daytime."

"Don't forget, I'm Fae. And Dark Fae, at that." I pointed toward Nate's computer. "So have you been able to find out any scuttlebutt about the Weres?"

"I'm still untangling the web of forums and lists they have. For an insular society, they're pretty damned chatty. I'm trying to sift through all the fluff to see what I can find. But you should be proud—and I say that sarcastically. You're trending on WereTalk."

I moaned. "Do I dare ask in what way?"

"Oh trust me, it's not flattering. Not at all. You're being demonized. Apparently you go around seducing everything with a cock, and then steal the money from them that was supposed to feed their poor starving families. Did you know you also have two vaginas?"

I blinked, stifling a laugh. "What?"

"Yeah, the rumor on one particularly nasty chat channel is

that you have two Vees…so you can have sex with three men at one time as long as they point their dicks right." He wasn't smiling anymore. "Lily, you need to be cautious. Someone plastered up a fake profile on one of the hookup sites that claims to be you, with your real address, stating that you want to be raped."

My amusement rapidly vanished. "You aren't kidding, are you?"

He shook his head. "I don't think Tricia posted that herself, but others following her lead and spreading dangerous rumors. I've been hacking into these sites and disabling everything I can find, but it's going to be awhile before I catch them all—if I can catch them all—and by then, they'll probably have reposted them. You have to do something about Tricia."

"I know." After a moment, I said, "Can you show me what you found?"

"No, Lily. Forget it. It's too ugly. I don't want you seeing what they had to say." He started to say more, then hesitated.

"Yes? What is it?"

"I sent the information to Archer, though. I figure he might have some contacts who can put a stop to this crap."

I wasn't sure whether to be angry or grateful. I hated being fussed over and treated like I couldn't handle my own business, but I had no desire to see the trumped-up posts that the Weres had been making about me. Feeling incredibly confused, I crossed to the refrigerator and pulled out bread and beef and mayo. I also managed find a tomato and some lettuce. My stomach had settled even more and now I was starving.

"You want a sandwich?"

"I could go for a nosh." Nate joined me by the sink, slicing the tomato as I spread the bread with mayo and mustard, and layered the beef on it. "Lily, these Weres…they mean business. I've seen Weres in grudgematches before and it's not pretty. You need to be careful." His voice was trembling, and I realize how afraid he really was.

"Boo!" Marsh suddenly appeared next to Nate.

Nate jumped. "Dude, do you have to do that? Can't you

announce your appearance before you show up? You could give a man a heart attack."

Marsh chuckled, then sobered. "I've been listening to what you've been saying about the vampires and the Weres. My first impulse is to say talk to the authorities, but the authorities are too afraid to do anything. Can't they just go out and eradicate the vampires? And arrest this woman who hit you?"

"As for Shayla, nobody's going to arrest her for smacking me. No witnesses and it's her word against mine. Oh wait, there *were* witnesses—at least at the food court. A few other Weres, who will side with her."

"As for the vampires," Nate picked up the thread, "the Deadfather has been investing heavily in a number of companies, providing a steady stream of revenue. This has probably been going on for years, but only recently out in the open. These corporations aren't going to want to lose their sugar daddy. They've been able to buy political seats because of this. Hence, the Deadfather controls some politicians. Vampires are slowly but surely making the laws."

"What do you make of the vampire rights bill? Surely it can't pass, not with all the worry over the increasing number of attacks." Marsh shook his head. "I don't understand people."

"Me neither. But the bill is bound to pass," Nate said. "Vamps have the right to legally marry now. It won't be long before every-thing else follows."

I nodded my agreement. "People don't want to see how dangerous they really are because as long as it's not their family member being killed, the money the vampires pump into the economy appears to be a good thing. You've got an entire sub-section of society who rallies for vampire rights because they are anti-oppression, but they don't realize that the vamps are looking at them as human juice bags. Then you have another subsection of society who's turned on by vamps and will do anything for them. The entire situation is a mess."

Nate rubbed his head. "I guess we can always leave and move

to Alaska. Vampires don't tend to congregate there. At least not for six months out of the year."

"All joking aside, Archer is right. We can't let ourselves be linked to destroying the Souljacker. We don't want a big fat target planted on our backs." I wasn't sure how we were going to manage that, but we had to find a way.

Marsh grinned. "In other words: walk softly and carry a big stake."

"That's about right." I cut the sandwiches in half and placed them on salad plates.

Nate rummaged through the refrigerator for a couple cans of soda. He handed me one and popped the tab on his own. He took a long drink, then set the can down as he leaned on the counter, staring out the window.

"It's really blowing out there. It's so beautiful." His voice trailed off as he watched the rising flurry outside.

I walked over to stand beside him in a comfortable silence. Nate leaned toward me, and we stood there, bare inches apart, watching the storm. Marsh was kneeling down by Mr. Whiskers, who rubbed his chin through Marsh's leg. The silence in the kitchen intensified, shrouding us in a muffled blanket. Outside, the snowfall picked up as huge white flakes piled up on the already significant snowpack.

"I think they're right—the weatherman. We're in for a real blow." Nate wiped his hands on a dishtowel. "Lily, please don't go out today. I have a really bad feeling…like you'll be caught in an accident or something." He was serious; I could see the concern in his eyes.

"I have to. This errand…I need to take care of something. I'll be careful. I promise."

"Nate's right. I don't think you should go either." Marsh looked up from where he had been wiggling his fingers in front of Whisky, who tried to catch them. It was better than a laser-dot toy, I thought.

I knew they meant well and I wasn't exactly sure what I could gain by talking to Tricia, but I had to try. Maybe she didn't know about the crass postings, that her anger had just fueled some of the more dubious members of their society. Inside, a voice whispered I was being stupid, but I knew that as long as Nate and Dani were in danger because of me, I had to do whatever I could to mitigate the situation.

"I don't like to sound obstinate, but I have to." I turned back to the table.

Nate shook his head. "If you won't budge, we can't stop you, but I still think it's a bad idea."

My phone rang at that moment, and I checked caller ID. I didn't recognize the name but the area code was from Wynter's land. The Fae court had its own area code. Granted, it was a small area, and the sovereign rights acceded it didn't include anything not in the favor of our current government, but it was step toward autonomy.

"Hello?"

"Vesper here. Wynter told you I'd be calling. I'm the director of the Aespions. I'm calling to set up your first training session. I will need to see you tomorrow afternoon at one o'clock. Be here, no excuses." Her voice was cold enough to freeze scalding water. I started to answer, but she hung up.

"Well, she's sure of herself." At Nate and Marsh's questioning glances, I told them what she had said.

"I think this will be good for you," Nate said. "I have a feeling that the Aespions are pretty freaking formidable. And, as much as I admire you, Lily, I have to say that you don't seem…um…all that in shape as far as defending yourself goes. Maybe you used to be a kick-ass traveler in the world, but I think you've kind of let your training go."

"I'm not sure if I should be insulted or not."

"Oh give it a rest. You never go to the gym and while you can eat like a horse and never gain an ounce, you aren't gaining muscle, either. Hey, do you think Archer will teach you how to shoot? He could get you licensed as a private investigator so that you can legally carry a gun."

I blinked. I had never touched a gun in my life and I really didn't feel comfortable doing so. Guns were illegal for the general populace to own, and so many had been melted down that they weren't easy for criminals to procure, either. But there were whispers about opening up gun licensing again, and the fury was loud and strong between the two opposing camps.

"Are you sure you would trust me carrying a gun?"

Nate shrugged. "Better you than Dani, to be honest. And with you working for Archer, it makes sense, for your own protection." He arched his eyebrows and grinned. "Somehow, I don't think you're a hothead who's going to go off her rocker and start shooting up the joint."

"We'll see. I'm not that comfortable with the idea, but perhaps if I trained with one I'd be more apt to agree. I'll ask Archer when I see him next." I paused as a knock sounded on the back door. "That's probably Dani."

As I opened the door, Dani rushed in, breathless and covered in snowflakes. "Have you heard the news?"

"What? What's going on?" She looked so worried that I hustled her over to the table and helped her take off her coat. "Tell us what happened."

"It's all over the airwaves. Turn on the news, quickly. I just heard it on the way over."

Nate quickly brought up a news site and turned up the sound on the streaming video. The announcer looked to be in shock as she read from the viewer in front of her.

"In what has to be one of the most startling pieces of news since the coming out of the Fae and Weres, President Darrington of the United States has revealed that he is instituting full vampire rights for the country, to be signed into law one week from today. Congress is convening now to discuss the ramifications of this executive order." As she went on to discuss the reactions coming in from all over the country and world, Nate muted the video.

I looked at the others. "Well, this is it. We're seeing the dawn of a new era, and it's going to be a bloody one. Vampires will have more rights than we do, given they're never arrested for their crimes now."

We fell silent—all of us. Once the order was signed—which it would be on midnight in one week, the newscaster said—staking a vampire would be considered murder, unless it was in self-defense. Which meant that in one week, the world would be a whole lot more dangerous.

CHAPTER 25

I glanced at the clock. "I need to…get my errands done. I'll be back in an hour or so. I promise, Nate, I'll drive safely." I jammed my feet in my boots and headed out the door before he could raise a fuss.

The drive to White Tower Center took about twenty minutes longer than usual, given the rapid buildup of snow on the ground and how slow I had to drive. The flakes were everywhere, driven by wind to the point that they were falling sideways. I wondered if Tricia was going to call off the meeting, but since I hadn't heard from her I figured she would be there.

I went over and over what I would say to her in my head. I would apologize, accept all responsibility as long as it wouldn't set me up for a lawsuit. I would beg her to blame me, not my friends, and stress how I had wronged her. I knew that there was no way in hell that would ever make it up to her, but right now she was the grieving widow and I was just the businesswoman who had lost a client. I'd play the part to the hilt to get Dani and Nate off the hot seat.

I eased into the parking lot, cautious because a sheet of ice had already built up on the asphalt. I pulled into a parking stall and turned off the ignition. I decided it was best to leave my purse in the car, so I took my keys and shoved them deep in the pocket of my jeans. I wasn't entirely stupid, so I armed myself with my dagger, slipping it into the thigh sheath before I headed over toward the underground entrance.

White Tower Center descended two floors belowground, and three above it. It was a thriving community center as well a shopping mall, though it saw its fair share of roughhousing and brawls. The elevators would take me to the front of the center, which meant a long walk around to reach the meeting spot, so I ducked into the hallway that led toward the stairwell going up. It would have been easier to meet in the parking garage itself, but then again, on a day as cold as this one, I understood her reasoning.

As I swung into the stairwell, I thought I heard a noise. Instantly alert, I stopped in my tracks, listening as carefully as I could.

There it was again—the sound of the door opening and closing somewhere in the stairwell above me. I waited. *One beat… two beats…three beats…*And the sound faded to silence. No doubt shoppers coming and going between the levels, but I still kept my attention focused around me as I resumed my ascent. No use in letting my mind wander when there were so many things that could go wrong. So many things were already going wrong.

Remember, a voice in my mind whispered, *it's almost sunset. Watch for vampires.*

I tried to shake the thought from my mind. I was wearing my silver pentacle, and that should protect me, but it wouldn't protect me against a gun or knife or sword or any other number of weapons. Vampires didn't just rely on their fangs anymore. They weren't that stupid.

Thoroughly spooked, I swung around the corner of the spiraling staircase and found myself facing a door. The word JANITOR was stenciled across the top of it. I was about to go past it when a hollow sound stopped me and I quickly turned, my foot still on the next stair.

The door slammed open and I found myself facing three large men, burly, with snarling faces. Instantly, their scent told me they were Weres. Probably weretigers. I jumped back, almost tripping as my heel caught on the stair runner.

"Who are you? What do you want?" I asked, praying they were run-of-the-mill muggers. I tried to keep my back to the stairwell wall as I inched toward the stairs leading down. They were closer to me than the ones going up, and offered the best chance of escape.

"Tricia sent us. Consider us her welcome wagon." But he sounded anything but welcoming.

A setup, and I had fallen for it.

"Doesn't Tricia have any honor?" I knew honor was a big thing among the Weres, so it seemed worth a shot at stalling them.

"Shut up, you whore."

Nate had been right, even though he hadn't known about what. I should have listened to him, but in my fervor to protect my friends, I'd let carelessness take the helm.

If I tried to talk my way out of this, I had a feeling my words would fall on deaf ears. Pressing my lips together, I eased my hand down to my thigh and smoothly withdrew the dagger, holding it in front of me. I had had many occasions in my life to defend myself, and while it'd been a long time and I was out of shape, muscle memory kicked in. I wasn't going to be doing any backflips, but if I was cautious I might have a chance at getting out of this unhurt.

"Look, she's got a toothpick!"

One of the Weres snickered.

"Do you really think that little pointy blade is going to do much damage to the three of us?" The tallest of the trio also seem to be the cockiest. Which meant that he was vulnerable. Too much ego always threw off your game.

I glanced at the other two. One was cheering on his brother, but the other kept his gaze on my every move. He was the one who was most dangerous, and by the glint in his eye I could tell he would have no compunction about flattening me out.

"So is Tricia paying you to kill me?" I might as well face them directly, although I didn't expect any answer.

"Oh, not necessarily to *kill* you. Just to convince you that it might behoove you to leave town for good. Pack up your shingle, sell your house, and move." Tall Boy snickered.

"What if I told you that I already shut down my business? Tricia won. She's already scared off most my clients and there isn't much I can do given the circumstances. In fact, I came here to apologize to her today and tell her how sorry I am. Does that make any difference?" I had my doubts, but it was worth a try.

The one who was keeping his eye on me shifted just enough to tell me they hadn't expected to hear that. But he looked no less dangerous, and I could tell he was tracking me by the way his nose quivered as he kept testing the wind. "And why would we believe you?"

I had managed to reach the edge of the first step leading down. I paused, gearing myself up to make a leap that would probably land me in a world of pain, but might just get me away from them without bloodshed.

"So you've already decided to hurt me even though I'm agreeing to her terms?"

"We have to have our fun," Tall Boy said. "And we hear you like it rough."

That was all I needed to hear. I decided to make a leap for it. I swung around, jettisoning myself off the top stair and out as far as I could go so that I wouldn't hit the steps when I landed. Flailing wildly with my arms, I did my best to soften the landing, bending my knees and tucking in. Muscle memory might work in a lot of cases, but this time it seemed to have a few holes in it. I landed on the balls of my feet all right, but before I could balance myself and stand, I fell forward and faceplanted on the concrete floor. Behind me, I could hear the weretigers scrambling for the staircase. I had just enough time to get my feet before they were halfway down and I ran for the door as quickly as I could, my feet slipping on the wet concrete in my haste.

I managed to slam open the door as I raced into the parking lot, but they were hot on my heels. The snowfall was so thick it was hard to see beyond the reach of my hand. The ice below the accumulation was especially slick.

As I made a beeline for my car, my feet went out from under me and I slid across the asphalt. Of course, the asphalt was covered with ice which, unluckily for me, broke my fall. And also felt like it broke my butt. I could hear the weretigers cursing behind me, and I guessed they were dealing with their own little slip-and-slide game.

I managed to right myself again and began to stagger toward my car. One knee was so bruised I could barely walk. Wincing from the pain, I tried to dig the keys out of my pocket as I lurched across the ice. But before I could make it, the weretigers had surrounded me. The parking lot was empty except for the four of us, and there was no help in sight. This was going to get nasty, and it was going to get nasty really quick.

I caught my breath, holding my dagger out. I was lucky I hadn't cut myself with it yet. But I couldn't keep an eye on all of them at once as they circled around me. My breath coming hard, I was frantically trying to think of anything I could to get out of the situation.

Tall Boy picked that moment to laugh. His high-pitched giggle made him sound like a prepubescent boy and my senses were primed enough to know that he was aroused.

"If you hurt me, my people will take revenge. The Fae are as tightly bound as the Weres. And I'm part of Wynter's court." Reduced to threats—and they weren't idle threats, even though they were doing me no good at the moment—I did what I could to stall.

At that moment, the sound of car entering the parking lot at high speed alerted all of us. Archer's BMW slid across the ice. It had barely come to a stop when Archer jumped out of the driver's seat, and Nate out of the passenger seat.

Startled, the weretigers turned. Archer pulled out a Tasmat, an extremely powerful stun gun that was more than effective on Weres. Most stun guns were powerful enough to take down a charging werewolf or weretiger, but Tasmats? They could take down an elephant. They were also notoriously illegal.

The moment they saw the stun gun, the Weres began backing off. I limped over to Nate's side, and he pushed me behind him. Grateful beyond measure, I forced myself to remain dry eyed. The last thing I needed to do was burst into tears. I had no desire for the Weres to report back that I was weak, even though that was precisely what I had let myself become.

"I'm giving you to the count three to get out of here. If you ever come near Lily again, if you ever lay a hand on her, if any of your friends ever lay a hand on her, I will hunt you down, take this Tasmat, shove it up your ass, and pull the trigger." Archer's voice was deadly calm, and his eyes glittered with an icy chill that I hadn't seen before. I realized right then that, as pleasant and fun as he could be, I wouldn't ever want to be on his bad side. A good reminder that beneath that handsome veneer, he was still a demon.

Nate escorted me to my car, forcing me to sit down so he could take a look at my knee, but it was too difficult considering my jeans didn't roll up that far, and I wasn't about to take them off in this weather.

"Can you drive?"

I started to say yes, but then realized that by the time I got the car home, I would probably be in massive pain, if I was lucky to make it at all. "No, I don't think I can right now."

By this point, the weretigers were screeching out of the parking lot, their low rider fishtailing on the ice. Archer watched them go, then hurried over to where Nate and I were.

"Are you all right? Did they touch you?"

I shook my head. "How did you know what was happening?" But even as I asked question, I knew. "Marsh. He was watching me, wasn't he. He let you know I was in trouble."

"You have a lot to thank that ghost for. Those thugs meant business. I doubt you would have left here in one piece. Tricia set you up, and you fell for it." Archer's voice was stern, and the harshness in it made me wince.

"No, I set myself up. I screwed up; I admit it. I just wanted to protect Nate and Dani from her. I should have known Marsh would have been watching me as I texted her about the meeting."

"Thank your lucky stars he was doing his job." Archer didn't let up. He continued. "You have to develop your instincts again, Lily. I know you have them—you couldn't have survived to the current century without them. Not the way you lived. And if you're going to work for me, we're going to have to get you in shape. Not just physically but mentally. I hate to say it, but I'm going to become the drill sergeant you love to hate. And…you have to stop trusting people so much."

"I know." I was hurting in more ways than one. My pride and ego had taken a huge hit with this blunder. "I realize that now. I have a feeling that my training with the Aespions will help. I'm supposed to start tomorrow. I guess Nate's right. I should learn to use a gun and a Tasmat. Now, can we go home so I can put some ice on this knee?"

"Let's get a move on. The snow is supposed to become a blizzard within a couple hours, and we don't want be out driving in it. Nate, can you drive Lily's car?"

"I've driven it before. You don't think the weretigers will be waiting to follow us, do you? I really don't want to tangle with them."

"Don't worry. They won't be coming after us for a while. But I don't think we're done with them yet." Archer lifted me, carrying me around to the passenger seat, where I stretched out my leg as far as I could.

With Nate at the wheel, we began easing out the parking lot. The drive home was harrowing. Several times we almost slid off the road, but luckily the streets were almost empty. Up ahead, Archer wasn't faring much better. But we finally made it, intact, and eased into the driveway.

So much for making peace with Tricia and the weretigers. I decided that I would have to go on the offensive, though I had no clue what to do. As for Tygur's death, I was just going to have to learn how to live with the fact that he had died in my home.

CHAPTER 26

The first thing I noticed when I got home was that the energy of the yard felt different. Oh, the wards felt steady, but something was off. I glanced around, trying to figure out what was different, but with the flurry of flakes and the throbbing of my knee, I couldn't pinpoint what felt askew.

Archer wrapped his arm around my waist as I draped my arm over his shoulder. He swept me up into his arms.

"My prince." I laughed, but that immediately turned to a grimace as my knee let out a bolt of I'm-not-happy pain. "Seriously, thank you. Without you and Nate…" I didn't want to think about where I might be without them.

"Shush. But you should thank Marsh. He's the one who did his job, who kept an eye on you. I wish to hell I had known what you were up to. I would never have let you go there alone." Archer sounded irritated.

"Are you mad at me?"

He blew out a long stream of breath. "No, not really. I'm just…damn it, I was worried as hell when Marsh popped into my office. *Our* office. He told me get my ass in gear and pick up Nate on the way. You're lucky traffic was so light, or we wouldn't have gotten there in time."

On the way toward the house, once again, the shift in energy hit me. I tapped him on the shoulder. "Stop, would you? Just hold still."

"What's wrong?"

"I'm not certain, but something feels off, and it's making me uneasy." Another moment and I still couldn't figure out what it was. "Oh well, I guess it's nothing."

Archer headed up the steps, cautiously making certain I didn't bump my knee on the railings. Nate had gone ahead to open the door.

I held my breath as we entered the kitchen, afraid of what we might find, but the kitchen was empty, and everything looked to be in place. Archer slid me into a chair and then quickly did a check of the house. Once he ascertained the bottom floor was clear, he headed upstairs. He had been gone only a moment when a woman's scream echoed down the steps.

I tried to jump up, but my knee hurt so badly that I jolted back to the chair. "Nate!"

"I'm on it." Nate rushed toward the staircase, but at that moment, Archer darted down them, a broad smile on his face.

"I accidentally opened the door on Dani as she was showering. She threw a bottle of bath gel at me."

"Damn you. You scared the hell out of me." I tried to catch my breath. "I'm so nerve racked I'll be jumping at shadows next thing you know."

Nate motioned to my leg. "Strip. We need to look at that knee."

"Hey—" I started to say, but he cut me off.

"Don't play coy. I've seen you in your underwear. You don't care who you dress in front of."

I gazed up at Nate's face. He was laughing. "What makes you think I'm wearing underwear? Go get me a pair of panties and a skirt from my room, please."

Stifling a smirk, Nate headed toward the stairs.

"Thank you, we'll be over in an hour. Please don't leave till we get there. It's important." Archer slid his phone back into his pocket. "Ray Bender is leaving early because of the storm. I told him we'd be there in less than an hour. So we need to get you fixed up. Either that, or Nate and I can go and leave you and Dani here."

"Nobody's going anywhere without me."

"All right. I put on some water for tea. It should be ready by the time Nate gets back. I'll be back as soon as I can. I'm going out to put chains on my car. We're not taking your gas hog—it may have the weight to hug the road, but there's no way in hell those tires are going to work. You need to change them, anyway. They're almost bald. I have my phone with me." Archer headed back out the kitchen door.

Just as I was about ready to attempt a trip over to the stove to remove the whistling kettle from the heat, Nate clattered back into the kitchen. He set the skirt and panties on the table next to me and headed over toward the range.

"I assume we're having tea? Dani said she'll be down in a few minutes."

"I think that was Archer's plan." I unzipped my jeans and, using the table for leverage, stood, bearing all my weight on my uninjured leg. My other knee gave a pop, sending another wave of pain through my leg. I let out a short cry, and dropped back into my seat.

"You're going to let me help you, and I don't want any arguments." Nate moved around to kneel in front of me, keeping his gaze clearly focused on my face and not lower down. "I'm going to have to look at that leg when I take off your pants. Just think of me as a doctor."

"I don't know why I feel so shy all of a sudden. You know that's not me." I wasn't embarrassed by my body in the least, but right now the last thing I wanted to do was to give Nate a crotch shot.

"Maybe it's because you're giving up your business? Or maybe it's just all the stress. Whatever the case, I wouldn't worry about it if I were you. Now, I'm going to ease your jeans over your knees. This is probably going to hurt, but I'll be as gentle as possible. I have to take off your boots first, though." Nate gently removed my boots, setting them to the side. As he was easing my jeans down my legs, a sudden glimmer caught my eye. I looked over to see Marsh appear by the sink.

"Where have you been? And thank you so much for letting them know I was in trouble. You saved my life, Marsh."

Marsh raised his eyebrows as he took in the scene. "Well, this is cozy. I've been out and about. I decided to follow the weretigers when they left the parking lot. Sure enough, they met up with Tricia Jones. They were having quite a *tête-à-tête*. She sure was pissed, I'll tell you that. They told her about Archer, that you are hanging out with a chaos demon. That went over like a lead balloon and after she nailed one across the face with her claws when he laughed, she stomped away, mad as a hornet. You know she'll be out for revenge now, so you—all of you—should keep on your guard."

By then, Nate had managed to get my jeans off. My knee was a throbbing purple mass of bruises, swollen double its usual size.

Nate let out a whistle. "You really bunged this up. Here, let's get your underwear and skirt on and then I will take care of this."

He had brought a pair of panties that had plenty of stretch in them, so it was easy to slide them up my legs without scraping my knee. Standing up to get them up over my butt wasn't quite as comfortable, and once again my knee twinged sharply. I winced, moaning as I leaned on the table hard, but at least I didn't feel so exposed now.

"Here, let's get this on you while you're still on your feet." Nate unzipped the skirt and gently slid it over my head as I raised my arms, one at a time so I could keep my balance. Then he positioned it at my waist and zipped it up. Relieved, and exhausted from the pain, I sank back into the chair.

"Teatime now." Nate took a moment to pour our tea, then pulled out the bread and popped a couple pieces into the toaster. While it was toasting, he found an ice pack in the freezer, and wrapped it in a towel.

"This is going to hurt, and there's nothing I can do to help that, but it will be good for your knee. Once you've got it flush against your knee, tell me what medicines you can have and I'll get them from your medicine cabinet."

I took the ice pack and gingerly placed it against the bruises. If I had thought the pain was bad before, the sensation of ice hitting my knee made me want to scream. I doubled over, wanting nothing more than to throw the ice pack across the room and then throw up from the pain.

"Breathe. Breathe deep, honey." Marsh was kneeling beside me. He reached up to pat me on the shoulder, but his hand went right through me and a look of consternation crossed his face.

"It's all right. Thank you for trying to help. It's my own fault; I got myself in the situation and I take full responsibility. I should have known better. I can't believe I was so stupid."

"Stop feeling sorry for yourself. We've all done stupid things," Archer's voice sounded from behind me. He had come into the kitchen door behind us. "I got the chains on. The snow is coming down so fast and thick that it's wiped out any sign of our tracks from when we arrived. I think we'll be okay heading over to White Tower Center, but after that we'd better hole up and stay home for the rest of the night."

The toast popped up and Nate moved to butter it. He slid the plate in front of me, along with the honey jar.

"You need to eat something. You've had a rough afternoon and your body is in shock. So start with that, and I'll see what's in the refrigerator."

I stared at the toast. "I'm not that hungry. I had that sandwich this afternoon."

"Just do as he says." Archer gave me a stern look. "I'm ordering you to eat—as your boss. Dig in. Now."

"Okay, okay." I bit into the toast, and the buttery rich flavor of the honey and bread hit my taste buds like a loaded gun. I moaned. "Maybe I am hungry."

Just then, Dani joined us, dressed, with fresh makeup and clothes. "That feels better. The news about the vampire rights bill made me feel slimy all over."

Archer glanced over at her. "What do you mean? What news?"

"You haven't heard? In one week, the president will be signing the vampire rights bill into law. Strike up another victory for the blood-sucker crew and the Deadfather." Her voice was icy, and she looked so angry that I was very grateful to be on her good side.

I was about to say something when she noticed my knee. "Good gods, what happened to you?"

"I screwed up. Thanks to Marsh, I'm alive. Well, Marsh, Nate, and Archer. But without them, I'd be in world of hurt right now." I briefly told her what I'd done and, when I had finished, she reached out and flicked me hard on the forehead.

"You idiot. Just…next time I'm going to smack you across the head, woman. What the hell were you thinking? Didn't you get it when I refused to let you pay for my shop repairs? We're all in this together, Lily. You, me, Nate, now Archer. Even Marsh. You're not fighting this battle alone. We won't let you. Remember: the Souljacker is after us as much as he's after you. And now we're going to head over to Nate's to make sure nobody has messed with his wards. After what happened at my shop yesterday, I thought it might be best. You'll be okay with Marsh for now, won't you? We'll be back soon."

"Of course. Go—it's a good idea." As they headed out the door, I glanced up at Marsh. "It's going to be a long night."

Marsh nodded. "I think I'm going to ask Mr. Whiskers if there's anything he can do. I may not be able to understand him, but he seems to be able to understand me." He hesitated by my chair for a moment, giving me a wan smile. "We'll find Charles, Lily. We'll find him before he finds any of you. Don't worry, please."

I wanted to believe him. I wanted to believe him more than anything. But it was getting hard to be optimistic. "Do you really believe that? Or are you just trying to make me feel better?"

Marsh shook his head as he headed over toward the stairwell. "Mr. Whiskers is upstairs. I'm going up to talk to him. You call me if you need me." He paused, and looked over his shoulder. "Lily, I don't know what I believe anymore. But we have to believe that things will work out. Otherwise what's the point of trying?"

As he vanished up the stairs, I leaned back in the chair and adjusted the ice pack. He made a good point. I just wished we had more than fumes to go on.

CHAPTER 27

While I was waiting, I put in a call to Vesper. She came on the line almost immediately.

"Vesper here. What can I do for you?"

"This is Lily O'Connell. I got myself banged up a little today. In fact, my knee looks like a giant blueberry. Should I still come out tomorrow afternoon? If I do, I'm going to have to have someone drive me out and they will need someplace to stay besides in my car." I found myself hoping she would tell me to wait and come out when I was healed up, but no such luck.

"You'll be here at 1 P.M. Bring whoever you need to; they can sit in the common room. If you can't walk, I'll have a cart waiting for you. There's plenty you can learn that doesn't require you to be jumping around. There's more to being an Aespion than just fighting. You've got a lot of book learning and class time to put in. And we have to get you signed up on the payroll. You get paid for your training as well, so if you don't show up, your pay will be docked." Her voice was gruff, but I detected the hint of a smile behind it. I had a feeling she was the type of leader who would enjoy breaking people in.

"I guess I'll see you then. And I will need that cart." I was determined to make sure she saw my bruises, so she wouldn't think I was slacking. I suddenly realized I already wanted to impress the woman. Which probably meant she was a good leader—inspiring your underlings was a skill and an art, not a given.

As I hung up, Nate, Dani, and Archer re-entered the room, the snow swirling in behind them. They were covered in thick flakes, and the chill and wind that burst through the door behind them was enough to make me shiver.

"How were the wards?"

"Good. Though it looks like somebody beat the crap out of Nate's mailbox, but that could have just been some driver who slid off the road in the storm tonight." Dani glanced at the window. "It's blowing pretty bad. Are you sure you want to chance going to White Tower Center?"

"We have to. We need to talk to Ray Bender."

"It's supposed to die down around three in the morning. Until then, the city is ordering all vehicles to stay off the road. So let's hope we don't meet any cops along the way." Nate began unloading a bag of groceries.

"We're not exactly the Donner party, Nate. I do have food here, you know."

He winked at me. "Yes, and we've eaten so much of it that I decided to raid my cupboards to replace some of what we've used up. Cookies, so stop bellyaching about it."

Archer poked around in the refrigerator. "You don't keep much real food here, do you? Mostly I see leftover takeout boxes that look a couple weeks too old."

I shrugged. "Hey, I cook. I bake cookies and cakes, and I make sandwiches. That's about the extent of my repertoire."

"Don't let her fool you," Nate said. "Lily is a damned good cook, she just doesn't like to do it."

"I see. So she pretends she doesn't know how in order to get someone else to cook for her. How often does that work out?" Archer was laughing, his hand on the cupboard doors as he peered inside.

"More often than not. Or it nets her dinner out." Nate began stowing the groceries away.

"What do you do for a living again?" Archer glanced at Nate. "I remember computer something…How good are you with those machines?"

"Good enough to be one of the highest-paid developers at

Modal Technologies. They were in a bidding war with two other software tech companies over me. I'd never told anybody this, not even Lily, but I have quite a reputation in hacking circles. MT hired me to break their systems as much as I could so they could tighten security. I'm the reason their software is trusted nation-wide." There was a flash of pride in his voice that I had never heard before, and it made me happy.

Archer cleared his throat. "I don't suppose that you're looking for a new job?"

"I'm not certain that you could pay me what I'm worth. I like my job, but I am available to freelance on the side as long as it doesn't conflict with what I do for MT."

I lifted the ice pack to examine my knee. It still looked like shit, but the throbbing had lessened some. I leaned over for a closer look, and winced. A knot had formed on the inside of my knee, and it looked like somebody had taken a sledgehammer to my leg. I poked at it, swearing loudly as my finger triggered a ripple of pain.

"Stop playing with it," Dani said. "The more you play with it, the more it's going to hurt. I wonder if you broke anything in there. You can't walk on it."

"I better not have broken it. Shattered knees take forever to heal, even for the Fae. I really should see a doctor about this." I let out a long sigh, not wanting to resort to drugs but realizing it was going to be a while before anybody could take a look at my injury. "Nate, I forgot to tell you. If you'll run up to my bathroom, you'll find a bottle of pills labeled Arnricat. If you would get them for me, I'd sure appreciate it. That's the strongest pain reliever I have in the house that I can take. And lucky for me, I can take it with a good glass of wine."

As Nate headed upstairs, I glanced over at Archer, who was stirring together the stovetop casserole. My stomach rumbled as the smell wafted past me.

"I had a rather disturbing thought a moment ago. What if the Souljacker and Ray traded tattoos? It's not uncommon for artists to ink each other. That would mean Ray's in danger. We'd better warn him when we head over there."

"Good thought. There are a lot of people who are in danger thanks to Terrance Schafer. If he'd let his son be properly taken care of, this wouldn't have happened. Of course, the situation was horrible, but a vampire isn't the person they were in life."

"I wish I could have staked Greg," Dani said in a soft voice. "I could live with the memory of that a lot easier than what I live with now."

Nate returned with my Arnricat tablets and brought me a glass of wine. I downed three of them, as well as the entire glass. They were an anti-inflammatory, used by the Fae like humans used aspirin and ibuprofen. "You really should eat more than toast."

"He's right." Archer knelt by my side. "Anytime you sustain an injury, your body uses extra energy to cope with it. I have no doubt you've used up your reserves. How are you doing on chi?" His frank question startled me.

I was about to answer that I was fine, but I stopped and assessed myself. I closed my eyes and listened for the hunger. It was there, hidden beneath the pain. "I think that I need to feed soon. It would help my injury as well. Chi helps us heal. It won't fix me up totally, but it would lessen the pain and probably reduce the swelling." I glanced over at Archer.

He caught my look and nodded. "Nate, do you mind making me some coffee? I'm going to need the caffeine." He glanced over at Nate. "So how did you and Lily meet?"

Moving to the cupboard for the coffee, Nate answered, "When I moved in, I saw Lily's sign. I decided to come over and say hello, given that I had no clue what she was doing here."

It was true—my signboard simply read LILY BOUND — A PRIVATE SALON.

"I invited Nate in for tea, and we got to talking. He seemed cool with what I was doing, and when I realized he was a computer tech, I thought it might be neighborly to hire him to set up my website. I had one, but it was pretty rudimentary. Nate showed me samples of his work and it was brilliant. He also set up my financial spreadsheets and helped me create ads to bring in business. We started having dinner once a week, and it didn't take long before he became one of my best friends." I glanced over at him fondly. "He worms his way into your heart pretty quickly."

Nate blushed, but finished making Archer's coffee.

"Do you have a girlfriend? Boyfriend?" Archer asked him.

That brought Nate's attention around. He glanced at me, then at Archer. "I don't talk about it much, but no. I haven't found anyone I really click with yet. Most women are attracted by my money, but when they find out that I'm…let's face it, I'm a geek who's married to his job. That turns most women off really quickly. I've had a couple of girlfriends, but it was a game to them. After a while they wanted someone who would fawn over them and go to parties, and I'm just not like that."

His voice was so sad that once again I vowed to find him the right match. I was hoping that Archer wouldn't make fun of him, and I wasn't disappointed.

"That's rough. It's not easy to find someone to love, no matter who you are. Are you open to nonhumans? I know a wide variety of people, and I might know a couple women you might hit it off with."

Nate blinked. "I've never really thought about it, but yeah—if you think we might hit it off, I'm willing to date outside my species."

"Will a kiss be enough?" Archer carried my plate to the sink as I popped a mint in my mouth. I needed to make the kiss as hot as I could. Sex was out of the question until my knee stopped hurting so much.

I grinned at him. "Oh, don't worry about me. A kiss will do fine. Come here, please."

He dragged his chair over beside me, so that he was well away from my knee. "How do we do this?" he started to say, but I leaned in and pressed my lips to his.

Drinking chi was like drinking wine—you could chug it down if it was cheap, but good wine? You wanted to savor.

I slowly drew his life force into me, like a thin wisp of mist flowing from his lips into mine. As I swallowed the heady taste of his energy, it filled my lungs and rolled through my body like a warm fog, filling all the empty spaces where the hunger rested, uncoiling like a snake rising up.

The energy soaked through my muscles and raced through my blood like a drug. Archer was strong and his energy carried that strength. As it reached my knee, the throbbing began to subside. My shoulders sagging with relief, I drew him closer, my arms around him in a fearsome embrace. Another moment, and the swelling begin to reduce, the inflammation fading to a manageable level. His joy and sorrow, his desire—it all flowed through me in the taste of his breath, and I reveled in it, soaking it in till it hit my very core.

Another moment, and I slowly released him and leaned back in my chair. Although I was satiated I could have continued, draining him until the last drop filled my body. Archer reeled back, pale but looking ridiculously happy. I could make it good or I could make it painful, and for him I had made it feel as good as I could. Because he was a demon, he would recharge quickly.

"That caffeine isn't going to be enough. You should probably eat something with sugar in it. Are you all right? I didn't take too much, did I?"

He shook his head. "No, I'll be fine. I'll have a cookie. How are you feeling?"

I stretched out my knee. It was still purple, and the knot was still there, but it looked far better than it had, and I was able to bend it without wanting to scream. I gingerly pushed myself to my feet and tested my weight on my leg. Not bad.

"I can't run yet, but I can walk. The swelling's gone down."

Archer grabbed a bag of cookies. "We need to roll if we're going to talk to Ray. Do you think you can make it?"

I nodded, testing my leg again. "It's sore, but if I don't have to run, I should be okay. I won't be able to wear my jeans. Dani, can you run up and grab me a pair of yoga pants? They'll at least keep me warm, and I can slide them on under the skirt." I was going to be oh so fashionable, but at least I wouldn't freeze.

She headed toward the stairs. "If I fit into your clothes I'd grab a pair for myself, but I'm far too short and curvy." She was wearing a long skirt that swept the ground, but it was gauzy, not exactly the warmest material in the world.

Archer was shoveling down the cookies, but he didn't look much worse for the wear, and I breathed a sigh of relief that my feeding off him hadn't left him too weak. Dani returned with both the pants and an elastic bandage. "Here, wrap this around your knee first. The compression will do it good."

"Good idea." I wrapped my knee, making certain the bandage wasn't too tight, and then cautiously slid on the pants, easing them up, under my skirt. "Dani, you stay here—"

"Oh, hell no. I'm not going to sit here worrying while you guys are out there. I'm coming with you." She jammed her arms into her jacket. "Deal with it."

"All right, all right." I glanced at Archer. "Okay with you?"

"There's room. But let's get on the road before we're stuck going nowhere. This storm's going to pack a punch before the night's over." He grabbed his keys and, with Nate and Dani flanking me, we eased down the now-covered kitchen steps and over to his car. "I'm glad I got the chains on," he added as we huddled in the BMW, waiting for the heat to come on.

Then we cautiously eased out on the road and headed to White Tower Center, hoping to find some clue as to what the Souljacker might be planning next.

CHAPTER 28

White Tower Center might as well have been a ghost town. It took double the usual time to make it there, given the storm and the slickness of the roads, and by the time we pulled into the parking garage, we were significantly late, but we had our choice of spots. We had called Bender twice, but our calls wouldn't go through either time and I didn't want to just not show up in case he was still waiting for us.

It was only a few minutes to seven, but the shopping center was nearly deserted by the time we got there, although there was one car in particular that I thought I recognized, but I ignored it as Archer pulled into a spot near the entrance closest to Ray's shop. Thankfully, it was a well-lit area.

"We're taking the elevator, with your knee."

I didn't like elevators, given how easy it was to be trapped in them, and I'd had that happen more than once, but he wouldn't take no for an answer, so we crowded in and I held my breath as the car began its shaky ascent. But it made it, and as the doors opened with a shudder, we spilled out onto the main floor.

We turned left and headed toward the center of the shopping mall. I hadn't been around this part of White Tower Center for some time. Most of the shops had closed up, though a few were still open and a handful of straggling shoppers still wandered through the mall, but I paid no attention to them, focused on finding the tattoo parlor.

"Ray's shop is supposed to be about seven stores down, on the right-hand side." Archer led the way, with Nate and Dani behind me. Marsh was next to me—he told me so even though he was keeping out of sight.

My knee wasn't particularly happy, but the more I walked, the easier it got. I had the feeling it was going to be stiff by morning, though, even with the infusion of chi that I had gotten from Archer. I still planned on milking the injury for all it was worth out at Wynter's court.

Nate craned his neck as we went. "This looks just about like any shopping mall." He sounded disappointed.

"You expected what? Harry Potter's Diagon Alley?" I stifled a snort at his glare.

"No, but...I guess...I expected something more dramatic or exotic. You know, specialty stores for Weres or Fae or...just something. Hell, there's a Car Jar—you can find them everywhere." He pointed toward the auto-accessory shop.

"Fae and Weres need to drive, too." I relented after a moment. "I promise, we'll all come back together later on and take you to see the places you're expecting. Though maybe we'll focus on Fae-oriented shops, given the current state of my relationship with the Weres. There are plenty of shops here like you were expecting, but they're interspersed with the ones for everyday life."

He flashed me a smile. "Thanks, Lily."

"I still can't believe you've never been here."

"You know...it's not a welcoming area to humans, and we stand out in a crowd."

He was right. Humans didn't give off the same vibe as Supes—it was an energy thing, and even those who were headblind knew it. So, when I thought about it, I really wasn't all that surprised. Nate was shy, and while he was built and in shape, he wasn't a fighter. All that compounded by being around people who made you feel like you were the one who stood out? It had to be difficult.

Archer pointed to the right. "There, Bender's shop."

As we swung in, I thought I heard something behind us, but when I turned, I only saw the back of a couple men, laden down with bags and packages, who must have come out of the shop next to the tattoo parlor.

Well lit compared to some of the holes in the road I had seen,

Ray's shop was spacious. He was a well-known artist in his own right. There would never be another Souljacker, or at least, if there was, they hadn't come forward, but Ray was a talented artist with a lot of satisfied customers.

Ray was nowhere in sight, but we heard the buzz of the tattoo gun as we entered the shop. I motioned toward the banquette to one side of the shop. As we sat down to wait, I breathed a sigh of relief for the break from walking. So far, so good, but I still hurt like hell.

The walls were covered with flash, as well as beautiful, macabre paintings of roses and elaborate sea creatures, and sugar-art skulls. Dani wandered over to one, glancing at the signature. She turned. "Bender's work," she said. "He's really incredibly talented."

"That he is." Archer glanced at me. "How are you holding up?"

"I'm all right. My knee aches, but the chi helped a lot. If you're up to it later, I wouldn't mind a top off." I grinned at him.

He reached out, and for a moment I thought he wanted me to hand him a magazine, but instead he took my hand and wrapped his fingers around mine and squeezed. "I'll always be happy to give you a top off."

I bit my lip, wondering just where we were going with this.

"What the hell?" Nate was staring at his phone in disbelief. He didn't sound happy.

"What? What happened?" I leaned around Archer, worried.

"I just got texted from a friend at work. They're going to fire me. He heard my boss talking about it. They say that program I wrote? The one I told you about that will automate services? They say it was done last year in China and that if we proceed, it will be a patent infringement. I swear, I didn't know! But Modal Technologies thinks I tried to steal the idea." Stricken, Nate just stared at his phone, his jaw hanging open.

"That's ridiculous. You aren't a thief."

"I know that, and you know that, but Modal Technologies apparently thinks so. This is so bizarre—how could this happen?"

Archer let out a soft grunt and let go of my hand. He rubbed his forehead, looking pained. "I think I know, and if I'm right, well…it's my fault."

"Your fault? How so? I only just told Lily about it two days ago."

I was equally as confused. "How on earth could this be your fault?"

Archer gave us a sheepish look. "Do you forget what I am? I'm a chaos demon. When I get involved in peoples' lives, chaos follows. I don't instigate it deliberately, but it happens. Not all the time, and never in the way I expect it to. I'm afraid that this off chance of them discovering a similar program isn't random—it goes against the odds, but that's what happens around me. Things that are a one in a million chance? Take cover, because sure enough, I'm a chaos magnet for beating the odds, in both good and bad ways."

Nate paled. "Crap. Then that means they're right—there is another program out there that's like mine? I didn't discover something brand new, but just…"

"The hundredth monkey theory," Archer finished for him.

Marsh's voice echoed from the other side of where I was sitting. "What's that?"

Startled—I had forgotten he was there—I said, "It's a theory that was proposed about the simultaneous eruption of a single idea among multiple groups. Basically, meaning that Nate and this person in China had the same idea at the same time, with no communication between them. And it probably means there are others who think they've discovered the same thing too."

Nate let out a long sigh. "I wonder if I can convince my boss of that. I guess I'll have to deal with it when I go into work. There's nothing I can do right now."

At that moment, the sound of the tattoo gun stopped. A few minutes later, Ray Bender emerged from the back. I had met him once or twice around White Tower Center, and recognized him right off. His client—a young Fae woman—winced. Her bandaged shoulder looked inflamed, but that was common given how big the piece seemed to be.

"You come back in three weeks and we'll see if we need to

touch it up. Meanwhile, here are your aftercare instructions. Don't get it wet. Don't scratch. Do use the ointment. Call me if you have any concerns." Ray waved her out and turned to us.

"I'm glad you made it. I'm heading out as soon as we get done talking." He paused, staring at me for a moment. "Lily? Lily O'Connell?"

I nodded. "Long time, no talk. Thank you for seeing us." I was about to ask if there was someplace private we could discuss matters, but realized that there was nobody else in the shop. "We need to ask you a few questions about Charles Schafer."

Ray Bender was a tall man, burly. His hair was long, pulled back in a sleek ponytail, and he had stretched ear lobes, with plugs made of sparkling crystals that were the size of buttons. He looked like the type of man you would think would have a beard, but he was clean shaven. His jeans and shirt were meticulous, even though he worked around ink all day.

"I'll help if I can." He pulled a rolling chair out from around the counter and wheeled it over to sit down opposite us. "I heard he's out. I heard about what's going on." He paused, then asked, "You all have his ink, don't you?"

I nodded. "Well, all of us except Archer. This is Archer Desmond, he's a private investigator. And I don't know if you've met Danielle Halloran and Nate Winston. The Souljacker did their ink. We were wondering if you'd heard about what happened, but you answered that."

Ray shook his head. "He and I were going to exchange ink, but before we got the chance, he was taken."

"Excuse me," Dani said. "Is there a restroom near here?"

Ray pointed toward the front of the shop. "Turn right, and about three shops down turn right again. There are restrooms and water fountains down that hallway."

"You want me to come with you?" I glanced up at her.

"No, save your knee the strain. I'll be right back. Something didn't sit too well with my stomach." Dani was out of the shop before we could stop her.

I turned back to Ray. "Tygur Jones was killed in my salon the other night. We're trying to find out where Charles is, since the police won't touch vampire executions."

"Cops won't touch much of anything anymore."

I let out a slow breath. "You've got that right. Which means we have to do the job for them, especially since you know he won't stop hunting his former clients until he has what he wants. We've figured out that Charles is after his art in the hopes of recovering his humanity. It's nuts. He's jumped the shark, gone over the edge, disappeared into la-la land. Call it whatever you want, he's lost all touch with reality."

"What are you planning?"

I closed my eyes, suddenly realizing how tired the past few days had made me. "You *know* what we need to do, Ray. If you have any information about where he might be, please tell us. I don't know if there's a code among artists but…"

"Oh, we have a code of sorts, but the artist is gone, girl. The real Souljacker? He died when that vampire turned him. If I knew where to find the creature that's out there now, I'd tell you in an instant. Like a rabid beast, you gotta put 'em down when they get dangerous." Ray leaned forward, his elbows on his knees.

"I will tell you, though, that you're not the only one looking for him. Not twenty minutes ago, a man—human as me—came through, and he was accompanied by four vampires. He was dressed to the nines. I know that was the Souljacker's father because I recognized him from the newscast about the escape."

Crap! Terrance had already been here. "What did he want?"

"He was asking questions about Charles. Wanted to know if I knew where he was. I was damned relieved to be able to honestly say I know nothing. I didn't like the looks of them. Beady eyes… dangerous. Vamps scare the fuck out of me, and not much else does. I've dealt with things that would make most people faint dead away. But vampires?" He shook his head.

Beside me, Archer stiffened. "You say they were here less than twenty minutes ago?"

"Yeah, they pulled me out of my session, which is the only reason I was still here when you arrived. I needed to finish up my client's piece, and the goons forced me to step outside to talk to them. At first, I was afraid they didn't believe me and were gonna rough me up."

Exactly what we didn't need. Terrance and his cronies…and then I froze. "Greg. I'll bet you Greg was with him. And if they are still in the shopping center somewhere…"

"Dani." Nate jumped up. "I'll go find her. She should be back by now anyway." He took off out the door.

I turned to Archer. "What do we do?"

"We'd better get moving. Find Dani and get the hell out of here before we run into Schafer and his posse. The last thing we want is for them to get wind that we're after Charles." He turned to Ray. "Please don't say anything about our visit. A lot of peoples' lives depend on secrecy."

Ray nodded. "I'll do what I can, bro. Now, if you'll excuse me, I need to get my ass home before the storm keeps me trapped in here all night." He paused. "You do know that there aren't any wards allowed in the mall, right? Not White Tower Center. Vampires are bound by an honor code not to feed here in exchange for being allowed to shop freely. It's not always followed, but for the most part, the Deadfather keeps to the treaty. However, someone like Charles…"

He didn't have to finish the thought. The Souljacker would no more abide by an honor code than a rabid badger would.

We were headed toward the entrance when a scream echoed through the wide plaza.

"That's Dani's voice." I tried to run, managing a fast walk, but Archer was already out the door and down the hall. I turned to Ray, a frantic look on my face. "My friend—"

"Come on girl, I've got you." He swept me up as if I weighed nothing and jogged into the mall, turning right. As the burly tattooist carried me along, I could only pray that Dani was okay, and that neither the Souljacker nor Greg had managed to find her.

CHAPTER 29

I draped my arm around Ray's neck, leaning into his chest as he carried me down the hall at breakneck speed and turned right, into a hallway. Up ahead, we could hear Nate's voice, coming through a set of swinging doors at the end of the hallway beyond the restrooms, which were to the left of the hall. Ray turned slightly as we came to the doors so that his shoulder met the doors and not my leg. As we burst through, we found ourselves in a wide hall, which I assumed was the back-alley portion of the mall. Still enclosed, it looked like where the shipping, receiving, and general behind-the-scenes work for the stores took place.

Archer was nowhere in sight. Nate was waiting for us, looking frantic. "Hurry! Archer's headed out to the loading dock. He's got her—the Souljacker. He has Dani. He was dragging her toward the door when I saw him."

"He must have been watching and followed us from the house." I wanted to scream or hit something, but instead, turned to Ray. "Please, can you help me get out there?"

He nodded and, without a word, followed Nate through a back door that led to a loading dock. We were just in time to see Archer crossing the street, heading toward the Underground's back entrance. Damn, the Souljacker was taking her into the labyrinth. I was frantic. I needed to be stronger, so I could run. I looked back at Ray. If I drank from him, I could manage it. Archer had given me a good start, but I needed more. But if I drank from him, I could easily kill him.

You can't do this, I thought. *You can't take his life just to save Dani's life. You don't know this man, he may have a family, a wife—*

kids. You aren't starving…if you drink from him, you'll be deliberately chancing his life.

"Damn it!"

My shout in his ear threw Ray off his game, and he stepped on a patch of snow that was hiding ice and we both went down.

"What the hell? What happened?" He shook his head, looking confused.

"I'm sorry, my fault. Dude, I…" As I searched for something to say, a noise behind us caught my attention. I turned in time to see two of the weretigers who had attacked me earlier burst through the door behind us. "What the hell? Are you guys stalking me?"

"Tricia doesn't like failure," Tall Boy said. "When we saw you walking through the mall, we decided to prove to her that we're not screw ups." As usual, he couldn't resist running his mouth off.

I groaned. Not this again. Not now. And then I realized that the car I had recognized had been the one in which they had sped away from the parking lot earlier.

As my mind flipped through potential outcomes to this scenario—all of which were bad—I suddenly had an idea. "You. Tall dude. Come here. I dare you. You and me—winner takes all. You've got an advantage, you know. I'm hurt already." I glanced at Ray and whispered, "Get on your feet and get ready to run like hell when I grab him. You do not want these men on your ass. Trust me."

He frowned, but did as I said, reaching down to haul me up with him. I stood there, motioning for him to move aside as Tall Boy sauntered toward me. Apparently, he and his partner were just about as bright as they had been earlier in the day.

Nate was frantically making tracks back to the stairs leading up to the loading dock. "Lily!"

Ray refused to budge. "I'm not leaving you alone with these thugs."

I sighed. "Just stay out of my way, okay? I know what I'm doing."

He frowned, but just then Tall Boy planted himself right in front of me, a cocky grin on his face. The oaf really thought I believed I could take him down.

"Okay, succuslut. You and me. Let's go."

As he made a sudden grab for me, I lunged for him, throwing my arms around his neck and planting my lips on his. As we toppled over, with me on top, I immediately began to suck in his breath, drinking as deeply as I could, as quickly as I could. Startled, he lay there like a pancake. I could make the experience hurt, and I did— draining his life force at the fastest rate that I could. Nate raced past me as Ray gave a shout and I heard a scuffle. I ignored the noise, focusing on draining Tall Boy of every ounce of energy that he had. He was struggling now, finally realizing just what was happening, but like a drowning man, there wasn't much he could do. He flailed, trying to push me off, but by now the flow of energy was so rapid that he was rapidly losing strength. Another moment, and he lay still.

I looked up in time to see Ray and Nate trying to hold down the other one. I jumped up, my knee feeling almost 100 percent, and unsheathed my dagger. As I headed over, I realized that from here out, everything would change. I had already gone beyond the pale, irrevocably cementing myself as an enemy to the Weres.

"What should we do with him?" Ray asked, straddling the prone weretiger.

I stared down into the man's face. There was no going back. He'd already tried to do me in once; this was the second time. He and his crony would have done whatever they needed to get back in Tricia's favor. I dropped to my knees next to him.

"Hold him for me."

Nate and Ray were doing their best to keep the bucking weretiger on his back. I leaned over and, once again, linked my lips to his. As the rush of energy flooded my lungs, I knew that I was changing, becoming someone new, and that whatever happened from now on, life would never be the same.

• • •

By the time the other weretiger was dead, I was fully able again. I rose up, turning to Ray. "You can go. We're headed into unsafe territory. I won't ask you to put yourself in danger."

He stared at me for a moment, wavering. "I have a wife and a daughter," he finally said.

"Take care of them. You don't need to be aligned with us. We aren't going to be very popular with the Deadfather after this. You don't need that hanging over your head." I nodded for him to go back inside. "Go. And next time I need more ink, I'll make sure to come to you."

Another moment passed, and he finally turned and went inside. Nate watched him go. "I hope he's okay."

"Me too. Come on, I can run now, so let's try to catch up to Archer."

Thoughts of Dani filled my head as we slid and slipped our way across the street. The snow was coming down so thick that we could barely see, and even the street lamps were just faint glowing masses in the midst of the whirl of flakes. Nate and I held onto each other. Even in the middle of the street, it would be too easy to lose track of each other in the blinding snow.

We managed to slog through, getting to the other side of the street without falling. The entrance to the Underground was right off the sidewalk—at street level, luckily, so there were no stairs here to navigate. There would be inside, but that was another matter.

I was so full of chi from the weretigers that it felt like I had taken a large dose of Hype or some other drug. My body buzzed and every noise seemed louder, every color a little brighter. As we stumbled in off the street, we stamped our feet on the wide mat and looked around.

The back entrance to the Underground led into a narrow hall that branched off every ten to twelve feet into another hall. It really was a labyrinth, and unless you knew where you were going, it would be easy to get lost. Considering those who hung out in the Underground, it wasn't a tourist trip I would recommend to anybody who didn't have a good weapon, be it natural or manmade.

"Where the hell did he go?" Nate looked around, frantic. "How are we going to find them down here?"

I thought, then stood back. "Marsh? Marsh! We need you."

Another moment, and Marsh appeared. "What should I do?"

"Go—search through and see if you can find Archer. Or Dani—especially Dani! Then come back so you can show us the way. If we start randomly trying tunnels and hallways, we'll get nowhere fast."

Marsh nodded, then vanished again. Ghosts could move through walls, zip along at an incredible speed—he could cover the tunnels far more efficiently than we could. I yanked Nate out of the way as a group of thugs passed by. I could smell the stench of werewolf on them—they were fresh in from a night out shifting. We weren't under the full moon, so it must have been a hunting party. My guess was they had taken a trip out to a meadow or rural park where they could race around in the snow in their natural forms. I thanked the gods they didn't know who I was, or we'd be in a lot of trouble.

The din from up ahead was getting louder, and I turned to Nate. "Stay here. I'll be right back. Don't move."

He nodded, wincing at the rising noise. I motioned for him to stand back against the wall, hiding in one of the nooks that pockmarked the place. Then I headed toward the noise. A moment later, I realized that I had entered one of the nightclubs from the back entrance. The bouncer turned to me and held out his hand.

"ID and fee?"

I shook my head. "Just wondering where exactly I am. I came in through the back way and am unfamiliar with the layout in this direction."

"You're at Belltower Mae's. Now either buy a ticket or sod off."

I could hear the veiled threat behind the words and slowly backed away. He was a vampire, and Belltower Mae's was one of the most popular low-life brothels around, catering to those who sought anonymity and compliance in their paramours. It was also a good place to pick up a disease that was a one-way ticket to the doctors, or worse. As I returned to where Nate was waiting, I glanced down each hallway, trying to place our whereabouts.

I didn't visit the Underground very often. White Tower Center was good for shopping and entertainment, but the Underground was a seedy underbelly to the mall, a parasitic symbiont that fed off the buried hungers of those who preferred life on the wild side. It wasn't that it was all bad—no, the wild boys and the satyrs howled it up in the depths, but there were too many vampires here, and too many who didn't know how to harness their darker desires. The Underground was a rich playground for them, and too often their playmates were unsuspecting and unwilling.

I made my way back to Nate, who looked visibly relieved when I showed up.

"This place scares the hell out of me, I don't mind telling you that. I wish Marsh would get back. Every minute that freak has Dani, is another minute he could be…" Nate trailed off, his voice sharp.

"I know, Nate. I know."

"Do you think…do you think he does it after he kills them? So it won't hurt?"

I had to take Nate's fear in hand. I was afraid too, but I was good at hiding it, and with Nate being human, any Were or vampire or even some of the Fae would be able to smell his panic. It acted like an aphrodisiac for some of them.

"Take a deep breath. You can't afford to panic here." I heard my voice—sharp and edged, and tried again. "You have to stay calm while we're down here, Nate. Please. For all our sakes." After a pause, I added, "I think he kills them first. It makes it much easier and that way…he won't chance ruining the tattoo, you know."

He thought about it for a moment, then nodded. "Where is—"

But, before he could finish, Marsh appeared. "I'm back. I found Archer and he said he's pretty sure he knows where the Souljacker's taken Dani. He remembered something while he was hunting around. Come on, I'll take you to him."

Grateful to be on the move again, and praying we were in time, I grabbed Nate by the arm and we followed Marsh over to a side door leading to a stairwell heading down. It was time to introduce Nate to the depths of the Underground.

CHAPTER 30

Two floors down, we met Archer by a diner that catered to sub-terranean Fae. I hadn't realized there was a call for such specialized niche cuisine, but apparently there was.

"You made it. Marsh said you would be on the way down, so I waited." Archer stared at me. "You're moving fast on that knee."

"We had to take down two weretigers. I stole their chi. It healed up most of the damage." I still felt unsettled over what I had done, but they wouldn't have had any compunction about hurting me, so it was what it was. "Do you know where Dani is?"

He let out a long breath. "Yeah, I think I do. As I told Marsh, I remembered something about the Underground that I discovered in a case I was working on last year. There's a discarded medical facility on this level. There were a couple of Fae healers here, but they vanished a couple of years back. I was assigned to track them down for Wynter, but we never did solve the case. But the rooms are still there. It would be the perfect place for the Souljacker to…" He stopped, his voice fading away.

I knew precisely what Archer was about to say but couldn't bring myself to say the words, but Nate did it for both of us.

"For him to strip the tattoo off Dani."

"Right. Let's go. It's down this corridor and then through a back passage. The place was well hidden from prying eyes. This part of the Underground is extremely dangerous, so be careful. There are some terribly unsavory creatures here, and not all of them fall into the Were or Fae category. Some are just out-and-out nightmares." He turned and led the way, away from the stairwell.

Archer was right. This area of the Underground was different than the two levels above. The walls weren't brick, but carved out of the rock—actual tunnels leading beneath the city. They were damp, which didn't surprise me, and the air down here was stuffy and slightly fetid. The narrow passages were lit by dim wall sconces that had been jury-rigged every five yards or so, and the light was so low and yellow that the shadows themselves took on an eerie life, flickering in a way that made it look like they were actually moving. The floor was composed of broken flagstones, set in concrete, offering a dry, if bumpy, surface.

Archer took the lead, and I made Nate go second. Now that I was back up to speed, I figured that I was a little more equipped—given my dagger and the pentacle—to handle any attacks that might come from behind us.

The tunnel passage wasn't straight, but it curved, branching off into other tunnels as we went. I began to appreciate just how labyrinthine the Underground truly was. Everybody assumed that it was mostly created from what had once been Underground Seattle, but the truth was, it went far deeper than that. For years the Fae and Weres had been working below ground, carving out a place where they could be safe, hidden away from a society that would have tried to kill them if they had come out before it was safe to do so. Unfortunately, darker elements had moved in, taken over parts of the Underground. The vampires for one, and other, even more deadly creatures had joined the mix and driven the others to the upper levels. From what I understood from Jolene, the authorities did their best to keep them from becoming common knowledge. The last thing we needed was for a group of teens to come gallivanting down, trying to prove how brave or tough they were. The vampires weren't the only ones not opposed to snacking on humans—blood or flesh.

Archer moved quickly and silently. I was surprised by how well he seemed to slip into the mode of hunter. He would pause to listen and peek around the corner before moving past each side tunnel that peeled off from the main corridor. We wound deeper—

the floor was sloping down at a mild gradient, and I realized it was spiraling.

As we went along, I noticed that the light was growing dimmer. More of the sconces were out—either broken or failed—and the shadows were deeper, the dampness more pronounced. I began to think about what might happen if we were down here during one of the big quakes that happened in the area every now and then. A tunnel system like this? Was the perfect place for a cave in should the land decide to shift and roll.

To take my mind off the possibility, I tried to focus on Dani, on how we would find her and she would be safe, and the Souljacker wouldn't have had the chance to hurt her yet. I struggled to keep the darker possibilities at bay, but images of Tygur kept flooding back.

Finally, desperate to clear my head, I whispered—because whispering seemed apropos—"Archer, are we almost there?"

He glanced back. "Yeah, another couple minutes, and we'll be at the turnoff."

"What ever happened to the Fae you were trying to locate, do you think?" Nate asked.

"I don't know, but chances are they were dragged off by something. I followed every clue I could fine, but nada. Nothing. One day they were there, and the next, they had vanished as if they were never born. There are things down here that have no resemblance to humankind, monsters in the dark. The mountains and land of this area spawn beasts and spirits. And this close to the Sound? Creatures come in from the waters." He shrugged. "What can I say? 'There are more things in heaven and earth, Horatio—'"

"'Than are dreamt of in your philosophy.'" Nate finished for him. "You're scaring the crap out of me, you know."

"You should be scared. Never, ever get complacent down here. You think the vampires are bad, and they are, but then you meet one of these critters and you'll realize the vampires are actually rather fun chaps compared to them." Archer stopped, keeping his voice low. "There, to the right—we turn there. A little ways into the tunnel, we take the first left into the chamber. So here's how it's going to play out. I'm going in first. I will come back and tell you what I see. If we all go clunking down the hall and the Souljacker has her, he might kill her to spite us, even if she's still alive. So wait here. Do nothing. Say nothing. I'll be back in a few moments."

"We could find Marsh—send him?" Nate suggested.

"I don't want to chance there being anybody there who can see him and warn the Souljacker. We're reaching areas where the creatures are powerful and the danger…well…it makes anything you've come through so far seem tame. We can't afford to screw up."

As Archer moved off, Nate huddled close to me. I wasn't exactly thrilled with our surroundings, either. A sudden thought occurred to me, and I stripped off one of my wristlets—the one on my right, non-dominant, wrist. I grabbed Nate's wrist and wrapped it around his arm, strapping it tight. As he looked at me, puzzled, I leaned close to his ear.

"Silver dragon scales. Against the vampires. Hold your arm up to your neck if you have to—it will keep them at bay," I whispered.

He smiled wanly, but I could feel him relax a little. "Thanks, Lily. I appreciate it." Then, after a pause, he added, "Do you think Dani's still alive?"

I stared at him, then shrugged, looking away. I didn't want to guess, didn't want to speculate in any way because my mind had the habit of running away with itself into the worst possible scenarios. At that moment, Marsh popped up beside me. I jumped, but managed to keep myself from yelping.

"Marsh, you have to be careful. You could give us away if you startle me too much. Go follow Archer, see what he's doing, and then come back and tell us so we'll be prepared." It occurred to me that it was better to make use of a ghost when you had him. It wasn't like he was a genie with a limited number of uses.

He nodded, vanishing without a word.

I strained to hear whatever I could. Archer could move silently, that was for certain, and much to his credit, he seemed to take things one step at a time without panicking. I, on the other hand, wanted to charge down the hall and see what we were facing. Every minute we hung behind was another minute the Souljacker had to hurt Dani. But luckily, it was only a moment before Marsh was back.

He glanced around, then motioned for Nate and I to huddle.

"Archer is searching the room there. There's nothing in sight, but as I was poking around with him, I happened to notice a lever. There's a secret passage into a back room and Dani's in there, strapped down to a table that's decked out with a number of scary restraints."

I didn't want to know why there was a table with restraints on it, nor what the original owners of the space had been using it for. "Is she alive?"

Marsh seemed to be taking too long to answer, but then he nodded. "She seems to be, but she's unconscious. I didn't see anyone with her, but Archer's struggling to get into the room now. There's someone coming down the corridor behind you, Lily. I can't tell who they are, but there are five men, and four of them have eyes that glow in the dark."

Crap. Vampires? Weres? It could be either, or something else.

I turned to Nate. "Come on. We can't wait here. We'll be sitting ducks. Around the corner and down the hall to where Archer is."

Nate didn't argue, just took off, with me following. Marsh stayed visible, slipping ahead to lead the way. As we came to the open door and burst through, we saw Archer putting his weight against one of the walls against the back of the room. I shut the door behind me as I came in, hoping that it would be enough to throw whoever was behind us off our track, if they were actually following us.

Archer motioned to Nate. "Get over here and help me."

Nate added his weight to the panel. "Marsh said there's a secret lever?"

"I flipped it, but the damned door seems stuck. I doubt it rusted shut; the Souljacker had to use the entrance to get Dani in there." Archer grunted as he once again shoved against the panel, bracing his feet against the floor to gain leverage. "Marsh, go through to the other side and see if there's anything blocking the door from opening, please."

Marsh vanished.

I looked around, trying to figure out what I could do to help. It was at that moment that I heard noises coming down the hall. Voices. The men Marsh had said were following us. I quickly scanned the room, trying to figure out a way to bar the door so they couldn't get in. The light was dim, once again provided by sconces scattered around the walls. There were lab tables covered with the detritus of what had once been beakers and dishes and what looked like some sort of a microscope. Then, as I looked over against one wall, I saw a chair that was the perfect height to fit beneath the door handle. I grabbed it, shoving it under the handle to try to brace the door shut.

Marsh reappeared. "The door seems to be nailed shut from the other side. I looked around the room and found another entrance from the hallway—it's hidden, so you won't be able to see it without a bright light, but I can show you exactly where it is. That one doesn't appear to be blocked as far as I can tell. I'm not certain how you get in, but there has to be a way."

"Any other entrances from the room?"

"No, but remember, vampires can turn into mist and go through walls and doors that way. The Souljacker could have gotten her in there through the door, shut it, and then changed to go out again." Marsh headed toward the door.

I pulled the chair out. "What if they're out there?"

"Who?"

"Whoever the men are that Marsh thinks were following us."

"Then I guess we just have to face them," Archer said. "We don't have much time. He could come back at any moment to kill her."

That got me moving. I yanked the door open and we hurried into the hallway. Marsh was up ahead, about four yards away, pointing to an area on the wall. There was no one else in sight, but I could hear noise coming from the main corridor.

"Hurry," I said pushing toward the front. "Marsh, did you notice any handle or anything inside?"

"Yes, it would be right about here." He pointed to one area on the wall.

I knelt, feeling around to try to find any sort of opening. The next moment, Nate had a thin pencil beam of light aimed at my fingers. He had a miniature flashlight on his key chain. I glanced up at Archer, expecting him to order Nate to douse the light, but he said nothing, just stood in front of the beam to block it from the hallway. It didn't take long with the concentrated light to see an unnatural indentation.

"Wait—" Archer started to say, but I had already, gingerly, reached.

Luckily, there was nothing there but a button. I decided to chance it—if the Souljacker had set a trap, then too bad; I'd be right in line. But as I pressed it, all I heard was a soft *click* and then the door slid back, revealing the entrance to the room Marsh had been talking about. I rushed in, Archer and Nate right behind me.

There, on a concrete slab stained with old, dried blood, strapped down with leather restraints, lay Dani. Her eyes were closed, and her neck had two fang marks in it, but she was still breathing. Archer was already by her side, working at the restraints tying her down. Near the table was a concrete counter with a sink in the center. There were rusty instruments on it, medical instruments that looked left over from some tortuous experiment.

I left Nate to guard the door and ran over to the slab. As I cradled her head, calling her name as I tried to bring her around, Archer managed to get her arms free. He went to work on the leather binding her legs.

"Dani? Dani...wake up. Dani? Can you hear me?" Not knowing what else to do, I slipped my purse off my shoulder and rummaged through it, bringing out a vial of a particularly strong perfume. It wasn't to everyone's tastes, but I liked it. Honeysuckle and rose, with hints of orange and jasmine. It was a vividly floral scent. I opened it up and wiped some on her nose. Her nostrils flared and then she coughed and shook her head as her eyes fluttered open.

"Dani, wake up. Please. Are you okay?" I reached down to examine the marks on her neck. Someone had fed on her, that was obvious, but she was still pink enough to tell me that not much blood had been drained away.

"What...where..." She struggled to sit up and I helped her, rolling her to a sitting position.

Archer was almost done with the last restraint when Nate suddenly shouted and raced over toward us. A black mist was seeping into the room from one of the inner walls. As it began to coalesce into its physical form, I recognized Charles. The Souljacker had returned, and he was carrying a set of surgical instruments. He had come for Dani's tattoo.

CHAPTER 31

The Souljacker stood there, clad in dark jeans and a dark turtleneck. Charles had been a quietly handsome man, but now he seemed to have an allure to him, a magnetism that was difficult to ignore. His hair had grown wavy through the transformation—it had a silken sheen to it that made me want to reach out and touch it. But his eyes had lost the gentle glow that had made Charles always seem approachable and caring. Instead, there was an unnatural shine to them, and a look that I hadn't seen in too many other vampires' eyes—a darting, almost rabid look. Predators notwithstanding, usually vampires were in touch with reality to some extent. The Souljacker was not.

Dani's scream echoed through the room as she scrambled to get off the table. Her gaze was fastened on Charles. "Get away from me, get away!" She clutched the wound on her throat, and stumbled behind Archer.

It was then that I realized we hadn't brought anything resembling a stake. Except…I pulled out my dagger. "Keep away from her." It occurred to me then that if he were unarmed, he couldn't attack me as long as I was wearing my dragon scale pendant. And my blade would work as good as a stake—silver dragon scales? Perfect, as long as I struck his heart directly.

The Souljacker paused, staring at the dagger, then up at me. I felt a pull as he locked his gaze with mine, but luckily, I was a succubus and had a glamour of my own. It didn't cancel out other charms and bewitchments, but it went a long way toward easing their effects. I managed to wrench my gaze away and shoved the dagger out a little further.

"I warn you, stay back." Without turning—you never wanted to turn your back on a vampire—I shot a question to Archer. "What the hell do we do now? He's between us and the door."

Archer held out his hand. "Give me your dagger. Just do it, and move Dani back against the wall. You too, Nate."

I handed over my dagger and slowly began to edge toward the back wall. Nate moved in, standing in front of us. I wanted to tell him to get behind me—I was less likely to get hurt than he was, but then I saw the wristlet I had fastened on his arm and let it be. He wanted to protect us, and the dragon scale on the wristlet would help keep the Souljacker away from him.

"Flank Dani," I whispered to him. "One on each side. Don't let him in to get at her."

He nodded, moving into place.

Archer took a step toward the Souljacker, then another, holding the dagger like a champion fencer. He had a perfect touch, I could tell the blade was balanced lightly in his hand, ready to pivot in whatever direction he needed it to.

Charles hissed, staring at the blade. He glanced beyond Archer to once again catch my gaze. Then, I realized he was trying to force Dani to meet his eyes. He had fed on her once and she was still under his influence and in a weakened state. It wouldn't be too hard for him to draw her in again.

"Close your eyes, Dani." I shifted to stand between Charles and Dani, so she couldn't see him. "Keep your eyes closed. He'll have less impact on you."

"I can feel him trying to draw me in." Her voice wavered, like a station flickering in and out.

Archer suddenly lunged, catching the Souljacker's hand with the tip of the dagger. Charles let out a muffled howl. He sounded like a wounded animal, primal and frustrated. The dagger couldn't kill him unless it pierced his heart, but the silver had burned, and for vampires, silver burn was like a cold white lightning bolt, jarring and painful.

Charles suddenly vanished, dissolving into a black mist.

Archer darted away as the mist bore down on him, raising the dagger to the side of his head to keep Charles from being able to grab him by the throat. But the mist moved past him, headed toward the three of us.

"Watch her," I shouted to Nate. "Here he comes. Dani, hold tight. Keep your eyes closed."

Dani was whimpering. "I can feel him in my head."

"Start singing. I'm not kidding—it will disrupt his ability to divert your focus."

Still crying, she began to sing. It was a children's song, a silly skipping song about frogs, but right now, it could have been the national anthem and done the trick.

"That's it—keep going." I shifted again as the mist neared, and, reaching for my throat, I bared my pentacle, holding it out from my chest so he could see it. If vampires could even see in their mist form. I had no clue about that, having never had the need to ask before.

Whatever the case, the mist stopped about a foot away from me. Archer had swung around and now came charging toward us, dagger out. But before he could reach us, Charles took form again, whirling toward the oncoming demon. He darted to the side, toward the table Dani had been tied down on, and Archer screeched to a halt. If he'd kept on, he would have skewered me.

I was about to suggest we run for the door when Nate screamed and stumbled to the side as the Souljacker sent a rusty scalpel that was on the counter into Nate's bicep. The blood was flowing freely, but it didn't look like Charles had hit an artery. But Nate was doubled over, cursing at the shock of pain.

I tried to push Dani further behind me, but the Souljacker picked up a wooden stool and used it to knock Nate to the side, hitting him over the head with it. So much for dragon silver—it couldn't protect against regular attacks unless it was worked into actual armor. Nate shouted as he went down, but the Souljacker was incredibly fast—vampires had most of us beat when it came to speed. He hit Nate again, bringing the chair down hard across his back.

Archer was racing full tilt toward Charles, but once again, the vampire anticipated him and—like some mad bullfighter—gracefully stepped aside.

I grabbed Dani and headed for the door, but, in a blur, Charles was there to meet us. He grabbed Dani's other arm and we began a horrible tug-of-war, with me trying to wrest her away from his grasp. Dani was struggling, trying to muster up a curse, but most of her witchery relied on charms and talismans, rather than on spoken commands.

Marsh blinked into view, directly next to Charles, and screamed in his ear, but the vampire merely took one mild look at him and went back to attempting to drag Dani out of my arms. I tried to hold on but vampires were strong, far stronger than most mortals or even Fae or Weres, and he finally managed to rip Dani away.

"Lily! Help me!" Dani slashed at him with her fingernails, raking her hand over his face. She left a long row of gashes, but he didn't even blink an eye.

I held out my arm with the wristlet on it and went barreling toward them. "Leave her alone, you freak!" I launched myself through the air—not the most graceful of moves—and landed against them both, smacking him hard across the side of his face with the wristlet. He shrieked again, shoving me back with a push so strong that I went flying against the concrete slab Dani had been tied on, hitting my side on the edge.

I couldn't breathe, I had landed so hard, and slid to the ground, moaning as my ribs shifted just oddly enough to tell me that one or two might be broken. Then, a second later, the pain set in and I doubled over, trying to catch my breath.

Archer had edged closer during my interaction with Charles and now he lunged forward, catching the vampire with my dagger. He shoved hard, driving the blade into the Souljacker's back, but unfortunately his aim was off and he missed the heart. As Charles let go of Dani and whirled around, Archer managed to keep hold of the blade, pulling it free.

Dani was scrambling to run, but with one lunge, the Souljacker grabbed her by the hair and yanked her to her feet. She screamed again, trying to kick him in the balls. I wanted to shout to her that it would do no good—not against a vampire—but I could barely breathe, let alone talk.

As he shifted his grip to her throat and hoisted her a good six inches or more off the floor, she began to sputter. Archer swung again, this time hitting closer. He tried to fall on the blade, to disrupt the Souljacker's grip on Dani, and while he didn't hit square against the back of the heart, he did get Charles's attention, pulling away again before the vampire could grab something to hit him with.

Dani once again dropped to the ground and she scrambled away, half crawling, half running. She managed to reach me by the table and I tore off my other wristlet, shoving it at her.

"Put this on, now!"

She fumbled for a moment, but managed to get it strapped around her arm. "How are we going to get out of here?"

Nate was struggling to stand, looking so woozy I knew that he was out of it as far as helping us went. There was no way he could manage any sort of attack, let alone a defense, and I was grateful I'd thought to give him one of the wristlets.

"Well, he can get his hands on us, but we can burn him with the silver. But if this keeps up for much longer, the racket's going to attract something much worse. And if he gets away, he'll only be that much more determined to target us. Twice burned, you know." I was trying to think, frantically scrambling from idea to idea.

Archer grunted. "The hell with it. You two grab Nate and get moving. Go as fast as you can back the way we came." And then he charged, driving forward. This time he wasn't aiming for the Souljacker's heart, but instead, he body-slammed him, knocking him to the ground.

I grabbed Dani and we struggled to our feet. Limping, this

time because of my ribs, we staggered over to Nate, and Dani managed to pull him up, draping his arm around her shoulder. The extra chi I had drawn from the weretigers was keeping me up and moving, but it couldn't guard against the pain that the concrete table had inflicted, though it flashed through my mind that if I hadn't topped off at the filling station, so to speak, I would be out cold right now.

We headed toward the door, past Archer and Charles, who were struggling on the floor. Archer had demon strength of some sort, though I wasn't certain how strong and resistant chaos demons actually were, but I had to believe he could make it through this and get out safely.

Dani was trying to keep it together. Nate was mumbling incoherently—the lump on his forehead where the wooden stool had hit him was as large as an egg. And I was just trying to breathe deeply enough that I didn't faint. We approached the door, hurrying as fast as we could, and I yanked it open, but shadows outside drove us back. There was someone out there—and they were headed our way.

"Crap. What do we do?" I glanced around, frantic. The only other exit was nailed shut.

"Get back," Marsh said, popping in again. He moved in front of us, but I knew that all he could do would be to try to scare whoever was headed through the doorway.

As we watched, five figures silently entered the room, all men. Four of the men were wearing dark suits—fancy, designer wear, and hats that hearkened back to Marsh's era. One of them was wearing sunglasses, and as he removed them, Dani let out a little cry. I gasped as the man stepped forward, a cunning grin on his face. It was Greg, standing there full as life.

"Well, hello there. Thank you for collecting our package," he said, motioning to the three men who were dressed like he was. They headed over to where Archer and Charles were fighting and dragged them apart, yelping as Archer slapped one with the blade. But they weren't interested in the chaos demon. Instead, they grabbed hold of Charles and dragged him over to stand in front of the other man—a man I recognized from his picture.

Dressed in a white suit beneath a dark coat, Terrance Schafer looked up at his son, and began to weep. "Charles, I've come to take you home."

CHAPTER 32

"You can't mean to leave him alive—do you know what he's done?" The words were out of my mouth before I realized what I was saying.

Terrance turned toward me. "I don't believe we've met, but I want to thank you for keeping my son occupied till we could collect him. We've been tracking him for some time, but he's a cagey one, aren't you, boy?"

The Souljacker struggled against his captors. "Let me go! You don't understand, you have no idea what you're doing—they taunt me—they're calling me. If I don't gather them back, they'll leave me forever. I have to have them back; they're what make me real. It's so stark in my mind, all black and white with no color except for the bloody red that flows forever through my thoughts." His voice was mesmerizing, it spiraled around us like a sinuous tendril of mist.

Terrance regarded his son with a quizzical look. "I really expected them to make more progress at the hospital."

"Hospital?" I couldn't help it; this was the most surreal scene I could imagine. "Your son was in an institution for the criminally insane. He's a *vampire*, Terrance. He's gone over the edge, beyond the pale. He's murdering his former clients so he can steal his art back. What don't you understand about this?"

Terrance slowly crossed the distance between us. I struggled to stand up straight, unwilling to show weakness to the man's face. He was as deluded as his son if he thought he could bring Charles around.

"My son may have made some bad choices in life, but we can rectify this one. He can come out of it."

"Choices? He didn't *choose* to become a vampire. In fact, your son isn't your son anymore. Don't you understand what vampires are like? That they aren't…" I stopped, suddenly aware that Greg and the other three vamps were staring at me, obviously too interested in what I was about to say. I swallowed the lump that rose in my throat. Maybe, just maybe, they'd let it pass.

It was then that I noticed Marsh was nowhere to be seen. He had vanished. Fine guardian he was, I thought, but then I brought my thoughts back to focus on keeping myself alive.

Terrance began to bluster, but Greg motioned to him and he fell silent. I suddenly realized that Terrance wasn't the one in power here, but Greg. Which could prove highly problematic. He moved forward, his gaze fastened on Dani.

"It's been a long time, Dani. Too long. I've missed you, my *wife*." He stopped a few feet from us, and his gaze moved toward Dani's wrist, where my silver wristlet wrapped around her arm.

She stood, frozen, Nate's arm still draped around her neck as she tried to hold him up. "Leave me alone. You aren't my husband."

"I recall we took vows. Made promises." Again his voice was silky smooth, but behind it lurked a hook, a sensuous lure that I understood all too well because, as a succubus, I had that same ability. I had used it in the past, but for so long now, I had hidden that side of myself away, unwilling to draw in anybody against their will.

"Vows that ended at death," Dani said, pulling back.

Nate tried to step in front of her, but I moved to Dani's side and eased him back. It was obvious we weren't going to be able to run at this point, so I made him sit down to rest. My own ribs were aching, and I coughed from the pressure they were putting on my lungs. Archer hurried over, a worried look on his face when I let out sharp note of pain.

"Lily…"

"It's all right." When he started to protest, I shook my head. "I said I'm all right." *Don't show weakness.* My years on the road were coming back to me.

Terrance was staring at Greg. "Excuse me, but I think we should get out of here. I don't want to wait too long. My son's cunning, and you let him escape once."

Greg let out a snarl. "I didn't *let* him do anything. The damned cur is quick. *You* told me he'd be pliable and obey me, but instead the pup turned into mist and disappeared."

"He shouldn't have. He promised me that if I helped him get out, he would do as I said." Terrance looked put out. "I have the silver cuffs. Perhaps I should put them on him now, before your men lose track of him, again?"

It occurred to me that Terrance was rapidly approaching the point at which Greg was going to lose his temper. If he didn't watch out, he and his son could do a father-son duet of *Vampire's Lament.* The song had hit the top of the charts; the musician, VamPyre, had actually been a pop star before he'd been turned.

"Just shut up and cuff him." Yeah, Greg had had enough.

Scowling, Terrance strode over to Charles and brought out the cuffs. The vampires holding the Souljacker captive thrust out his arms, and Terrance slapped the silver wrist cuffs on him, then went to fasten the attached silver collar around his neck.

Charles screamed and began to fight them.

I winced. It had to burn, and though I wanted to see Charles staked, I didn't necessarily want to see him tortured. I turned to Archer, intending on burying my face in his shoulder. Instead, he forcefully pulled me to him and whispered in my ear.

"We need to make a break for it while they're occupied with him. I'll help Nate. You and Dani run for it the best you can. But we have to go now. I doubt they'll leave us alive."

I nodded. There was no other choice. I quietly pushed back away from him and reached for Dani's hand. She took it, looking at me with a question in her eyes. Archer subtly shifted so he was next to Nate.

The Souljacker was still thrashing as Terrance struggled to

get the collar on him. Greg's attention had been diverted by the ruckus, and he moved to help the others hold Charles still.

Archer nodded at me, and I held tight to Dani's hand and, ribs burning like hell, ran for the door. Archer scooped Nate up and followed. We were through before the vampires realized what we were doing and began shouting all at once.

"Don't look back, keep on running," Archer said behind us.

Dani and I raced down the hall the way we had come. I said nothing to conserve my breath, which was hard, given the injuries to my ribs. I couldn't even slow down to see how Archer and Nate were doing. I had to just go on trust. From the noise behind us, I knew that at least one of the vampires was on our tail.

We reached a juncture and, behind me, Archer shouted which direction to turn. Dani and I skidded around the corner. I could tell she was crying but we were running too fast to talk, and I knew she was feeling pretty punk still from being drained. Thankfully, at every twist and turn, Archer would shout the direction for us to go. I never would have remembered the way if left on my own.

We were almost at the area where the diner was when Archer shouted—and this time it didn't sound normal. I skidded to a stop and turned, in time to see him grappling with one of the vampires. Archer shoved Nate toward us, and I motioned to Dani. "Take Nate and go on. I'll help Archer. Get up to the main level and out of the Underground!"

Feeling helpless, I raced toward Archer and the vamp. He was swinging with my dagger, but the vampire had him down, and was managing to avoid the blade. I charged over, ribs aching, and pulled my pentacle off my neck, holding it out in front of me. As I came within reach, I slammed the pentacle against the vampire's forehead as he looked up, startled, and he screeched as the silver burned into his flesh.

At that moment, another sound back by Dani startled me—more shouting. Still holding tight to the pendant, I turned, thinking that one of the other vamps had gotten to Dani and Nate. But instead I saw four very burly Fae men come racing down the winding stair from the upper levels, carrying silver stakes. Behind them, I saw Marsh, looking pleased as punch.

"Move!" one of them shouted.

Dani dragged Nate to the side, and I dove out of the way too. The men barreled past, and one of them managed to catch the vamp as he flew off Archer and staggered back in surprise. He drove the stake through the vampire's heart and *poof*...so much dust and ashes.

Archer rolled to his feet, dusting himself off. Before I could ask where the men had come from, they were facing the hall behind Archer. There, we saw the other three vamps—Greg at the helm—marching down the hall with Terrance at their side. The Souljacker was in their grasp.

The four strange Fae were bearing down on them.

Apparently, Greg seemed to recognize them and let go of Charles, backing away, his eyes wide with what I could only read as fear.

"You're on your own, Schafer! Retreat!" He and his men fell back and, before the Fae could reach them, the three vampires turned into mist and disappeared.

Terrance Schafer looked horrified as the Fae reached him and his son. One of the men tackled the business mogul, knocking him to the ground and holding him there. The others surrounded Charles.

"Don't let him get away," I said, running toward them, wincing as every step jarred my body. "Don't let him go!"

"He can't turn into mist, Lily." One of the men turned to me. "Not bound in silver like he is. What do you want to do with him? Wynter ordered that we give you the decision, if at all possible."

I stared at him. "Wynter? How did she know we were in trouble?"

"You have me to thank," Marsh said, appearing at my side. "I went to ask her for help when I saw what was going on with the others."

I stared at him, then back at the Fae who had asked me what

to do with Charles. "Who are you, then? And how did you get here so quickly?"

"My name's Dextra. Not all of Wynter's warriors live out in her court. We are always ready, always on call. It was a quick trip from where we're stationed." He smiled. "So…it's up to you. Wynter said that you were charged with this man's fate."

I stared at Charles, realizing with horror that the Fae weren't going to take care of this for me. While I had killed before, and killed vampires in the past, I had never had to face someone who had once been a friend and run a stake through his heart. But I couldn't ask anybody else to do it and retain Wynter's respect. She had given me the task of destroying him.

"Don't kill my son! Don't…please…" Terrance was crying now. "He can be redeemed."

I knelt beside him, staying out of his reach. He couldn't hurt me, given he was being restrained, but still, I had learned never get too close to an enemy.

"Terrance, listen to me. There's nothing that can bring your son back. That creature is no longer your son. He's a murdering predator, who is in terrible pain—his delusions are just that. They aren't grounded in reality. Nothing will ever take away his vampirism, or make him the boy you remember. Charles died the day the vampire killed him and turned him."

Then, ignoring Terrance's hail of abuse and anger, I turned back to Dextra. "Hold him, please. Hold him very tight. I'll put him out of his and everyone's misery."

Archer crossed to my side. "Do you want me to do it, Lily?"

I shook my head. "This is something I have to do. Charles… we can't let him go. He'll just kill again and again…and Dani and Nate and I are on his list. My dagger, please?"

Archer handed me the blade, kissing my forehead. "I'll help Dani and Nate."

I took the dagger and turned to Charles. His gaze was darting from face to face. The pain from the silver was obvious and I wanted to tell them to take the cuffs off, to give him a moment's peace without the burn of the silver, but the danger was too great.

"I'm sorry," I whispered to him. "I'm so sorry. You were…" But there, I stopped. Like I had told Terrance, the artist was long dead. Only the body remained, housing a monster. Better to focus on that. I drew back my blade and aimed for his heart as the Fae warriors held the Souljacker's arms back, giving me an easy target.

"Good night, Charles, wherever you are." With one thrust, I plunged the blade into his heart, surprised by how easily the silver ran through cloth and flesh. It was like a hot knife on butter, and as the tip penetrated the Souljacker's heart, there was a moment's hush, and then his body exploded in a soft puff of ash and dust, which clouded the area. As the cloud began to settle, Terrance let out a loud wail. Charles was gone for good.

I turned to Dextra. "I'm hurt, Dani and Nate are hurt…we need to get up top and then somehow make it home through the storm. I don't want him following us." I nodded to Terrance. "We can't…I don't know what to do with him."

"Leave him to us. We'll keep him contained till you are long gone. But Lily, this man has a lot of power and influence. I'd be very careful, if I were you. Are you sure you want to leave him standing?"

I realized that Dextra was asking me if I wanted Terrance killed. I shook my head. "We can't. We just…I can't justify it. But if there's any way to cloud his thoughts…to maybe wipe his short-term memory?"

"There are drugs. They aren't foolproof, but they may help. Leave him to us."

One of his men led us back to the entrance to the Underground, then walked us over to our car. The storm had truly taken on white-out proportions, but with a little luck and every skill at navigation Archer had, we made it back to my place. It took almost an hour instead of fifteen minutes, but we made it in one piece.

CHAPTER 33

Sorting out the aftermath is always the hard part. Nate and I were both banged up. What I thought were broken ribs were, luckily, only severely bruised ones. Nate had a concussion. Dani was anemic thanks to the blood drain. Archer managed to come through without much of a scratch beyond a few bruises here and there.

Vesper called me to tell me training would be delayed at least a day given the storm. Dextra got in touch with me, exchanging phone numbers and hinting that he wanted to keep in touch, given I was going into training as an Aespion.

All said and done, everybody crashed at my place that night, and we drank ourselves silly. The next morning, the world was blanketed with white, and the sun came out for a few minutes to sparkle against the new snow. Everything felt recharged, and I stared out the kitchen window, grateful that Archer had volunteered to shovel off my steps. Whisky was on the counter beside me, rubbing against me. I scritched his chin.

"Hey, I don't know how you did it, but does Marsh have to leave now that I'm safe from Charles? He's kind of fun to have around."

As if in answer, Marsh appeared. "I heard that. And no...I'm still here, so...I guess I'm free to do what I want. I don't have that overwhelming drive to watch over you now, though I have to say, I didn't mind it so much." He paused. "How are you? And Dani?"

"Dani's in a bit of shock after seeing Greg. She told us what happened at the mall. The Souljacker had tracked us there, and when she went to the bathroom, he grabbed her. When he got her in that room in the Underground? He apparently realized he had forgotten his surgical instruments—he was muttering about them loud enough for her to overhear. So he left her there to go get them. When he got back, of course by then we had found her." I stared at the sink for a moment. "He fed on her, though. At least he didn't make her drink any blood in return, so she won't have to worry about that."

When a vampire forced you to feed on them, if you didn't die right away, you would still turn into one once you did meet your fate. You could live for fifty years as a normal mortal, but the moment you died, the change in your blood would be waiting for you. Researchers were working on a cure, but so far, nothing.

"How about Nate?" Marsh leaned over Whisky, running his hand through the cat. Or rather, Whisky stayed still as Marsh's hand passed through his body. I had the feeling the two had bonded in a way they never had when Marsh was alive.

"Nate's a little shell shocked over the whole mess, but he'll be all right, once the lump on his head goes away. But…he's talking about moving out of the Blood Night District now. He's more afraid of vampires than ever, and I don't blame him. He's afraid Terrance will take revenge on all of us."

"Makes sense." Marsh turned to stare at me. He crossed his arms, a soft smile on his face. "Now, what about you? How are you dealing with all of these changes?"

I thought about his question for a moment. "Let's see. The Weres hate my guts right now. I've lost my business. I've been conscripted by Wynter into her secret service, so to speak. I'm bruised up, banged up, have been beaten right and left the past few days by weretigers and vampires. Chances are the Deadfather's going to be looking into what happened to Terrance, so there's potentially a field of mines to navigate there…How am I? Just peachy, I guess."

As flippant as I tried to sound, I couldn't fake a smile to go along with it.

"I wish I could help." Marsh frowned, staring at me.

"Hey, you saved our asses, Marsh. You did help. And…if you can…stick around. I like talking to you. I like having you back in my life again. I missed you."

He laughed, then. "Oh, Lily. I'm glad I'm here too, ghost or not. You'll be okay. You'll navigate all those problems because you're you. You have your friends to help you. And…you have Archer. He's good for you, Lily. I watch the two of you, and I think, you look like you belong together."

I started to speak, when Archer popped into the kitchen. "Hey, come watch the news. They're talking about Terrance on it."

Hurrying into the living room, I settled down beside Archer on the sofa. Dani was in the rocking chair, Nate in the recliner. The television had a picture of Terrance splashed on it. Archer turned up the sound.

"In other news, business tycoon Terrance Schafer was found wandering in the blizzard early this morning, suffering from exposure and amnesia. When questioned as to what happened, doctors say Schafer mumbled something about the Underground and vampires, but that was all he could tell them. It does not appear that Mr. Schafer has suffered any injuries due to vampiric activity, and police say he may have taken some medication that affected his behavior or caused sleepwalking. There were no traces of drugs or alcohol in his system. In other news, opponents to the vampire rights bill are massing to ask the president to reverse his decision—"

Archer turned off the television. "So, Terrance can't remember much about last night."

"I hope whatever they did to him lasts." My phone dinged and I pulled it out, checking my texts. "What do you know?" I stared at the screen, surprised. "Wynter has given her seal of approval on me working with you, Archer."

"Good. Because we start bright and early tomorrow morning. Or maybe the day after, if the snow's still too deep." He laughed, pulling me into an easy embrace. "I hope you don't mind, but even though the Souljacker's taken care of, I want to stick around in your life." He was staring into my eyes, his voice soft.

My mind whirled. I didn't dare use the word…I couldn't even hope to use it yet, but something in my heart jumped for joy as he gathered me to him, kissing me deeply. His lips were soft and for the first time in a long while, I felt safe.

"Get a room," Nate said, laughing, and Dani threw a pillow at us.

But I didn't care. I kept kissing Archer, because with all the panic and fear and violence in the world, it seemed like the perfect cure to my melancholy. As I leaned into his arms, a faint movement on my leg startled me. I glanced down, thinking a fly or spider had crawled on me, but to my surprise, the phoenix tattoo had shifted, the tail feathers unfurling a little wider, the colors a little more vivid. Charles was dead, but his work hadn't been in vain. And it appeared that as we changed, so would the tattoos that mirrored our souls and hearts.

PLAYLIST FOR SOULJACKER

I listen to music a lot while I write, and always try to include my playlists in the books for you. So, here's the list for *Souljacker*:

Adele:	"Rumour Has It"
Amanda Blank:	"Make It Take It"
	"Might Like You Better"
	"Big Heavy"
Android Lust:	"Stained"
	"Saint Over"
Beck:	"Think I'm In Love"
	"Nausea"
	"Loser"
	"Sexx Laws"
	"Mixed Bizness"
	"Broken Train"
	"Devil's Haircut"
	"Hotwax"
Black Angels, The:	"You on the Run"
	"Indigo Meadow"
	"Evil Things"
	"Don't Play With Guns"
	"Young Men Dead"
Black Mountain:	"Queens Will Play"
Cobra Verde:	"Don't Play with Fire"
Crazy Town:	"Butterfly"

Eels:	"Souljacker Part 1"
Elektrisk Gonner:	"Uknowwhatiwant"
Faithless:	"Addictive"
Fergie:	"Fergalicious"
Finger Eleven:	"Paralyzer"
Fleetwood Mac:	"The Chain"
	"Gold Dust Woman"
Garbage:	"#1 Crush"
	"Queer"
	"Only Happy When It Rains"
	"Bleed Like Me"
	"Sex Is Not the Enemy"
Gary Numan:	"Stormtrooper in Drag"
	"Dominion Day"
	"The Angel Wars"
	"I, Assassin"
	"My Shadow In Vain"
	"Voix"
	"Soul Protection"
	"My World Storm"
	"Pure"
	"Here In The Black"
	"Everything Comes Down To This"
	"My Breathing"
	"Sleep By Windows"
In Strict Confidence:	"Snow White"
	"Tiefer"
Justin Timberlake:	"SexyBack"
Kills, The:	"You Don't Own The Road"
	"Sour Cherry"
	"DNA"
	"Wait"
	"Future Starts Slow"
	"Satellite"
	"U.R.A Fever"

	"Nail In My Coffin"
	"Dead Read 7"
Kirsty MacColl:	"In These Shoes?"
Lady Gaga:	"Paparazzi"
	"Paper Gangsta"
	"Poker Face"
	"Teeth"
Larry Tee & Princess Superstar:	"Licky"
Lord of the Lost:	"Sex on Legs"
Lorde:	"Royals"
Peaches:	"Boys Wanna Be Her"
Pink:	"Lady Marmalade"
Pussycat Dolls, The:	"Don't Cha"
	"Buttons"
Rob Zombie:	"Living Dead Girl"
	"Never Gonna Stop"
Róisín Murphy:	"Ramalama (Bang Bang)"
Rolling Stones, The:	"Gimme Shelter"
	"The Spider and the Fly"
	"Lady Jane"
Shriekback:	"Intoxication"
	"Over the Wire"
	"New Man"
	"Big Fun"
	"Dust and a Shadow"
Stone Temple Pilots:	"Atlanta"
	"Sour Girl"
Tom Petty & the Heartbreakers:	"Mary Jane's Last Dance"